WHEN ALL ELSE FAILS...

She began to peel her peignoir off as she pleaded, "Please believe me, darling, I swear it wasn't me. Do I look like a gunfighter?"

As she sat there, naked, with the soft folds falling around her firm, rounded hips, Longarm sighed and said, "You look more like Delilah must have looked to Samson. You're as deadly too..."

She reached out to take one of his hands. "Don't you want me, Custis?"

"I'd be a liar if I said I didn't," he said...

Also in the **LONGARM** series
from Jove

TABOR EVANS

LONGARM

AND THE
STALKING CORPSE

A JOVE BOOK

First Jove edition published October 1981

First printing

Printed in the United States of America

Jove books are published by Jove Publications, Inc., 200 Madison Avenue, New York, NY 10016

Chapter 1

Longarm crossed Larimer Street feeling mighty cross with himself that Saturday morning, for he saw he was going to be late getting to the office again. While this would come as no great surprise to his boss, U.S. Marshal Billy Vail, Longarm knew he faced a longer-than-usual chewing out. The office was only open half a day on Saturday, and with the federal courts closed, business would be slow. So the marshal would have time at his disposal to discuss his tall deputy's shortcomings in tedious detail.

The cool dry morning breeze sweeping into Denver from the nearby Front Range was clearing Longarm's head of the cobwebs he'd picked up the night before in the Black Cat Saloon, along with a right athletic gal who'd answered to the name of Sue. As he squinted in the painfully bright morning sunlight, Longarm was still walking sort of stiffly, but he figured he was sober enough to ponder out an excuse for oversleeping, which was a right polite way of putting what he and old Sue had been doing when he'd heard the bell on City Hall ring nine times.

He didn't think Marshal Vail would accept a morning quicky

1

as a valid excuse for his being this late. Old married gents like Billy Vail tended to forget that it was important for a man to leave a lady purring contentedly while he shaved. So, as Longarm got to the corner of Arapaho and 17th, and spied the blue uniforms of the Denver P.D. amid a milling crowd down the block, he grinned and headed that way. As a professional peace officer, it was his simple duty to assist others in the same line of work, and he could see that the Denver coppers were up to something he might be able to say he'd found more important than checking in with the durned old clerks at the Federal Building.

When he reached the scene, he saw that coppers and civilian passersby had gathered about a man in bib overalls, who was spread like a bearskin rug on the sandstone walk. The man was groaning too much to be hurt badly, and as Longarm nodded to a copper he knew, the gent on the ground asked someone to help him to his feet. But the copper told him, "Lay still till the ambulance gets here, dang it. I already told you, both your durned ankles are busted or sprained."

Longarm asked the copper what had happened. The man in blue pointed up with his chin and said, "Suicide attempt. As we put her together, that farm boy throwed hisself out that open window up there, landed on the awning yonder, and somersaulted to the pavement to land on his fool feet, which must have stung some. He ain't hurt bad."

Longarm stared up at the open window of what he now saw was a cheap hotel and mused aloud, "Suicide leap, from a second-story window?"

"I never said he was smart. I just said he leaped. Two stories likely seem high, to a furriner off a farm."

The injured man sat up, groaning some more as he clutched one of his ankles with his knee drawn up to his chest. Longarm didn't think Billy Vail was going to like this excuse all that much unless he did something important. So he dropped to one knee beside the farmer and said, "Don't try to stand. Let me have a feel of that ankle before you go busting it up worse."

"Are you a doctor?"

"I'm better than some doctors when it comes to horrible injuries. I'm a deputy U.S. marshal and I see more of them

2

than the average sawbones does."

He put a hand gently on the man's ankle and added, "You ain't hurt all that horrible, despite the swelling. Can you wiggle your toes and does it hurt when you try?"

The man shook his head and said, "My foot feels all right, but I can't bend my ankle."

"Don't try, then. It's sprained or maybe busted a mite. They'll take you to the dressing station directly and wrap you right. Sprained or busted, you ain't going to run after any trains for a while. Why in hell have you taken to diving out windows of late, pilgrim? Don't you know a gent could get hurt that way?"

"I noticed," the farmer groaned. "It was a sudden feeling that come over me as I faced a dismal future, broke and sober. I don't reckon I'll do her again. As I've been laying here, it's passed through my mind that I was trying to kill the wrong fool. As soon as I'm able, I aim to get me a gun and do it right."

"Shooting yourself is against the law, friend."

"Ain't fixing to shoot *me*. Gonna shoot *him*, the man who robbed me! Mary Lou ain't never going to speak to me either way, after the way I lost the wherewithal to marry up with her. But at least I'll have the satisfaction of putting the man who ruined my life in his grave."

Longarm grimaced and informed the farmer, "There's a local regulation against that, too. Man could wind up in jail, putting folks in graves. I've heard the part about you being broke, and from the red in your eyes I'd say you've been drunk as a skunk in recent memory, too. Things may look brighter after you simmer down with some plaster around your ankles."

One of the coppers craned his neck to demand, "Where's that infernal meat wagon? I can't stand here all day guarding this lost sheep. I got me a beat to walk."

Longarm smiled to himself as he added that to the excuse for Billy Vail. He said, "You boys can go on about your business and leave this poor victim of circumstance to me, seeing as how I'm a peace officer too, right?"

They nodded but stayed put, the bastards. Longarm decided he'd better investigate further. The farm boy had said he'd been robbed, and no peace officer worth his salt would walk away from a tale of robbery before he'd heard all the facts. Even old Billy Vail knew that.

He asked the farmer to tell his tale, and then, as the latter did so, the tall deputy's eyes glazed over, for the man's story, while sad, was all too familiar.

"There was this street hawker, selling soap off a barrel down on Larimer when I come outten the bank after cashing the check for my produce yesterday noon. He said it was good soap and I meant to buy a bar for my Mary Lou. But business must have been slow, for the hawker unwrapped a bar and said he aimed to put a ten-dollar note around one bar, to make the sale more exciting."

Longarm glanced up at one of the coppers, who winked at him and said, "Let me guess what happened next. The soap salesman rewrapped the bar and mixed it with the others on his barrel, saying the bars were all a dollar apiece and that the lucky gent who bought the one with the ten-dollar bill around it would be taking home a fine bar of soap and a nine-dollar profit."

The farmer on the pavement winced and said, "Gosh, that's just what happened. Are you gents saying he's done her afore in Denver?"

"Many, many times." Longarm said. "I'll tell you what happened next. You bought a bar of soap, right?"

"I did. I said it was for Mary Lou and the hawker told me it was from France. I never expected to get the bar with the ten-dollar bill wrapped around it, but I did."

Longarm nodded. "That's what I just said. Naturally, since you were nine dollars ahead of the game, it only seemed right to buy a second bar for your sweet Mary Lou, and you were surprised as hell when you won a second ten spot, weren't you?"

"Surprised, deputy? I was plum thundergasted! I've never been very lucky at gaming, but guess what happened when I plunked down a dollar for the *third* bar of soap!"

"You won again. I told you we knew how it works. He must have spied you coming from the bank. After beating him three times in a row, you must have felt right friendly toward this gent, right?"

"As a matter of fact I felt sorry for him. He looked so flummoxed, and when I whupped him another time he confessed I'd cleaned him out and that the game was over. He said he'd never seen anybody so lucky. He said he only did that trick with the ten-dollar note to drum up business, and that he'd never expected anybody to beat the odds like that. He said he was not of a mind to buck a man who was on such a lucky streak."

Longarm looked up at the copper he knew and asked, "Reckon it's old Soapy Smith?"

"Has to be," the copper replied. "Most of 'em ain't that generous with their flash money. Modest street cons palm the bill and just use the temptation to sell nickel bars for a dollar to the great unwashed. Smith's the one who plays it for high stakes."

Longarm nodded, turned back to the injured man, and said, "You likely know how you were suckered, pilgrim."

The farmer groaned and said, "It come to me, just afore I jumped out the window. The soap hawker asked me if I'd buy him a drink, since I'd about cleaned him out. I figured it was only Christian, since he was being such a sport about losing thirty dollars so sudden. He said he knowed a place across the way where we could drink in private and maybe get some gals to sit on our knees. But I said I was fixing to marry up next week, so a drink or two would have to hold him."

"Right, and after you got to the Silver Dollar and settled down comfortable, old Soapy Smith just happened to notice some other gents playing monte across the way, correct?"

"Well, it was blackjack and not monte they was playing, but I see you are ahead of me on brains. It only come to me recent that them other gents must have been in on it with, uh, what'd you call him? Soapy?"

"Soapy Smith, one of Denver's better-known educational institutions. I'll tell you what you did with your produce money, pilgrim. You let Soapy sucker you into the game, full of good cheer and feeling smug as hell about the winning streak he said you were on. The details get tedious after that. Suffice it to say you won the first few hands and then, as you were fed congratulatory drinks, things went sort of fuzzy until you came to your senses this morning, short of cash."

"I was swindled outten my whole spring crop, and now I'll never be able to face Mary Lou again. But as soon as I can walk, I'll get me a scattergun and we'll see who's laughing last around here!"

The horsedrawn ambulance came around the corner and Longarm said, "No you won't. I told you it's unlawful. I know where they'll take you in yon meat wagon, so no matter what the sawbones say, stay put there until I come by with your purloined cash. Are you listening to me, old son?"

"You mean it? You reckon you can get them rascals to give me back the money I was meaning to marry up with?"

Longarm rose, dusting off the knees of his brown tweed pants as he readjusted the cross-draw rig under his frock coat and asked one of the coppers, "Where's old Soapy staying these days? I doubt like hell he'd be at the Silver Dollar."

The copper shrugged and said, "He drinks in Henry's, down by the stockyards, when he ain't working the street for marks. But I don't see what we can do about this gent's misfortune, Longarm. Arresting Soapy Smith seems to be a waste of time as well as a mite dangerous. He's sort of nasty for a con man, and when you *do* get the drop on him, he's got more damned witnesses on tap than you can shake a stick at. This farm boy's tale rings true to me, but you know it'll never hold up in court."

"I ain't figuring on arresting anybody," Longarm said amiably. "Ain't sure that what he done comes under federal law, in any case. I just mean to have a friendly word with Soapy Smith."

"Want us to come along?"

"Wish you wouldn't. It might not be *that* friendly."

"Oh." The copper grinned.

Longarm was grinning too, as he retraced his steps to the west and consulted his pocket watch. He was now so late that Billy Vail would be losing interest in chewing him out, and starting to worry. The boss would know that when Longarm was really late, he was onto something. It really wasn't any business of the Justice Department, but Longarm was sure there was something, somewhere in the Constitution, that covered keeping Miss Mary Lou from dying an old maid.

Henry's was a serious drinking place for cowhands, railroad

workers, and such, down near the Burlington yards. There were no fancy gals and no piano to distract gents as they wet their whistles at the long bar running the length of the single narrow room. It was early, so the stuffed buffalo head over the bar stared down on only one customer as the elderly barkeep read the *Police Gazette* spread on the mahogany. The customer was a tall, dapperly dressed gent with a mustache rivaling Longarm's. The pearl grips of a serious-looking sidearm peeked out from the shoulder holster under his left armpit. He ignored Longarm as he stood facing the bar and the bottle of redeye he'd ordered, with one booted foot hooked over the brass rail.

Longarm nodded to the bartender and drew his pistol as he stepped up to the solitary drinker with no preliminary remarks. The man stiffened at the unexpected move and went for his own weapon, but didn't make it. Longarm pistolwhipped him across the face, knocking him to the sawdust-covered floor, and then kicked him in the head to stretch him full-length on the floor, dazed and moaning.

The bartender knew who both of them were, so he went on reading as Longarm sat on the chest of Soapy Smith to relieve him of his pearl-handled Walker Colt and toss it in a corner. Soapy Smith shook his head to clear it as he muttered, "I'll kill you for this, as soon as I can figure out who you are and where I might happen to be. What the hell did you hit me for? I ain't done nothing to *you* in recent memory, stranger!"

"Let's put this down as a friendly negotiation, Soapy," Longarm said. "I came here to discuss a pilgrim you took advantage of last evening, and I said I was sure you'd be a gent about giving his crop money back. I sure hope I told him true."

Soapy Smith said, "Dammit, get off my infernal chest and let me have some air. You weigh a ton."

"Old son, you haven't felt my full weight yet. You see, this farm boy needs the money to marry up, and I'm sure you wouldn't want to stand betwixt a bride and groom, now would you?"

"Look, I suckered that yokel fair and square. I never pistolwhipped him and sat on his chest. I takes pride in being a gentle grifter, and it seems to me your methods border on sheer highway robbery, stranger."

7

Longarm shoved the muzzle of his .44 in one of Soapy Smith's nostrils and agreed, "I'll admit to a certain high-handedness this morning, as I am in a hurry and you have a rep for being testy to folks who approach you gentle. But, friendly or firm, I mean to recover that poor fool's roll, so where's it at? Do I have to run my hands over your shrinking flesh, or do you aim to hand it over polite?"

Soapy Smith rolled his eyes toward the bartender and growled, "Dammit, Henry, are you going to just stand there and watch a man get robbed at gunpoint?"

The bartender answered, "He ain't robbing me, Soapy, and if I was you, I'd give him the money. Modesty may forbid him to say it, but the man sitting on your chest with a double-action .44 in your nose answers to the name of Longarm. So, if it's all the same to the two of you, I mean to stay out of this discussion entire."

"Longarm?" Soapy gasped. "Hell's bells, why didn't you say so? Get off my chest and let's drink to it!"

"About that pilgrim's money, Soapy—"

"Shit, I'll give it back if it means all that much to you. I thought you were just some fool *mortal*, Longarm! Let me up and we'll do this friendly."

So Longarm rose and holstered his .44 as he extended a helping hand to the bruised and battered Soapy Smith. The latter moved to the bar, poured himself a stiff one, and downed it before he wheezed, "I got the money here, in this roll."

He took out a roll of bills wrapped in a rubber band and added, "I figure I took that chump for a rough eight hundred. I'll just count it out and we'll say no more about it."

But Longarm reached out, took the whole roll, and stuffed it in his coat pocket, saying, "He never gave exact figures, but I'm sure you'll agree a wedding present is in order, Soapy. After all, it ain't like you don't have a trade."

Soapy Smith's eyes widened as he saw his whole roll vanish and Longarm added sweetly, "I'll pay for the bottle there. It's only fair."

"Goddammit!" protested the con man. "There's over a thousand in that roll, and I only took the chump for eight hundred!"

"I'll take you at your word. The extra two hundred's for

8

damages and maybe a ribbon bow for Mary Lou."

"Dammit, I don't like being robbed of my own gold, Longarm."

Longarm said soberly, "Few people do, Soapy. But if I know you, you'll go on robbing them anyway. It's been nice jawing with you, but I have to get to the office before it closes for the day. So adios, you son of a bitch."

Longarm turned away, dropping a coin on the bar as he headed for the swinging doors. Behind him, Soapy Smith stared in confused rage for perhaps a full second. Then he growled deep in his throat and darted across the room toward the gun in the corner. Longarm turned with a weary smile, and as the con man dropped to one knee and snatched up the pearl-handled Walker, the more businesslike .44 in Longarm's big fist coughed a round into Smith and bounced him off the wall. Soapy Smith lay facedown, moaning in pain, and the bartender observed, "You only winged him, Longarm."

Longarm nodded, walked over to pick up the con man's gun again, and placed it on the bar, saying, "Better put this away and make sure no more kids play with it." He kicked Soapy gently and added, "I can see you'll likely live. Henry, here, will see about getting you a doc. Are you listening to me, Soapy?"

"I ain't going to forget this, Longarm. You've robbed me and I'm shot in the breast, but if I live, I'll come looking for you, hear?"

"That's what I wanted to talk to you about. You ain't shot in the breast. I aimed for your shoulder and that's what I hit. I didn't kill you just now, because killing folks in Denver is tedious as hell, with all the paperwork and such involved. But by now you ought to have learned I *could've* killed you if I wanted to. Are you paying attention, old son?"

"Go ahead and crow, you bastard. This day is your'n, but mine will come as soon as I'm up and about again."

"They were right," Longarm said. "You are one testy cuss, considering your chosen profession. What I was about to say, Soapy, is that I don't want to see you in Denver anymore. I was polite this time, because I figured eight hundred wasn't worth a killing. But it's come to me, as I've gotten to know you better, that you're a mighty worthless specimen. So I don't want to see you around here anymore. I have to get back on the job, and you'll likely want to bed down somewhere and nurse that shot-up shoulder. But as soon as you're up and about, I want you on a train to other parts. You've made your brag and I'm taking you up on it. So the next time I see you in Denver, even in church, I mean to gun you down like the dog you are."

"What if I gun you first?"

"Old son, you just had a chance to try that, so you know how dumb you're talking. You're leaving town, Soapy Smith. I ain't asking you, I'm telling you. Why don't you go to Canada, or better yet, Alaska? I doubt I'll ever be sent to Alaska, and I'll kill you sure the next time we meet. So, seeing this is the last time we'll ever be talking man to man, let me leave you with a piece of advice. You're going to have to cool that ornery temper of yours, Soapy. It ain't natural in a con man. Most marks tend to forgive a *jolly* con man, if he gives 'em back their gold with a sheepish smile. But your surly manners are going to get you killed. If not by me, by somebody else."

"You can just up and fuck yourself, you grinning bastard!"

Longarm chuckled and said, "That's what I mean, Soapy. I already said adios, so I'll be leaving. Don't ever let me see your ugly face again, for, like the Lakota say, I have spoken."

Billy Vail accepted Longarm's excuse, not because he liked it all that much, but because it was getting late and Billy had a lot on his mind. As Longarm sat in the red leather chair across the desk from his boss, the balding and pudgy chief marshal said, "I know you expected the afternoon off, but tell the ladies it'll have to be another time. You remember that gent called Timberline that you said you killed over in Salt Lake City a while back?"

"*Said* I killed him, hell! I killed him deader than a turd in a milk bucket. We shot it out on the marble steps of the Salt Lake Federal Building, and he rolled to the bottom with a busted neck as well as my lead in him."

Longarm fished out a cheroot and reflected, "It was an interesting case, as I think back on it. Timberline got his nickname from being taller than any gent has a right to grow. His real name was Cotton Younger, and they say he was kin to the

Younger Brothers, so when I figured out who he was—"

"Dammit," Vail cut in, "I know who Timberline was, or is. I sent you on the case in the first damn place."

Longarm struck a match and was about to light his smoke as Vail's last words sank in. Holding the flaming match, he frowned and repeated, "*Is*, Billy? Don't you mean *was*? I had it in my report about our shootout, and like I said, he lost."

"That's what I thought, too," said Vail. "But it seems we were fooled, for Timberline's alive and kicking and making more mischief than you can shake a stick at!"

The match burned down to Longarm's fingers as he stared, slack-jawed, at the serious florid face of Marshal Vail. He cursed and shook the flame out. He knew Vail didn't josh much, so he was likely serious. Longarm shook his head and said, "Somebody's telling fibs, Billy. I didn't just shoot that tall drink of water. I shot him in front of federal employees, and the way I know he busted his neck on the way down those marble steps is because I was at the autopsy."

"Did you see him buried, Longarm?"

Longarm took out another match, did it right this time, and blew some annoyed smoke out of his nostrils as he replied, "You know I caught me a train back to Denver right after the gunplay, so I can't say I acted as one of Timberline's pall-bearers. But, buried or stuffed, I left him cold and dead on a zinc table in the Salt Lake City Morgue. I don't know who's been raising Ned in the name of the late Cotton Younger, but it can't be him. Like I said, I killed him fair and square."

Vail picked up a flyer from his green blotter and read off, "'Suspect around seven feet tall, has pale, rabbitlike eyes and snow-white hair, although he appears to be no older than thirty.'"

Longarm nodded. "Yeah, he had his hair died black when we last tangled. That's why I didn't know who he was right off. They used to call him Cotton because of that cotton top. He's likely a part albino—or I mean he *was*."

"A man answering to this description just shot up the Aurora post office, Longarm."

"Do tell? Aurora's just outside the Denver city limits, Billy."

Vail looked disgusted and growled, "Tell me something I don't know. Tell me how many gents answering to a freak

11

description like that there might be west of the Big Muddy, old son."

Longarm took a drag of smoke and observed, "Well, giants ain't all that unusual . . ."

"Albino giants, robbing post offices and such, when they could make a good living in a tent show?"

"Hell, Billy, maybe this new freak is sensitive about his appearance. Whoever he may be, he can't be Timberline! You want me to ride out to Aurora and see if I can get a line on what this new owlhoot may be using as his handle?"

Vail shook his head and said, "Deputy Grenoble and some postal dicks are working on it in the first place, and we know what to call him in the second. He was with two other riders. The holdup went sour and they had to crawfish out. Witnesses say one of them called out to somebody named Timberline about getting out sudden and alive. So, as I study on this, Longarm, we have us a gent who looks like Timberline, who's called Timberline, following the family trade of the James-Younger clan that Timberline was raised to follow. How do you like her so far?"

"Not much. I'll allow that finding a double for Cotton Younger would be a chore, but bringing the original back to life would be too. I don't want to upset your stomach just before you go home to eat, Billy, but I was there when they cut him up on that autopsy table, and even if I was bragging about my bullet in him, *that* should have finished him!"

"Maybe he was tougher than he looked. He was a big tough jasper, right?"

"Billy, nobody comes that tough! I'll bet my life and throw in my retirement that the man I gunned in Salt Lake City was Cotton Younger and he was killed permanent. Some old boy who read about it in the paper is having some fun with us. Remember me telling you how I've always suspected there must be two or more runty jaspers bragging they are the one and only Billy the Kid? The Kid can't be all the places people have seen him, so—"

"You're not after that rascal, Longarm. You're after Timberline. He's working in my backyard and I feel foolish as hell about the way I marked that case 'closed' after you told me you'd nailed him."

Longarm's face went wooden-Indian and his voice took on a coldly polite tone as he asked quietly, "Are you accusing me of lying, Marshal Vail?"

Vail knew his tall deputy well enough to reply hastily, "Don't get your bowels in an uproar, old son. I don't doubt for an instant that you thought the man you gunned over in Salt Lake was Timberline. But you admit his hair was black when you shot him, right?"

"*Dyed* black, like I said. It was white at the roots when we looked him over careful, on the table. Aside from looking like Cotton Younger, let us not forget he was acting like Cotton Younger when I caught up with him. If you'll dig out that old report, you'll see he was shooting folks a lot as I hove into view."

Vail sighed and said, "I was reading your report just before you got here. The man you gunned surely had a gunning coming. But if we can assume he's dead for certain, what we have is his twin. Do you remember anything like that, Longarm?"

Longarm blew a thoughtful smoke ring. "No. I spent enough time on the trail of Cotton Younger to know him pretty good. He was an only child. I reckon his poor ma didn't have it in her to birth more than one such critter. He hailed from Clay County, and was distant kin to both the James and Younger lads. He rode on a couple of early jobs with the gang and then joined the army to avoid discussing his recent activities with the law. He deserted the Seventh Cav just in time to miss the Little Big Horn. He was up in the Bitter Creek country pretending to be an honest cowhand when you sent me after him on a false lead that turned out lucky. The man in those parts that everyone thought might have been him was somebody else, but seven-foot gents are sort of rare, and between one thing and another, I figured this other tall galoot fit better, so in Salt Lake, when I tried to arrest him peaceful—"

"Dammit, Longarm, I told you I've just been going over the report on that case. Back up and reconsider that first lead. What if the one we had down as Cotton Younger was Cotton Younger after all?"

Longarm looked disgusted and said, "He wasn't. And even if he was, he's dead too. Timberline shot lots of folks to throw me off. So everybody connected with that old case has been

13

cleared or buried." He blew another smoke ring and added, "I just came from a discussion of razzle-dazzle with a professional called Soapy Smith. I'd say someone was trying to con us, Billy. You'd hardly expect a man holding up a post office to use his right name, would you? Besides, lots of tall cowhands are called Timberline: It's a natural nickname for a man walking about with his head in the sky."

"What about the albino hair?"

"Snow on the peaks? How the hell should I know why a man has funny hair? Maybe he bleached it. The real Timberline dyed his white hair black so's we'd overlook his past. Maybe some old boy who thinks he's cute heard about the recent rider from the James-Younger gang and reversed the trick with a bottle. One thing's for sure, we won't find out by sitting here and jawing about it!"

Longarm rose. Vail asked where he thought he was going, and Longarm answered, "Out to look for the rascal, of course. How many seven-foot men with white hair could there be in Colorado at a given moment?"

Vail shook his bald head and said, "I have other deputies keeping an eye peeled here in Denver, Longarm. I'm sending you over to Salt Lake City."

"That's crazy, Billy. They just held up the post office in Aurora, not a serious ride from right here!"

Vail nodded, but insisted, "I told you the other deputies could handle it if this spooky big blond gent is dumb enough to spend even a day in our fair city after a holdup attempt. I want you to run over to Salt Lake and eliminate a possibility. My clerk has your tickets and travel vouchers and he's typing up an exhumation request for the Salt Lake law, so—"

Longarm bit down hard on his cheroot and swore under his breath. "I don't like gazing on folks who've been buried awhile, Billy. But wait a minute. Did you just say an *attempted* holdup? They didn't get anything from that post office out in Aurora?"

"No. I thought I told you they rode off in considerable dismay. The postmistress out there showed some spunk, and when they told her to open the boxes she produced a loaded pepperbox instead."

Longarm grinned wolfishly. "I am beginning to see the light. This lady running the Aurora post office wouldn't by any

14

chance be young and pretty, would she?"

"She might not curdle milk by smiling at it, but I told you other deputies are interviewing her and the other witnesses."

Longarm noticed how innocent his boss was looking; that meant they didn't want him anywhere near a gal who was a knockout and likely single. He said, "I'm surprised at you, Billy. Have you ever known me to commit forcible rape on any of the fillies working here in the federal building?"

Vail smiled benignly. "Well, maybe not forcible. But stay the hell away from that gal in Aurora anyway. She's already had a dismaying experience and the men who scared her are long gone. That's not the reason I'm sending you to Salt Lake, although, now that you mention it, I owe it to a fellow federal employee. I'm dead serious about wanting this Cotton Younger pinned down as dead or alive. So hold your nose as you have a look, and we'll play her by ear from there."

Longarm shrugged and went out to confront the pasty-faced male clerk playing the typewriter for Billy in the office out front. His papers weren't ready yet, so Longarm said he'd come back at noon for them. There might not be time to get out to Aurora and back, but he could wet his whistle before leaving on such a fool's errand.

Longarm knew it was ridiculous to ride all the way over the Rockies just to make sure a man he'd shot was dead, but that was the trouble with lawmen who spent too much time behind a desk. Billy had never seen the late Cotton Younger, alive or dead, so he wanted it official.

Chapter 2

Leaving the Federal Building, Longarm headed for a saloon he'd long known on a certain side street. The other federal employees who drank weren't supposed to do it during duty hours, either, so none of the regulars at the bar acknowledged his presence, and he returned the favor by pretending not to see them. He wasn't a man who needed strong drink to steady his nerves, but on the other hand it seemed dumb to face a meaningless mission cold sober. He studied his own reflection in the mirror over the bar, wondering if he was getting too old to take up cow-handling again. A top hand made almost as much as a deputy marshal, and the work wasn't much more boring. He hated that damned train to Salt Lake City. It would be a long enough ride to make a man stiff and too short to investigate any females he might meet. He'd see if there was any action along South Fourth Street before coming back, of course, but he doubted there'd be all that much. Mormon gals were sort of snooty, and there weren't many other gals worth looking at in the City of the Saints. He didn't much relish exhuming the late Cotton Younger, either. Timberline hadn't been down there long enough to be just bones, but he'd been in the ground too long to smell as fresh as a daisy. As he was trying to remember Timberline's face, he saw it, in the *mirror*! A man at least seven feet tall was in the doorway, staring sort of wildly at Longarm as he reached for the gun at his side!

Longarm spun and dropped on one knee as he got his own weapon out, and folks all about started yelling and milling like sheep. Some fool got in his line of fire as Longarm threw down on the doorway. When he had a clear shot again, the man was gone. Longarm sprang to his feet and tore out into the street, dropping behind a watering trough as he swept his surroundings with his gun muzzle and steel-gray eyes. The only figure near enough to matter was a short man in a derby hat, standing by a box camera set on a tripod. Longarm rose with a frown and asked, "Did you just see a tall galoot with white hair, mister?"

"I sure did," the photographer said. "He had a gun in his hand. He run north and around the corner." Then, as Longarm nodded curtly and started that way, the photographer added, "You'll never catch him now. But I got a picture of him."

Longarm took another step before he stopped, turned with a frown, and asked, "You *what*?"

"Took his picture. Just now. I can't say why, for he surely never asked. But as he bore down on me, looking mean and holding a gun, I squeezed the bulb by reflex. The camera ain't aimed anywhere in particular. I generally only take pictures of tourists and such when they ask, but—"

"Never mind how and why, dammit!" Longarm cut in, adding in a calmer tone, "I'm a deputy U.S. marshal, and the Justice Department will pay you for any picture you may have. How long does it take to develop those plates?"

"Only a few minutes, but I'm out here to make money, and if I have to go all the way down to the lab on Larimer—"

"I'll run the plate to a closer lab, if you'll unload that box. How much do I owe you?" Longarm cut in.

The street photographer slid the sealed plate out, but looked dubious as he said, "Gee, I don't know. I generally get two bits a shot, but if this is important—"

"It is." He handed the man a silver dollar and grabbed the plate from him with no further bartering. He remembered he'd left his change on the bar in the saloon, but he didn't go back for it. He'd only had a glimpse of the man in the doorway, and a man does not study features at such times. But if his would-be attacker had been caught on this plate, which was probably too much to hope for, they'd know better what they were looking for. They said the camera didn't lie, unless somebody retouched the negative, and this plate was a virgin!

He almost ran to a photo shop he remembered near Welton and Broadway, a few blocks away. A nice-looking gal wearing her brown hair piled high and her skirts in a Dolly Varden gasped in surprise as he tore in, waving the sealed photographic plate and yelling, "This is for Uncle Sam, and I need it developed pronto!"

Despite his unseemly entrance, the gal nodded and said, "I can see it's some sort of emergency, sir. The darkroom's back this way."

He followed her. Sure enough, it was dark as hell in the back. A candle stub glowed in a ruby jar, allowing him to see enameled trays and such as his eyes adjusted. The girl took the plate from him, slid the gelatin-covered glass from its metal container, and plopped it in a tray as Longarm asked her how long it would take and if he could smoke.

She said, "Give me twenty minutes or so, and smoke outside if you must. You'll ruin the negative if you strike a match."

Longarm grinned sheepishly and said, "I knew that. I wasn't thinking. I haven't met many ghosts and I'm sort of shook up."

Naturally she asked, politely, what the hell he was talking about, so he filled her in, learning in the process that her name was Elanore and that she owned the spread. For some reason she seemed a mite annoyed when he opined that it was unusual to find a gal running her own business.

"What's wrong with a woman owning her own business?" she asked frostily. "Are you one of those men who feel a woman should be kept pregnant in the summer and barefoot in the winter?"

Longarm chuckled. "Well, I don't hold with making a gal go barefoot in the winter."

She suppressed a smile and said, "It's developing, and it was a lucky shot. A little off center, but the face is all there."

Longarm peered over her shoulder as she fixed the image in another tray. "It's all black," he said.

"Of course," she replied. "It's the negative. Just let it set a moment and I'll run off a positive."

Her hair smelled nice and she hadn't gone all flustery when he'd risked a bawdy remark, but he was more anxious to get a better look-see at that gent who'd tried to gun him than he was to find out the details of her private life. She moved the plate to a box and pulled a cord, flooding the room with sunlight from an overhead skylight. As she opened the top of the box, she explained, "This will fix another image in reverse, and then when we develop that—"

"I savvy some about photography, Miss Elanore," he cut in. "While we're on the fine points, though, I'd like to get some suspicions out of the way. You might say being suspicious is my job."

She closed the box, saying, "That's enough," and drew the curtains again before she asked, "What do you suspect me of, Marshal?"

"I'm only a deputy marshal and I don't suspect *you* of anything, Miss Elanore. I ran this plate over here instead of to the lab that photographer used for a reason. I remembered passing this place, and it didn't seem sensible that you could be in cahoots with him."

Elanore blinked in surprise and asked, "Cahoots? What on earth is there to be in cahoots about?"

He said, "Photographers. I know the camera ain't supposed to lie, but ever since I found out the photographer who took the one official picture of Billy the Kid was a personal friend of his, I've always wondered. None of the descriptions we have match the dumb-looking boy in that picture, and you can see, if you look close, that the picture was flip-flopped to make the kid look left-handed, which I know for a fact he ain't."

Elanore pursed her lips and said, "Oh, I see. You're wondering if that street photographer could have tried to trick you, right?"

"It didn't hit me right off, but yes, ma'am, it did strike me a mite odd that a man with a box camera just happened to be there as the man I was chasing tore by. Is there any way a sneaky gent could set things up so's a picture was already in the camera, if you follow my drift?"

The girl took the positive plate from the lightbox and put it in the developing tray as she mused aloud, "I don't see how.

20

If the plate was already developed ahead of time, I'd have noticed. I can assure you it was a fresh and undeveloped plate when I started. Look, we're starting to see a positive now."

"Yeah. Try it another way. Suppose you had an old plate, taken of some old boy while he was still alive, only you waited until long after and—"

Elanore shook her head and said, "It wouldn't work, Mr. Long. You told me this man you're after has been dead for some time, right?"

"Yeah, and any pictures he sat for would have been took a lot earlier, for he'd been hiding out a few years in the mountains when I caught up with him. How long does an undeveloped plate last?"

She thought a moment before she replied, "In this dry climate? Six weeks at the most. The gelatin emulsion on the glass dries out and starts to flake if you don't use a wet plate soon after it's prepared."

"And that photographer was using wet plates, right?"

"Yes, it's still the cheapest process, although the print I'm making for you is on new paper that lasts much longer. I see it's about ready to fix, too."

She moved the positive print to the last tray, swished it about, and opened the blinds again. Longarm stared down morosely at the face in the photograph. He could see the cornice of a typical Denver walkup in one corner of the background, which was mostly sky. The camera had been aimed up at the moving gunman, giving his features a sinister cast they really didn't need. The man in the picture was Timberline, or Cotton Younger. Longarm never forgot a face he'd swapped shots with at close range. He sighed and said, "I sure wish you could tell me this was trick photography, Miss Elanore."

"I'm afraid I can't," she said. "Is that the man? The one who's supposed to be dead?"

"Yep. Some other folks saw him, I just saw him, and now we have an infernal photograph of him! So the ornery cuss is alive and kicking and seems to be gunning for yours truly. It's no secret that I visit that taproom regular, and had I not been admiring myself in the mirror when he busted in loaded for bear, we wouldn't be having this discussion on the matter. While I don't know how *he* done it, I suspicion that when I

21

get around to dying, I'll likely stay that way!"

"Brrr," she said, giving a little shudder. "It's spooky to think about either way. This picture proves he's alive, but I don't believe in ghosts, do you?"

"Ain't met many who allowed themselves to be photographed on the streets of Denver in broad daylight, ma'am. I'd best pay for your time and trouble and run this over to cheer up Marshal Vail. I do so hate a man who says I told you so, but he's like that, at times."

She looked sort of wistful as she said, "I won't charge the U.S. government for doing so little, Mr. Long. Uh, do you have a first name?"

"Yeah, more's the pity. You can call me Custis, when and if I get back from Salt Lake City."

"Oh? Do you have to leave right away?"

"I sure do. If Cotton Younger's up and about, some imposter is occupying his grave over there, and it's time we found out who the skunk is . . . or was."

The banjo clock on the oak-paneled wall of Marshal Vail's office said 12:35 when Longarm came in. Behind the desk, Billy Vail wore his bushy eyebrows in a deep frown as he snapped, "Where in hell have you been now? I promised my wife I'd make it home for dinner by one, and you have a train to catch!"

Longarm hooked his rump over the corner of Vail's desk and said, "I know," as he took the sheaf of prints out and spread them like a card hand on the green blotter. They were all the same picture of the same man. "Had these printed on that handy new paper. You'll want to spread these around to the boys, and tintypes are tedious to carry."

Vail picked up a photo, scowled at it, and said, "All right, who might this jasper be, dammit?"

Longarm blinked, then said, "Oh, that's right, you never saw the rascal in the flesh. That's Cotton Younger, alias Timberline. We just met up again in the Parthenon Saloon. A street photographer caught him as you see him, on the fly. I thought it was impossible too, so I went back to the scene of the accident and hunkered down like I was a camera. That corniced building

22

you see in the right-hand corner of the picture is really there, and a savvy young lady tells me the plates were genuine in the first damned place."

"Yeah," Vail said, "I can see he's a moose, and I see the white hair under that throwed-back sombrero. It's funny, but I had a different picture of Younger in my mind."

"I know the feeling," Longarm replied. "That's why it took me some time to kill him the first time. No matter how good a description we have on an owlhoot, we never picture him exactly right in our heads before we actually see him. I remember this one galoot I was after a few years back. The wanted flyers said he had a tattoo on his wrist. So there I was, drinking with him like a big-ass bird, when he raised his arm and I saw it sudden. I mean, anyone who'd ever seen him before would have spotted him on sight, tattoo or no, but—"

"Don't tell your granny how to suck eggs," Vail interrupted. "Fill me in on how you came by these infernal photographs."

So Longarm brought Vail up to date. When he'd gotten to the wistful parting from Elanore, Vail said, "I see it all. About this killer, that is. This may come as a great surprise to you, but I don't care if you made a date with that she-male or not. And you're right about it being generally known that you drink at the Parthenon during duty hours, and I've been meaning to talk to you about that. What I can't figure out is why Cotton Younger come gunning for you in the first place."

"Maybe he's sore at me for killing him the last time we met?" Longarm suggested.

"That's my point. In the first place, you must have gunned someone else, and in the second, you're good. After trying that stickup just outside the city limits, any man with a lick of sense would know he's hotter than a two-dollar pistol in these parts. That big albino moose must look in the mirror once in a while, for you can see he's clean-shaven. So why in thunder would a man who stands out in a crowd ride out of a holdup and into the center of town to gun the last lawman anyone in his right mind would try to?"

Longarm reached into his coat pocket for a smoke as he said, "That's easy. He ain't *got* a lick of sense. Though, come to think on it, the last time I was after Cotton Younger he was slick and sneaky. What would I have been doing this coming

Monday, had you not sent me over to Salt Lake to dig up graves?"

Vail looked up and said, "Don't talk dumb. You know you won't be going now. The son of a bitch is here in Denver, and identified for certain."

"I know I ain't going to Salt Lake just yet. But I told that clerk out front that I was, when I picked up my travel gear. I sent him home, by the way. He said he was late for a date with his true love. I told a mess of other folks I was leaving on the Salt Lake train in an hour, too. One of 'em was right pretty and I suspicion she likes me. But duty comes before pleasure. You still ain't told me what I'd have been assigned to this coming week, Billy, were it not for spooks popping up out of the past."

Vail thought and said, "Hell, nothing important. Things have been sort of quiet of late, and I had you slated to lend to old Donovan down the hall."

"Federal Prosecutor Donovan?"

"Sure. You've escorted prisoners to court for him before, remember? It's one of the jobs we do, in case you've forgotten the dull parts. He's trying a case next week and the scoundrel he's trying to jail can't make bail, so I figured you'd sit next to him in court and make sure he pays attention to the judge instead of flying out the window."

Longarm picked up one of the pictures and put it in a breast pocket as he asked, "What's this federal trial about, Billy?"

"How should I know? We never made the arrest. I think it was Treasury agents who brought the rascal in. But U.S. marshals get the boring court duty. What difference does it make?"

Longarm glanced at the wall clock and said, "Don't know. I'll ask old Donovan or the folks in his office, if they ain't all lit out by now." He rose and added, "After that I aim to work the street, sort of sneaky, so if anybody asks, I'm supposed to be on my way to Salt Lake."

Vail nodded, but asked, "Where will you be, in case I need you? Checking out no-questions-asked roominghouses and such?"

Longarm said, "I'll try that too. Denver's a big town, but how many albino giants can there be on one block? You get on home before your dinner cools, Billy. I'll get word to you if anything comes up over the weekend."

"Right. You coming to work Monday? It's hard to tell, some mornings."

Longarm pursed his lips and said, "Monday's a long ways off, Billy. Lord willing and the creeks don't rise, I'll be one place or another by then. You'd best carry me on the books as on the road. I hate to be a creature of habit with some gent gunning for me."

Vail agreed, and Longarm left the marshal's office to walk down to that of the federal prosecutor, at the end of the hall. He tried the door and found it still open, despite the hour, so he went in.

A radiant blond was playing the typewriter inside. She filled out her lace dickie right nicely for such a slim-waisted little gal, and sat her stool atop what he couldn't help picturing as two scoops of vanilla ice cream. She made his mouth water and he remembered that her name was Nancy Moore, although he'd been trying to forget it. Nan looked up with a more-than-friendly smile and said, "Why, Custis, what a nice surprise! I'm afraid Mr. Donovan has left for the day, but I stayed late to type this brief, so we have the office all to ourselves."

Longarm kept his face sober as he said, "I came by to ask about this here trial you folks wanted me to lend a hand on. I am on my way to Salt Lake City, but if it's important I could make sure Billy Vail replaces me with someone sensible. Who's your boss trying to put in jail, and why?"

"Oh, it's just a land fraud, Custis," Nan said. "Some piggy cheated Uncle Sam by filing on more land than the law allows, using proxies. It's open-and-shut. We have the scoundrel dead to rights."

Longarm frowned, puzzled. "You need an armed guard and you're holding the land hog without bail?"

"He seems a rather primitive type," she explained. "Shot our process server in the thigh when he was invited to come in peacefully. It took a team of Treasury agents and some leg irons before we convinced him he should stand trial."

"Sounds dumb. What's his name?"

Nan thought and said, "Hansen. Gus Hansen, I think. He's

some kind of foreigner and doesn't speak much English. But English or no, it's against the law to file false homestead claims."

She rose and stepped around him to close the door he'd left ajar as she added, "Let's not worry about the trial next week, Custis. I told you before, I believe in living for today, remember?"

Longarm remembered. He had a firm and sensible policy about messing with gals where he worked, and he'd been having one hell of a time keeping that in mind around Miss Nancy Moore. This was the second time she'd caught him alone, and he figured there was something wrong with her glands or something. She was as pretty as a picture and built like the well-known brick edifice, but up till now he'd defended his virtue. So this time Nan didn't wait for him to make the first move. She walked up to him as bold as brass, snatched the lit cheroot from his surprised lips, and planted a saucy kiss in its place.

Being human, Longarm kissed back as Nan wrapped herself around him. But eventually he came up for air and gasped, "Dammit, honey, we are smack in the middle of the U.S. Federal Building!"

"So call me patriotic. Everyone's gone home for the day, you fool!"

"No they ain't There's guards and janitors and such all over the damned premises, and besides that—"

She kissed him again, and reached out with one hand to lock the door behind him. His body was betraying his good sense, and he could only hope she'd think that was a hidden gun she was rubbing her pelvis against down there. He could tell from the way she moved that she felt it.

The next time they came up for air she purred, "Oh, you do kiss nicely. Pick me up and carry me, Custis. It's more romantic that way."

"Carry you?" He frowned. "Carry you where? We're in an infernal *office*, girl!"

"Haven't you ever made love on an office sofa? There's a big one in Mr. Donovan's chambers, darling. I told you he's gone for the day."

She saw he had no intention of sweeping her off her feet, so she took him firmly in hand and started dragging him to his

26

doom as she pleaded, "Don't be shy, darling. The door's locked and we have this place all to ourselves until Monday morning."

Longarm knew he was in trouble now, no matter what. It was dumb as hell to romance where you worked, but if he let her down at this stage in the proceedings, he was going to have a plate of hell-hath-no-fury facing him on a pretty steady basis. Given a choice of consequences, he figured he might as well pick the one that would likely feel the best.

She led him into the inner sanctum of the federal prosecutor, and he could see that Donovan rated better with the taxpayers than poor old Billy Vail did, for the prosecutor's chambers were downright luxurious. Nan pulled him down on the big leather sofa. He noticed that the blinds were already drawn. He didn't know whether she'd been expecting him or whether the blinds were drawn to spare the furnishing from Denver's harsh sunlight. It was broad daylight outside, and he could hear the clang of a streetcar mocking him as Nan started to unbutton her blouse, saying, "I don't know what's come over me. I don't generally do this sort of thing on such short notice, you know."

He said, "Well, look, if you'd rather hold out for a ring . . ."
She laughed. "All of us are looking for a ring, but a good time will do if nobody offers."

"Oh? So a good time will be had by all?"

"Not all. Just the pretty ones."

"I didn't know I was pretty, Nan."

"I don't know how pretty you are, either. Why don't you take off your pants and let me see?"

He laughed, feeling a bit more sure of himself now that he understood the rules of the game. It was still against his policy to mess with gals this close to home, but Nan was an older hand at office romance than he'd suspected. While she was an obvious little bawd, it didn't show during business hours. He'd thought, the first time she started up with him, she was one of those gals who'd want to take a gent home to meet her mother after a little slap-and-tickle. But he could see from the way she was shucking herself out of her duds that Nan enjoyed sex for its own sake, like a sensible old pard. So, since she was getting ahead of him in the first place and had less to take off in the second, Longarm proceeded to peel. He let his duds

27

fall any old way they wanted and was working on his infernal tight boots as Nan lay back, naked save for her high-button shoes and striped stockings, to moan, "Oh, hurry, won't you? I'm so hot I can taste it!"

"I noticed," he said as he kicked off the last boot and got free of his wool pants and longjohns. He rolled over, naked, to mount her. She spread her thighs in welcome and dug her nails into his buttocks as he entered her with a hiss of pleasure. Nan hissed too, and said, "Oh, nice. I like big men, no matter how tall they are!"

Her rollicking rump really was as round and white as two scoops of vanilla ice cream, but there the resemblance ended, for her flesh was as warm as melting butter. He came fast, as any man would have, and then settled down to a steady lope to let her catch up. He knew he'd be able to peak at least three times without stopping, in anything this nice, but as he settled in, some of his wits returned and he couldn't help wondering how many times she'd done this very thing on this very sofa, and with whom. Her boss, Mr. Donovan, was sort of nice-looking in a distinguished-older-man sort of way, but he decided it wasn't likely. Nan would doubtless go for it, but old Donovan looked too smart to mess with the hired help. Besides, if she was screwing her boss on a regular basis, she wouldn't be so anxious to seduce fellow workers, and she acted as though she hadn't been getting as much as she needed of late.

As if she'd read his mind, Nan said, "Oh, let me get on top. I had no idea I'd be this randy. You should have done this sooner, you brute!"

Longarm laughed and rolled off to exchange places with her. Nan got one bent knee against the back of the sofa and placed her other foot on the rug for leverage as she eased onto his erection, closing her eyes with a satisfied sigh as she settled herself on it to the hilt. She leaned forward with her weight on her locked elbows and her amazing torso at a forty-five degree angle, her ample breasts bouncing all over as she began to move up and down in a rotary motion. Longarm raised his lips to kiss a turgid nipple and she laughed and said, "Your mustache tickles, but I like the way your lips feel. Is that why you go around with those dreadful cheroots in your mouth all

28

the time? I can still smell that cheap tobacco of yours, even in here."

Longarm sniffed and stopped what he was doing to observe, "So can I. Where did you put my smoke after you snatched it?"

She rose, twisted teasingly, and slid down his shaft as she purred, "I don't remember. Who cares, darling?"

He sniffed again and said, "I do. I smell something burning, and it ain't a cheroot! Let me up, gal. I think we've set the building on fire!"

"Don't stop, I'm coming!" she pleaded as Longarm braced an elbow under himself to rise and investigate. He didn't just *smell* smoke now. He could see that the room was filling with it! He swore and swung his feet to the rug, with Nan's arms and legs wrapped around him as she went on with her orgasm or whatever the hell she was doing. She was a little gal, so he just got up and headed for the front office with her clinging to the front of him like a limpet. He would have found the new position more enjoyable had he not seen the flames from the wastebasket in the corner near the hall door.

"Jumping Judas, turn me loose!" he yelled as he strode over and kicked the metal wastebasket on it's side with his bare foot. The room was filled with blue smoke from waist-level up. When he tried to bend over and put the fire out, he lost his balance and fell to the tile floor atop her, driving his shaft deeper and making her cry out with mingled pain and pleasure. He reached out and stood the wastebasket on its head to smother the flames, while Nan sobbed, "Oh, harder, harder, harder! I love it on the floor! The tile is so cold . . ."

Just then, somebody started pounding on the door and even Nan froze as a voice called out, "Anybody in there? Where's the fire?"

Nan whispered, "Oh my God, it's the hall watchman!"

"I know," Longarm said. Then, still mounted on the blond, he called out in a jovial tone, "We noticed the smoke, thank you. It's coming from outside, I think. We just got around to closing the windows."

"That you, Mr. Donovan?"

"Yes, I'm working late," Longarm replied, thrusting deeper

29

as Nan bit her lip and shook her head at him pleadingly.

Out in the hall, the watchman jingled his keys and said, "Well, just so the fire ain't in any of these offices. Can I fetch you anything, Mr. Donovan? Cuppa coffee or such?"

Longarm started slowly and deliberately to screw Nan harder as he called back, "No thanks, we've got all the comforts of home in here. You just run along, old son. We're sort of busy."

As they heard the watchman's footsteps fade away, Nan suddenly laughed hysterically and said, "Oh my, you have played this game with someone in the next room, haven't you?"

He said, "Not more often than I've had to, but since we're old friends, I'll confide to you that it calls for a cool head in an emergency, like Daddy waking up. Don't ever throw a lit smoke in the wastebasket again, girl. Aside from almost burning down the building, you came close to getting us both fired!"

She laughed again and said, "I know, but wasn't it fun? Listen, I have a room up on Lincoln, near Colfax. I'm not supposed to have visitors after dark, but as I see you're a man who can keep his wits..."

He said, "Like to. Can't. I'm supposed to be on the Salt Lake flyer at this very moment. We'll have to put off any further fornication after we finish this here session." He moved experimentally and added, "Speaking of which, could we go back to the sofa? This tile floor ain't doing a thing for my knees."

She smiled up at him and said, "It's even harder on my tailbone, now that the novelty's worn off. Let's get up, but forget the sofa. There's something else I'd like to try."

He dismounted and helped her to her feet, running his eyes over her copious curves with renewed admiration in the brighter light of the front-office gaslight.

Nan led him to her typing desk and said, "Sit down."

He did so, with a frown, but said, "This is silly, Nan. I can't think of a thing I want to type in my birthday suit."

"I'll do the typing," she said, and, suiting actions to her words, sat in his lap, guiding his semi-erect shaft into her soft interior as she did so. He leaned back, bemused, as he felt himself rising fully to the occasion. Nan arched her back to take it deeper and began to type. He laughed and said, "This is surely a crazy way to write a letter, Nan."

She began to bounce in time to her typing as she said, "I know. I'm sort of warm-natured, as you may have noticed. Sometimes, sitting here in this molded wood chair, I get all hot and bothered. There's that sort of high ridge in the seat, meant to fit between your cheeks."

"I feel it agin my tailbone, now that you mention it."

"It rubs right against me as I'm trying to type. Sometimes it makes me so hot that, well, you won't believe this, but I sometimes come, sitting here and typing like butter wouldn't melt in my mouth."

He laughed and said, "I believe you. I had this teacher in school, back in West-by-God Virginia, who used to look sort of funny as she sat on the corner of her desk, sort of scrooching about as she scolded me after class. She used to keep me after class a lot, for some infernal reason. I was growed and gone before I suspicioned why."

Nan stopped typing, gripped the edges of her desk, and bounced harder as she closed her eyes and observed, "I'll bet I know why, too! Did you ever to do this to your poor, frustrated teacher?"

"No, more's the pity. She was sort of nice looking, as I study back on it. But you know how old everybody seems to you when you're a schoolboy."

He closed his own eyes and pictured the almost-forgotten young woman in that long-ago-and-far-away little red schoolhouse. Like most men, Longarm always remembered the ones he *hadn't* had with more longing than some he'd had. He'd forgotten that schoolmarm's name, and he was still mighty riled about the way she'd picked on him for no reason at all. But even as a boy he'd been uncomfortably aware of the wild look in her eyes and the earthy odor of her body as she'd loomed over him, alone in the classroom. As it all came back to him he pretended he was back there, sitting on a hard school seat, with that dark and sort of broody-looking teacher bouncing on him instead of that corner of her desk.

As he came he murmured, "You should have told me sooner, teacher, for between us we sure wasted some good times on your desk and my schoolboy fist!"

Nan joined him in orgasm, lowering her golden tresses to the keyboard as she moaned and sat quietly pulsating. Longarm

31

knew that when a man was keeping it up by thinking about other gals it was time to stop; from here on it was more showing off than pleasure. He knew the naughty typist expected compliments on her performance, as well she might, so he said, "I'd sure like to do this some more, Nan. But that infernal flyer will be pulling out for Salt Lake any minute."

"Can we do this some more when you get back?"

"Hell, try and stop me! But we're sure going to have to be careful next time. Does your boss have any notion you're so casual in your ways?"

Nan laughed and said, "I told you, butter wouldn't melt in my mouth when I have my clothes on. Don't worry, darling. The old dear thinks I'm as pure as the driven snow."

"Let's keep it that way, then. Mum's the word here at the Federal Building, and we'll try and work something out at my place. I've a furnished room across Cherry Creek. My landlady don't allow visitors either, but she's a sound sleeper."

"Oh, that sounds adventurous! The other side of Cherry Creek's supposed to be highly improper. I've never been there. When will you take me?"

"I'll let you know. After I get back from Salt Lake I may have a few things to tie up before I run off with you."

This seemed to satisfy Nan, and it wasn't exactly a lie. He did have some things to take care of before he could smuggle her to his furnished room. One of them was named Sue, and as far as he knew she was still waiting for him there.

Sue wasn't. He'd forgotten where she said she worked, but at the Black Cat she'd allowed that she was a working gal, and when he'd asked if she meant the kind of working girl one usually met in the Black Cat, she'd seemed sort of anxious to prove she didn't charge. She likely could have, and made a fortune. But she did something else for a living, and that was likely where she'd lit out to, without leaving a note. The small furnished room still smelled of her perfume and other odors but, praise the Lord, the landlady hadn't been up here to make the bed yet. Longarm opened the window to let some of Sue escape. There was a gentle breeze from the mountains, so he knew the room would soon smell more like Denver. Denver smelled like burning leaves. He'd never figured out why. It made sense for a town to smell like burning leaves in the fall, but Denver smelled that way all year. He spied a hairpin on the rumpled sheet and put it in his vest pocket. There was nothing much he could do about the spots on the sheet. The landlady never commented on them, if she noticed. Sometimes Longarm's landlady looked at him sort of funny in the hall, but even the time he and that Mexican gal had busted the bedsprings, she'd never said anything about it. Of course, his paying for the damage might have helped. He had a steady job and it was likely harder to collect regular rent over in this neighborhood. But he tried to keep his nocturnal activities down to a roar. He hoped his landlady appreciated his efforts as much as he appreciated hers.

As long as he was here, Sue or no, Longarm changed his shirt and underwear, leaving any lingering traces of Nancy Moore for the Chinese laundry to worry about. He checked his .44 and derringer, got a fresh supply of smokes, and let himself out.

He wondered why he felt wistful as he retraced his steps along the cinder paths of the Cherry Creek shantytown. Sue had been nice in bed, and her black hair and athletic, big-boned body had been an interesting contrast to the vanilla ice cream he'd just had. But it was mighty early for a man to be getting horny again. What the hell was the matter with him? Two gals in less than twelve hours were more than enough for any man; such overindulgence was likely dangerous to his health. Yet, between them, Sue and Nan had left him broody and unsatisfied. Like most knockaround gents, Longarm had a secret romantic side. Both women had treated him just the way every man said he'd like a gal to treat him, with no bullshit about moonlight and roses. And he couldn't think of a thing either woman could have done to pleasure him more. But as he crunched along in the afternoon sunlight, it seemed as if neither event had ever happened, as though he'd just come out of a cathouse after a quick roll with some uncaring gal whose name he didn't know.

"Howdy, Longarm," a voice was saying, and Longarm looked up to see a uniformed beat cop coming his way, twirling his billy and looking hot and stuffy in his high wool collar.

Longarm recognized him from earlier and replied, "Howdy

your own self. Did that pilgrim ever get home to Mary Lou with his money?"

The copper nodded with a chuckle and said, "I heard what you done to Soapy Smith too. It's all over the railroad yards. If I'd been you, I'd have finished the sidewinder then and there. That Soapy Smith's a bad one."

"I noticed. But I hardly ever kill anyone unless I'm forced to. I sort of promised to finish him off the next time I see him this side of the Wyoming line."

The copper said, "Heard that around the yards too. Old Henry told his other regulars all about your discussion with Soapy Smith. Henry thinks you're playing with fire. Soapy has a rep he's proud of, and he's either got to crawfish or kill you now. They do say he don't like to crawfish much."

Longarm took out two smokes, handed one to the copper, and lit up before he said, "It's my sincere hope that Soapy is just blowing bubbles. Do you know a street photographer who hangs out near the Parthenon Saloon?"

The copper took a drag on his own smoke and answered, "Sure. His name's Stubbs. Flash Stubbs. They call him Flash because he has this pan of flash powder for taking pictures in the dark, and—"

"Never mind that part. I just wanted to make sure he belongs in the scenery hereabouts. I bought a picture off him earlier today, and it ain't often we get that lucky."

Longarm took out the photograph of Cotton Younger and showed it to the beat man. "This gent was fixing to gun me in the back when he had second thoughts and ran by Flash Stubbs and his box camera. Does his face mean anything to you?"

The copper frowned down at the picture and shook his head. "Can't say I've seen him around town. Of course, I don't get out to the fancy parts east of the Capitol grounds, but this white-haired gent rings no bells with me in the parts that white cowhands frequent."

Longarm nodded as he considered how a seven-foot albino dressed in rough trail duds would stand out in the parts where either Mexicans or sissy types hung out. He said, "Well, he just scared hell out of me near the center of Denver, and in case you're wondering, he's Cotton Younger, alias Timberline and other things too dirty to mention."

The copper's jaw dropped as he studied the picture again and said, "So that's the Timberline that tried to hold up the Aurora post office? Funny, I had him pictured different."

"I know. We're sending copies of this out to other lawmen. Ought to make it easier, knowing his features better. But even allowing for the mind's eye not being perfect, we're still left with how a seven-foot cowboy with white hair seems to move about so invisible."

"Hell, you saw him, Flash Stubbs saw him, and the folks at the post office in Aurora saw him, didn't they?"

"Yeah. But where the hell has he been between times? Do you reckon there's a hotel or cathouse in Denver who doesn't know we're looking for a giant with snow-white hair?"

"I doubt it. But some folks are shy about going to the law about a customer."

"Bullshit. There's a mess of reward money on that snow-white head, and he's not a Colorado rider."

"He must have some friends in town. There was others riding with him when he tried to rob the post office, remember?"

Longarm started to shake his head. Then he nodded and said, "You'll make detective any day now. He has to be hiding out in some private home, for he'd have been spotted by now in the usual drift-through places. It's been nice talking to you, but I have to catch a train."

"Oh? going someplace?"

"Salt Lake. Federal case," said Longarm, walking on with no further explanation. He didn't know whether he'd missed the flyer or not. It didn't matter, since he wouldn't be on it. But the more folks thought he was out of town, the more folks might be surprised to see him turn up.

He came to the steel-frame bridge spanning Cherry Creek and headed over to the main part of town. Longarm suspected that the man who'd named Cherry Creek had been drunk at the time. There were no cherries growing anywhere near it, and the term "creek" seemed a little grand for it, too. On the rare occasions when it rained on the Arkansas Divide, Cherry Creek could overflow its banks, but most of the time it was a sort of sluggishly moving series of puddles running toward the Platte over flat wet sand.

As he crossed the bridge, Longarm saw some schoolboys

playing on the creek bottom. Kids in Denver never took their shoes off to play in Cherry Creek. The idea was to hop from one sandbar to the next without getting wet. Doing it barefoot would have been even more pointless, as the water in the deepest parts was barely ankle-deep. The kids waved up at him and he waved back, for he'd been a kid at one time, and he figured it must be as frustrating today as it was then.

He'd just made it to the north end of the bridge when one of the kids yelled out, "Hey, cowboy, look out behind you!"

Because he'd been a kid once, the tall deputy sensed that it wasn't a game. He dove forward, grabbed a rail post, and spun around as he dropped to his haunches just in time for a bullet to pluck the pancaked Stetson from his head.

His own gun drawn, Longarm yelled to the kids, "Get clear, dammit!" as he rose gingerly with the slim steel post between him and the gunfire. But though a haze of blue smoke hung between the silent buildings on the far side, there was nothing there worth shooting at.

The three schoolboys had run up the north bank, and while two hung back, one kid in corduroy knickers and wet shoes came toward him, calling out, "Are you shot, cowboy?"

Longarm bent to pick up his hat, glanced at the bullet hole in the crown, and said, "Not serious. I'm not a cowboy, either. I'm a lawman, so I'd take it kindly if you could give me a better notion of who just tried to bring me to an untimely end."

The boy said breathlessly, "Gosh, a lawman! The man who shot at you was over yonder, aiming from the corner of that house with the green shutters. He was pointing a rifle gun at you. He's likely behind that house right now, right?"

"Wrong. There's a copper up the street a ways, and if the bushwhacker didn't know it, he soon will. He'd still be shooting if he was dumb enough to hang about after missing. But you say you saw him, and I thank you. So tell me what the rascal looked like."

The boy thought and said, "Gee, I dunno. He was a grown man. Dressed cow, like you."

"I'll have you know this is a store-bought suit. But I follow your drift. Listen to me, boy. I know all grownups look a lot alike to you, but was he taller or shorter than me?"

"Uh, I can't say. He was peering around a corner at you.

36

He looked big and as mean as you."

"Thank you. Did he by any chance have white hair?"

"White hair? He had on a cowboy hat. I couldn't see what kind of hair he had under it."

Longarm spotted the copper he'd talked to earlier, coming their way at a trot, on the far bank. He told the boy, "Look at that copper, and as he passes the house with the green shutters, tell me if he's taller or shorter than the gent with the rifle."

The boy nodded, and as the copper waved his stick and headed across the bridge to join them, the boy said, "The man with the rifle was taller, way taller."

The copper slid to a halt and looked confused, so Longarm said, "The rifle shot you just heard was aimed at me. As you can see, it missed. Is there a candy store around here?"

"Sure," the copper replied, looking even more confused, "a couple of blocks up Curtis, that way, but this is sure a peculiar time to think about candy, Longarm!"

Longarm holstered his gun, reached in his pants pocket and said, "You're likely getting old and set in your ways. This young gent here just saved my hide and, even better, got a look at Cotton Younger. How tall are you, six feet?"

"More like five-eleven, but what's that got to do with candy stores?"

"The boy here says the bushwhacker was taller, way taller than you. I reckon you didn't see any giant toting a rifle on the far bank, so he lit out after missing me a second time."

Longarm handed the boy a coin and said, "Listen, pard, I want a promise from you about this here reward money, hear?"

The boy blinked down at his palm and said, "Mister, this here is an eagle! It's ten dollars in gold!"

"Hell, I knew that. I'd give you more, but it would only lead you into temptation. You'd likely save it. Are you listening to me, pard?"

"Wow, a ten-dollar eagle! What do you want me to promise, mister?"

"You have to spend it foolish. A present ain't a present if it's sensible. You have folks to feed and clothe you, as I can see, so you can't tell 'em about our deal. I want you and your two friends to run up to that candy store and blow it all on

37

total useless pleasure. If I ever hear about you wasting a dime of my hard-earned wherewithal on anything sensible, I'll be sore as hell."

The boy grinned from ear to ear as he asked, "Do we have to spend it all on candy, mister? There's this box kite in the window, and—"

"Box kites are within the law, and you can buy all the tops and marbles you've a mind to. Just so you and your pals spend it all on kid stuff."

The boy turned and ran over to his friends, yelling, as the copper said, "That was right decent of you. We'd best report what happened."

Longarm said, "You report it all you want. I *know* what happened. It's a waste of time looking for him over there now, and since he seems to have a hard-on for yours truly, we'll likely meet again anyway. I'm sorry to keep parting like this, but I still have a train to catch."

As he turned away, the boy he'd rewarded came shyly back, saying, "I forgot to say thanks, and I got a question."

"Question away, son."

"Well, I know you said we were to spend it all on ourselves, but I got this pesky kid sister, and there's this rag doll over to the store that she might like, so would that be fair?"

Longarm put out his hand and said, "What's your name, boy?"

"Larry, Larry Wilson."

"Well, I'm Custis Long and from now on we are pards. You go along and buy that dolly for your pesky sister, Larry. But for God's sake don't make a habit of it!"

Chapter 3

The town of Aurora was no more than a wide spot in the stage route, six or seven miles east of the Denver city limits, occupied mostly by horny toads and jackrabbits who hardly paid enough city tax to matter. But the little town hung on, serving as a post office and shopping center for the spreads and homesteads in the area. There weren't many of those, either, for the rolling prairie due east of Denver was drier than the more favored parts closer to the mountains, and no farther from town.

Longarm knew the horsedrawn streetcar line didn't extend that far east, so he rode out to Aurora on his own McClellan rig and a buckskin gelding he'd borrowed from one of his few friends in town who didn't think he was partway to Salt Lake by now. He'd forgotten how small the place was until he got there. A man riding fast could have passed it thinking Aurora was a big headquarters spread. The cluster of frame buildings stood stark on the prairie. Most of the paint or whitewash they might once have boasted had been bleached and blasted off by the wind and sun. Longarm reined in by the diminutive post

39

office and tethered his mount to a sun-silvered hitching post. The post office was no bigger than a railroad workman's shanty. Since the stage no longer passed through, it was more a sub-station for the Denver post office than anything else. Yet three grown men had tried to hold it up. He wondered about that as he mounted the wooden steps and went inside.

A little gal wearing spectacles and a mop of brick-red hair was sorting letters behind a counter dividing the post office's single room. There were no bars between her and the public, as there were in most such places. Behind her on the wall were arrayed a rack of pigeonholes and a bank of locked post office boxes. She looked up warily and Longarm saw that she was pretty, save for the way she held her jaw, tightly, as though she were daring someone to punch her in it. He held out his open wallet, displaying his federal badge and identification, and the little redhead's expression softened somewhat.

She read off his name and asked, "What can I do for you, Mr. Long? You likely know I'm Kathleen Mahoney, for I've jawed with other lawmen about them desperadoes until I'm blue in the face."

He put the wallet away, took out the photograph of Cotton Younger, and placed it on the counter top, saying, "New evidence, ma'am. Does this white-headed rascal look familiar to you?"

The little postmistress picked up the print, adjusted her glasses, and said, "It could be the big one. They were wearing kerchiefs over their faces when they busted in here like Jesse James. But I remember that funny hair, and the hat and duds look familiar too."

He put the picture away, managing not to swear in front of a lady, but she must have noticed the look in his eyes, because she asked, "What's wrong? Did I say something silly?"

He shook his head and said, "No, ma'am. You called it as you saw it, which is more than can be said for many a witness. But there was nothing about masks in the report I read. So we're right back where we started and I've rode out here to Aurora on a fool's errand."

"Oh? And what's wrong with riding out to Aurora, you Denver big shot?"

"Now let's not get our buh . . . whatever, in an uproar, Miss

40

Mahoney. I never said word one against your budding metropolis."

"Don't get snotty with me, you durned old Denverite! I'll have you know that someday Aurora will be a real town, with paved streets and all. You Denver rascals sit over yonder by the water, laughing at us, but——"

Longarm cut in to insist, "Just one cotton-picking minute, ma'am. In the first place I hail from West-by-God Virginia, and in the second, I never rode out here to discuss civic rivalry. As to any cruel remarks about Aurora, I don't remember hearing any."

"I'll just bet. What *did* they tell you about Aurora, seeing as you're a furriner in these parts?"

He shrugged and said, "I disremember anyone in Denver saying anything about your fair city. Hardly anyone's ever been out here, have they?"

"No, they're too stuck up. They think we're only a one-horse prairie town."

That sounded fair enough to Longarm, but he said, "Well, at least most folks must know why you named Aurora such. Aurora was the Goddess of Dawn or something in the old country, and since you folks are due east of Denver, the Denver sun rises from these parts, right?"

She smiled wearily and said, "I didn't think you read much. But if we are Denver's dawn, Denver is our sunset. All the business hereabouts gets sucked into Denver, and since the stage stopped coming through we can't even afford new paint."

"I noticed. But you're likely right about this being a bigger town one of these days. You may have to settle for playing second fiddle to Denver, but at the rate the state is growing, I'd expect them to run the gas and streetcar lines out here most any day. Meanwhile, no offense, I'm sort of curious about the reason for them jaspers trying to hold you up. Don't get riled, but you don't do a lot of business here, do you?"

She shook her head and said, "I've been wondering about that too. We neither get nor send mail direct from here anymore. The mail sacks come and go via the Denver post office, on a buckboard, if you follow my drift."

"I do," he said, "and you're smarter than some lawmen who

41

seem to have missed it. Why risk a stickup in any size settlement when you could road-agent a buckboard on the open prairie, coming or going?"

"I think those three men were after something besides the U.S. mails," she said.

"That sounds reasonable. What do you reckon it might have been, Miss Mahoney?"

"That's where I get stuck. We only service a few of the surrounding spreads, and nobody I've talked to remembers sending or receiving anything you could spend. One of the hands at the Bar Eight sent a money order to Monkey Ward for some spurs he fancied in their catalogue, but it wasn't a big one."

He started to reach for a smoke, caught her eye with an unspoken question, and when she nodded he put a cheroot between his teeth and struck a light before he said, "I met a farmer in town who said he'd just been paid for his cash crop. It must have been truck vegetables, this early in the season."

Kathleen Mahoney shook her head and said, "Nobody out this way has sold anything important recently. Beef outfits have long since unloaded spring veal."

"How about the smaller nesters?"

"Oh, this close to Denver they don't do any business by money order. We're on windmill water out here, so the few farms are hardscrabble. Big cash crop is barley, for the breweries in town, and that isn't ready to harvest. For jingle money a farmer may run a hog or some hens in to the Denver market, but they get paid in cash. So, like I said, those desperadoes made a mistake if they thought I had much cash back here."

He spotted a sign over her head and said, "You do sell money orders, though. So Uncle Sam must back your play with a little dinero, right?"

She smiled wanly and pulled a cigar box from under the counter, saying, "He does, and this is it."

She opened the box, and Longarm saw there was maybe forty dollars in it, in bills and change. He said, "Ain't you supposed to keep that in a safe?"

"I would if I could," she said. "But the safe over there under all them mail sacks hasn't been opened since it got here. They shipped it out to us without the combination. Sometimes, when I have nothing better to do, I hunker down and fiddle with the dial. But I've never been able to find the right combination, and I've tried a mess of 'em. I suppose you'll ask next why I haven't written the post office about my problem?"

He chuckled. "Nope. I work for the government too." Then he glanced down at the box again and said, "There's hardly enough there to justify a holdup. For that matter, there's hardly enough to justify your defending it instead of just turning it over to them."

She put the box under the counter and produced a pepperbox pistol that belonged in a museum. "I drove the rascals off with this," she said. "I had some help, of course. When I started yelling and the hounds outside started baying, some of the boys over to the general store across the way ran outside, yelling, and that's when the three of them lit out. I reckon we showed them Aurora is a tougher town than it looks."

Longarm managed not to burst out laughing as he pictured the scene. The owlhoots must have been more confused than scared. Nothing they'd done made much sense. What in thunder could have possessed them to try such a dumb robbery and then light out, scared skinny by a bitty redhead with a pepperbox? He asked, "Have you ever fired that thing, Miss Mahoney?"

She looked sort of sheepish as she replied, "No, I've never had the nerve. My late father brought it from Ireland, having heard about Indians and such. I don't think he ever fired it, either. I'm not sure it's loaded."

Longarm held out a hand, and as she gave it to him he observed, "You don't talk Irish, Miss Mahoney."

"That's because I'm American, most likely. My father always talked sort of Irish, but my mother was from Iowa and raised me to talk proper. Can you tell if that gun will shoot or not?"

He held it up to the light, tried to turn the cluster of barrels, and said, "It's rusted solid and the nipples have fallen off. There could be some powder and ball in some of the chambers, but I'd get rid of this thing if I was you. You'll never fire this old gun on purpose, but sometimes old powder goes off on its own. You're lucky as hell those three owlhoots didn't take you up on your invitation to a gun battle. What on earth made you act so ornery?"

She lowered her eyes and said, "I was afraid they might, you know, be after my virtue. One of them right out and called me 'honey lamb' when they came in here, waving them durned pistols."

Longarm clamped down hard on his cheroot and swallowed an impolite laugh. He'd heard of men riding out of their way to ravage a pretty maid. In fact he'd gunned some who'd been doing just that, up Canada way one time. But the nester gal he'd saved had been alone at an isolated homestead, and the would-be rapists had known her long enough to build up to the notion. That was an idea, but he discarded it. Had anybody seven feet tall and sporting snow-white hair been lusting after this little redhead for long, she'd have known him. The reports said others in the tiny town had seen the men ride out, so they weren't local lotharios. And who else would have known that a reasonable-looking white woman would be in here alone?

She didn't know how to take his silence. She blushed almost red enough to match her flaming hair as she said, "I reckon you think I'm stuck up about my looks, but I don't have a harelip or a hunchback, and I have been asked more than once to dance, over to the Grange hall."

"I think you're very pretty, Kathy," Longarm said, taking the liberty of addressing her by her first name, "but I misdoubt that was what brought those owlhoots here. If it wasn't money, either, then they must have been after somebody's mail, and that takes us back to the buckboard and the easy way, don't it?"

He had the sense that she hadn't really been listening, and this was confirmed when she said, "Do you really think I'm pretty, Custis?" Obviously she hadn't objected to his familiarity, since she seemed willing to keep things on a first-name basis. She went on, "My best friend, Pru, says I'm a spinster 'cause I'm stuck out here in this infernal little town. She says I'd likely be fighting men off with a club if I was living over Denver way."

This line of discussion didn't have much to do with the U.S.

mails, but it seemed only polite to reassure her. "Your friend is on the money, Kathy. Why, I've seen gals not half as pretty as you are, whistled at on the streets of Denver."

She bowed her head and said, "I don't think I could stand being whistled at, but it does get tedious out here, with all the young men either married or ugly. Do you have a sweetheart in town, Custis?"

"Uh, nothing you'd call serious..."

"How come?" she pressed on. "I'd think a man like you, working in Denver and all, would meet up with a lot of girls."

"Well, my job keeps me pretty busy," he said as he took out his watch. It was getting on toward suppertime and he could make it back just after sundown if he started now. He was supposed to be out of town, but if he stayed to the side streets and bedded down somewhere far from his usual haunts, like maybe that widow woman's place on Sherman Avenue...

Kathy was saying, "It's getting on toward closing time, and it'll soon be Saturday night. Is Saturday night in Denver as lonesome as Saturday night out here?"

He didn't see how it could be, but he said, "Saturday or any other night can be lonely anywhere, Kathy. It depends on who you're with."

"Are you fixing to be with somebody tonight, Custis?"

He shook his head and said, "No, I'm on duty until we catch the rascals who tried to hold you up. I can see they ain't here, and since I'm being paid to look for them, I'd best be on my way."

She reached out and put a hand on his sleeve. Then she drew it back, flustered, and stammered, "Please don't go! I mean, that is, they told me some lawmen would stay out here to guard this place, only they never. When I allowed there was only forty dollars in the place, they sort of seemed to lose interest, but what if those desperadoes come back, to find me alone and undefended? You just said my daddy's gun wouldn't shoot, remember?"

"Yeah, but look, you'll be locking this place up until Monday morning, won't you? You can take the money with you and hide it under your bed in case they come back. Do you live far from here, Kathy?"

She said, "Just out back. That mustard-colored frame house with the sunflowers. I, ah, live alone since my mother was took by the ague, Custis."

So there it was, and what was he to do about it? The Good Lord had no right to put so much temptation before a man if He didn't want to be taken up on it. Longarm knew that even if Billy Vail found out about it, he was within the bounds of duty. What the hell, they had promised the girl protection and she was a material witness and he was supposed to be hiding out and—

He warned himself silently to forget it. The girl had to be a virgin, and even if she wasn't, shooting at sitting ducks was considered unsporting. The poor lonesome little thing would be putty in the hands of any cuss ornery enough to trifle with her, and then what? How did a man ride off, buttoning up his britches with a grin, after taking advantage of a poor little critter like Kathy? Longarm knew he'd horsewhip any other gent who betrayed her trusting heart. Since hardly anybody was big enough to horsewhip him, he'd have to make sure he didn't deserve it.

He meant it too, and he was going to leave, when a man in a straw hat came in, saying, "I was afraid you'd closed for the weekend, Miss Kathy. Got me a letter to mail, here."

Kathy sold him a two-cent stamp as she introduced the two of them. The straw hat belonged to one Hiram Sloats, who raised hogs a couple of miles closer to Wyoming. He said he'd heard about the attempted holdup. That came as no great news to Longarm, but the next thing the farmer said did. "Funny thing, about it being three riders, I mean. My oldest boy hailed three men this afternoon, out in our west forty. They was dressed like cowhands and headed east. Boy said when he yelled an invite to coffee up, they rode off faster, not looking back."

Longarm frowned. He knew that few riders on honest business passed an isolated homestead without accepting a cup of coffee and some polite gossip. He asked, "Did your boy say if one of the men was sort of tall in the saddle, Mr. Sloats?"

The farmer scratched his head and answered, "Matter of fact, now that you mention it, he did. Said the rider's legs nigh dragged the ground as he was setting a scrub pony. Paint pony, he said. Others rode a bay and a roan. All scrub stock, like you hire from a livery. Boy's interested in cowhands, no matter how often I whup him. So he's likely right when he says they wasn't riding decent cowponies. You don't reckon they could have been the rascals who come here earlier, do you?"

"If they were," Longarm said, "they sure get around. I tangled with the big one earlier today, twice. What lies to the east of your spread, Mr. Sloats?"

"Nothing. Not for forty miles, leastways. It's all open range, only there ain't even cows on it at the moment. Used to be the Double Slash cattle outfit, but they got tired of pumping water and moved north to Wyoming Territory after the Indians settled down, the way I hear tell. It all happened afore I got to these parts. Why do you ask?"

Longarm said, "Thought they might have been headed someplace. But if there's nothing that way, they ain't. Nobody aiming to ride far and serious would do her on scrub mounts. So try her this way. Say they aimed to ride hull-down over the horizon until nightfall, and then circle back."

Kathleen Mahoney gasped, "Oh my God, they're after my body!"

Sloates said, "Jesus Christ! Sorry, ma'am. I'd best round up some of the boys and when the rascals ride in we'll dust them good!"

Longarm held up a hand, palm outward. "Now let's just eat this apple a bite at a time, folks. In the first place, we don't know they're headed for Aurora, and in the second, most of you men out here are married men who know more about raising crops and stock than raising Ned with professional gunslicks. We'd best keep this notion to ourselves for now, Mr. Sloats. I'll make sure Miss Kathy's protected. I can't hardly do that with all sorts of men I don't know milling about in my gunsights."

"But you're one man and, no disrespect, there's three of them and you just allowed they was gunslicks," Sloats objected.

"I'm pretty slick with a gun, too, and I'll be behind cover with this .44 and my saddle rifle if push comes to shove. I have another reason to swear you to silence, Mr. Sloats. I'm not playing solitary because I'm a hero. I'm doing it because I'm a lawman and I want those rascals. If we alert the town, they'll know it long before they play their hand, whatever it may be. I don't even know if they're coming here. But if they are, I want 'em to ride in feeling smug, if you follow my drift."

Sloats said he did and left, looking sort of pale. Longarm smiled at the redhead and said, "All right, let's lock up and get ourselves and my buckskin under cover at your house."

"Oh, Custis, do you mean to spend the night with me?"

He said, "Can't say, yet. You, ah, understand that I ain't making any advances, don't you?"

"You mean . . . *improper* advances, Custis?"

"Any kind of advances, dang it! I mean for you to stay upstairs whilst I mount guard downstairs with my Winchester. And I mean you are to stay put up there. It makes me broody to hear folks walking about in the dark when I'm on the prod."

"Can't we have supper first, and maybe talk some?"

"Well, we can sup, for I doubt anybody will pay us a call before it's really dark out."

She smiled and moved down to open a leaf in the counter to join him, taking his hand as she added, "It's Saturday night and I'm not alone!"

As she led him out, he was sort of glad he'd have to stand guard in his boots and britches whether he wanted to or not. He didn't see why any owlhoot, dead or alive, would return to the scene of the crime. But there was one crazy chance in a hundred, and that would likely be enough to keep him from temptation . . . goddammit.

Chapter 4

Kathleen Mahoney was as good a postmistress as the town called for, but she was one godawful cook. She seemed proud of the dreadful meal she placed before him on the kitchen table, though, so Longarm ate it wondering what it was, and washed it down with something she said was coffee. It must have started out as coffee, for he saw the Arbuckle label on the can she took it from. How she got it to taste like iodine and old socks by putting it on the range for a spell was a total mystery to Longarm, and in his day he'd drunk some funny brews. He'd have suspected the local wellwater of being alkilied, if the coffee alone had been bad. But it took serious mistakes to fill a supper plate with whatever she'd started out with. It chewed like india rubber, tasted like glue, and looked like a steaming cow turd. When she asked him if he'd like dessert, he patted his stomach and said he was so full he'd bust if he ate another bite, so she didn't get to poison him further. She put the dishes in the sink and suggested they watch the sunset from her porch swing. He said he'd rather not. He didn't know how many of her neighbors knew there was a man in the house, and he aimed to keep it that way. Not only for her reputation, but to encourage anyone aiming to pay a night call, uninvited, on a woman alone.

That was about the only thing that made any sense to him, now that he'd had time to study on it. The owlhoots had had time to notice that Kathy was right handsome, as they were trying to hold her up. They would have cased the job ahead of time and so they'd know she lived alone. He could see them going over the botched job in hindsight, likely rawhiding one another about whose fault it was, until one of them suggested going back and maybe having some fun with that spunky little redhead. That had to be it.

He carried his Winchester to her sitting room and joined her on an overstuffed davenport, facing the window to the east and the open prairie that way. There was no law saying the outlaws couldn't come from some other direction, but the route from the east was the best one, and in any case it would soon be too dark for it to matter. At his direction, Kathy had barred the doors and shuttered all the other ground-floor windows. If they were dumb enough to knock on any door, he'd show them how nicely a .44-40 slug went through wood. If they had sense enough to circle the house, he'd be waiting for them at the only obvious entrance. He lit another smoke to get the awful taste of Kathy's cooking out of his mouth and sat back, leaning his rifle against the windowsill. He'd left his hat and frock coat in the kitchen. It figured to be a long, tedious wait, so he unbuckled his pistol rig and hung it over the arm of the davenport on his side. Kathy was staring out at the soft evening light on the prairie as she sighed and said, "This time of day makes me feel so forlorn. How about you?"

He said, "I like the gloaming. Makes everything sort of soft and pretty-looking. Be nice if the light could stay that sort of salmon-and-purple shade all the time. But we'd likely get used to it and start noticing things like summer-killed grass and fences that needed paint."

"Saturday nights are the worse of all," she insisted, adding, "Saturday nights is when a woman alone feels old and ugly."

He laughed gently, and said, "Stop fishing for compliments, girl. You know you'll never be ugly and you can't be all that old."

"I'm almost twenty-four . . . If I tell you something, will you promise not to laugh?"

"I never laugh at friends, Kathy."

"Well, I know you won't believe this, but I've never been kissed."

"You're right. I don't believe it. You told me you've been to the dances at the Grange hall and, dammit, everybody's been kissed."

She shook her head miserably and said, "Never. Save by my folks, of course. My daddy was the postmaster, before he passed away. I took over for him to support my ma, for she was poorly. It was my ma taught me how to cook and who taught me, uh, the facts of life."

"I see. You do know the facts of life, don't you?"

"You mean about getting married up and where babies come from? Of course. I read books too, and some of what that Miss Woodhull writes is downright scandalous. I know all about the ways of a man with a maid, Custis, but somehow nothing like that ever happens out here and, dammit, I'll be twenty-four this fall!"

He saw that it was getting darker and a star was out. He figured he'd puke if she said something dumb about wishing on it, but she didn't, so he just sat quiet, letting her prattle on. It helped to pass the time and it steeled his resolve to remain platonic, for if there was one thing he needed less than a lovesick spinster, it was a lovesick *virgin* spinster!

Another star winked on, and while he could still see the horizon, it was almost gone. So he said, "You'd best go on up to bed, Kathy. I don't want anybody in my line of fire if things get hectic down here."

She said, "All right. But will you do me a favor first?"

"If I can. What is it, Kathy?"

"Would you kiss me? I mean, the way they do it in them romantic stories? I know it ain't proper, but I know you're a gent and I've always wondered what it felt like."

He started to say something. Then he realized anything he could say would sound cruel. So he reached out, drew her to him gently, and kissed her in as brotherly a manner as he could manage. Her lips were tightly pursed, like a little girl's. He

51

kept his own lips closed and made his hands behave. She sort of shuddered, then went limp in his arms as her lips softened and responded instinctively, as a grown woman's. He removed his lips from hers and said quietly, "That's about all there is to it, Kathy."

For a moment she didn't answer. Then she said, "Your mustache didn't tickle like I thought it would. Can we do it again? I think I'm getting the hang of it."

He chuckled and said, "Well, just one more time."

As they kissed again, her tongue entered his mouth and she took his wrist to move a hand up on her breast. He could feel her heart fluttering like a trapped bird in there and he drew back, saying, "Hold on there, didn't you just tell me you were, uh, pure?"

She gasped weakly and said, "I am. Oh my, that felt so exciting!"

"I should think it would. Where in thunder did you learn that other stuff, honey?"

"You mean French kissing, and your hand on my breast? It was in this book I read. It was ever so romantical."

"I'll bet. Don't ever kiss any other gent like that, Kathy, unless you're up to a wrestling match or tired of being a virgin."

"Do you mean I made you passionate?"

"Close enough. Look, kid, there's some facts of life your ma left out. You can't kiss gents like that unless you're dead serious about going all the way."

She flinched and pulled away primly, saying, "Oh, I *couldn't*!"

"That's what I mean. You kiss like we did the first time and wait for the gent to propose, if you aim to marry up a virgin. That other stuff is cruelty to animals, unless you're serious. And now that we've discussed the birds and bees, you'd best get upstairs and behave yourself."

"Will you kiss me good night, then?"

"No. One of us has to behave decent, and you don't know no better."

He rose to pull her to her feet and send her on her way. She laughed and said, "I'm so proud I made you passionate. I bet if I was willing to be wicked, you'd want me that way, wouldn't you?"

52

He turned her around, slapped her on the rump, and said, "I never said I wouldn't, and you are purely tempting fate. Get up them stairs, you saucy wench!"

She left, laughing like a little girl. He rubbed his palm on the tweed of his pants. Damn, she sure had a nice little ass. He knew that some night, stuck alone with a hard-on, he was going to kick himself for passing this one by. But he'd be kicking himself a lot sooner if he took advantage of the poor loony gal. So he sat back down to wait, knowing it was a hundred-to-one shot and that he couldn't even smoke.

A million years went by as the sky turned to star-spangled ink. There was no moon, so the prairie lay under the stars even blacker. Somewhere in the night a distant door slammed, and somewhere a dog was barking. It was too far off to concern him or his guns. It had been a long day, and this night figured to be longer. Kathy had been right about Saturdays being lonely when you were alone, and dammit, he was missing out on all sorts of good things in town. He didn't see how he'd possibly ever get the dark Sue and the blond Nancy in the same bed at the same time, but wasn't that a pisser to study on?

He told himself to cut it out. It was one thing to daydream about sex alone on the prairie, but another thing entirely to work yourself up when you knew a good-looking gal was right in the same house, likely undressed and in bed by now. He heard something. He stiffened and reached for the holstered .44 at his side as he strained his ears, wondering what he'd heard. There it was again, the sound of a soft footstep. Where the hell and who the hell? He held his breath and there it was again. *Inside the house!*

He slid off the davenport to face the doorway leading in from the central hall. It opened. He raised the gun as he spotted what looked like every kid's nightmare picture of a ghost in the dark. He said, "Freeze, and I'll only say it once!"

"Custis, it's me. Did I startle you?"

He got to his feet, forgetting his manners as he replied, "Startle me? Hell no, you scared the shit out of me! I damn near gunned you, girl! What in the hell is wrong with you? You got worms or something? I told you to stay upstairs, goddammit!"

She sobbed and said, "Please don't be cross with me. I

couldn't sleep. I was wondering what you were doing down here."

"As you can see, I've been having a sex orgy with Miss Virginia Woodhull. For God's sake, get back up those stairs and play with yourself or something."

"Oh, how can you speak so cruel to me? Is it because I kissed you so naughty and made you passionate?"

He started to deny it. Then he grinned and said, "Yeah. I reckon so. But seriously, honey, I want you to promise me you'll stay put up there. Is it a deal?"

"Well, if you'll kiss me good night again," she replied, stepping over to him in her nightgown. He shrugged and took her in his arms, gun still in hand, and decided that as long as she needed a kiss to settle her down, he might as well scare her good. He hauled her in tight, flattening her breasts under the thin cotton against his chest as he bent to tongue her hot and deep. Kathy's knees buckled and she would have fallen in a heap, but he carried her to the davenport and sank to it with her. He put the gun to one side and ran his hand over her body as he kissed her some more. Then, since she didn't resist, he ran his hand down her flank and went for broke.

That did it. She pulled away and moaned, "Oh, stop, I don't want to go *that* far! Leastways, I don't *think* I want to go that far, and . . . Custis, what are you *doing*!"

Longarm wasn't sure he knew, himself. One part of him warned him that it was time to stop as he got his hand between the trembling thighs under her thin gown and cupped her groin. Another part wondered if he *could* stop as he felt the hair between her legs and started rubbing, picturing how red it must be. "I feel so queer and you're touching me where you oughtn't!" she gasped.

He kissed her again, feeling the moisture of her excited body through the thin cotton. She placed a hand on his wrist to move his hand away, but either he was stronger than usual or she wasn't really putting her back into it. She suddenly went limp again and began to tongue him back as he started moving the hem of her gown up an inch at a time.

Then a shot rang out and a coarse voice called out, "*Wahooo!* Powder River and let her buck!"

So Longarm rolled off Kathy, snapping, "Upstairs and bolt

54

the door, pronto!" as he moved to the rifle near the open window.

Behind him he heard the redhead move out in her bare feet as he raised the Winchester silently. It sounded as quiet as a tomb out there now. Then a familiar voice called out, "Hey, Longarm. We know you're in there, you son of a bitch!"

Longarm called back, "I figured you might. That you, Timberline?"

"You know it, old hoss. Want to come out for a better look?"

"Not hardly. Why don't you come in, Timberline?"

There was a low, nasty chuckle, then the unseen tormentor replied, "I don't reckon I'd better. You're ornery enough *without* cover, as I remember."

Longarm shouted, "I remember killing you, too. Would you be good enough to explain that, Timberline?"

"Why, I'd be proud to, Longarm. Come out here and we'll talk about old times. You know that gal you stole from me up in the Bitter Creek country? Well, she's married up now. Ain't that a bitch?"

"I figured she might be, Timberline. What has she to do with this current discussion?"

"Oh, didn't you know? After I gun you, I aim to pay a call on her and her new hubby. Of course, if you think you can stop me, I'm waiting out here for you. How about it, old pard? Just you and me, fair and square, like the last time?"

"Not hardly, you spooky skunk. In the first place, you have two men with you, and the last time we fought you sort of disappointed me. It ain't usual for a man to get up after I gun him dead. How the hell did you manage that?"

Before anyone could answer, another distant voice called out, "What's going on out there?"

Overhead, Kathy threw her window open to yell, "Help, help, them bandits are back and we're about to be murdered!"

Longarm muttered, "Shit," as he heard the sound of hoofbeats galloping off. It sounded like one horse. Had Timberline, Cotton Younger, or whoever come gunning for him alone? The last time they'd tangled, Timberline had been a sneaky but brave fighter. Maybe being able to rise from the dead made him feel self-confident.

But that was crazy. Longarm didn't believe in ghosts, even when one seemed to be haunting him. Kathy came back in the room to cry out, "The neighbors are coming, darling."

"I noticed," he said. "You'd best put some duds on, lest they think we've been acting improper."

She gasped and said, "Oh dear, you're right!" Then she laughed and asked coyly, "But *weren't* we doing something improper when that Timberline interfered just now?"

Longarm said, "Yeah, the son of a bitch, and I'll never forgive him."

Now that the fat was in the fire and the whole town of Aurora was on the prod, there wasn't a chance Timberline would be back, and Longarm wanted to leave, but he couldn't. Neither he nor anyone else would ever forgive him if he let anything happen to Kathy, and Timberline had said he had nasty plans for at least one of Longarm's old girlfriends. It was midnight before everything simmered down and a bunch of local heroes insisted on helping him guard the redhead with their lives. So he couldn't have started up with her again if he'd wanted to, and now that he'd had time to reconsider, he didn't want to.

Kathy went back to bed and Longarm stretched out on the davenport downstairs to catch some sleep too, as the volunteers walked up and down outside, challenging every passing night bird to mortal combat.

Kathy awakened him on a cruel gray Sunday morning, threatening him with breakfast and church, in that order. He said, "I'm taking you into Denver. It's not likely that spooky rascal will come back here again, so I can't search for him here."

"Then why are you taking me with you? Are you getting passionate at me again?" she asked.

"Not if I can help it," he replied. "I'm going to leave you with my boss, Marshal Vail, and he won't get passionate, either, with his wife looking on. I doubt you're in danger here, but we can't take the chance. So let's get you aboard a pony and be on our way."

It was a short ride into Denver, but Kathy made it tedious by asking fool questions about the conversation she'd heard the night before. She asked what Timberline had meant about

Longarm's old girlfriend, and it was easier to tell her than to avoid it.

As they rode side by side along the wagon trace to town, he explained, "There was this widow woman named Kim Stover, trying to run a bitty cattle spread her husband left her after some cows stomped him flat in a thunderstorm."

"Oh? Was she prettier than me, and were you passionate with her?"

"Nobody's prettier than you, and there's things a gent don't say about no lady, pretty or otherwise. Matter of fact, she was a redhead, like you, only she was more carrot than brick and maybe a mite taller in the saddle. She sure rode a pony right. Anyway, it was up in Wyoming Territory at a place called Crooked Lance, and—"

"That Timberline said it was Bitter Creek, Custis."

"I know what he said. I was there. Bitter Creek is the only town up that way too big for a frog to cross in one hop. They call everything roundabout there the Bitter Creek country. It's near the South Pass. You want to hear what happened or do you want a geography lesson?"

"I'll be good," she promised. She likely meant it too, dammit. Longarm liked redheads no matter what color hair they had. But a man had to draw the line somewhere.

"Cotton Younger was wanted for everything but smallpox," Longarm went on. "So he was hiding out up there, working as a foreman with his hair dyed black. The other hands had took to calling him Timberline because he loomed over them so high. He was courting this Kim Stover, and he'd have had it made if she'd said yes. Who'd ever have found him if he'd settled down as the owner of a spread in a remote mountain vale?"

"But last night he said you stole his sweetheart, Custis. That must have made him very angry, huh?"

Longarm replied, chuckling, "I reckon it must have. I never rode up there to steal his gal. I was sent on a false lead to catch Cotton Younger. The suspect turned out to be another outlaw only half as bad, but other lawmen had gotten the same tip and . . . well, it's too long a tale to tell in detail, for it did get a mite complicated, and by the time we all got done chasing and double-dealing one another we wound up down in Salt

Lake, where I unmasked the real Cotton Younger and shot it out with him. Up until damned recent, I was of the professional opinion I'd won, too."

"Brrr. Did you kill him, the last time you fought?"

"I sure thought I did. I sent him down a flight of stairs with a fatal wound and a busted neck. I got the part about the busted neck from the Salt Lake City coroner's office. It ain't delicate to tell a gal how they figured this out. Suffice it to say I'm pure disappointed in that coroner's report, right now."

"Is that when you got passionate with that other redhead?" Kathy asked.

He didn't answer. Why was it that gals were less interested in tales of blood and slaughter than they were in each other's sex lives? Kathy wouldn't know Kim Stover if she woke up in bed with her—which was a very interesting picture, when you studied on being in the middle if it ever happened. She insisted, "I'll bet you went as far with her as you did with me, right?"

"Wrong." He grinned. It was the simple truth, for he hadn't stopped at stealing a feel off the widow woman. They'd spent two weeks together and if there was anything a man could do to a woman that they hadn't tried, he couldn't think of it. He said, "Old Kim went back to herding cows and I came back to Denver, and I'll take Timberline's word that she's married up now. Soon as I can get to a telegraph wire, I mean to warn her and her new husband about his threat. It's coming back to me that Timberline was a moody, jealous gent when it came to Kim. You may have noticed he holds a grudge past common sense."

"How come you never married up with that old redhead if she was so nice?" Kathy asked.

"We talked about that, on the train back to Wyoming. Neither a priest, a soldier, nor a lawman has any business getting married. Kim had been made a widow once, and didn't like it much. So we parted friends and said no more about it. I'd better wire the Salt Lake coroner too. I can't for the life of me see how both of us made such a mistake. If that gent I shot on those stairs wasn't Cotton Younger, who the hell was he? He sure as hell *looked* like the rascal in that photograph, and if he'd been anybody else, we wouldn't have been shooting it out."

They went on talking in circles as they rode straight into Denver and reined in at Marshal Vail's home on Capitol Hill. Vail's wife was pruning roses in the garden and, being a motherly type, she took Kathy under her wing to show her where she could "freshen up." That was what gals called taking a leak after a trail ride. Billy Vail took the opportunity to fire a couple of verbal rounds at Longarm as he was tethering the ponies in the back. "Dammit Longarm," he said, "I told you to stay away from that little postmistress! She's said to be a nice girl, and I know about you and redheads!"

"Simmer down and listen, Billy. I swear I fetched her in as pure as the driven snow. As to why, old Timberline returned to the scene of a damned dumb crime last night, so I likely saved her from a worse fate. Can she board here until we catch the varmint again?"

"Of course, but for God's sake bring me up to date! You actually met up with Cotton Younger again, face to face?"

"Nope. Would have been suicide to take him up on his invite to come out and dance with him. We exchanged some surly words, though, and the voice goes with the pretty picture. He's riding with at least two others, and since they know the area well enough to circle around sneaky, it's a good bet he's hiding out between times in some private house here in Denver."

"Let's go inside and open a jug," Vail said. "It's Sunday morning and the streets should be near deserted, which gives us an edge if he pokes that snow-white head of his out again today. I had more prints run off from the negative you left at the shop down the street. Every lawman in town has a picture of the rascal pressed to his breast."

They clomped up the back steps into the kitchen. Longarm took a seat as Vail opened a bottle of Maryland rye and placed it between them on the table, with two glass tumblers. He poured and observed, "The rascal can't get far now. While you was out in Aurora, did you ever figure out what they were after? Report says there wasn't enough cash on hand to justify the efforts of three grown men."

Longarm said, "There wasn't. I don't think they were out to rob the post office. It was Timberline's way of announcing his intentions. He knew our office would investigate any federal crime, which robbing a post office is. The little gal's pepperbox never drove them off. They was funning us."

Vail sipped his own drink, grimaced, and asked, "What's the point?"

Longarm said, "Ain't sure. But I'm beginning to suspicion that *he's* stalking *me*. He knew I was out there at Miss Kathy's last night. Just like he knew where I lived and where I drank during office hours. But anyone would know the last two. Did you tell anybody I'd be staking out the Aurora angle?"

"Hell, not a soul. I didn't know it myself. I've told the few people who might be interested that you're in Salt Lake right now."

"Hmm, and who might have been interested, Billy? I got reasons for asking."

Vail thought and said, "Well, some gents from the Denver P.D. dropped by to give me a tip on Soapy Smith. They said he's back on his feet and making war talk about you, Longarm."

"Shoot, he couldn't take me even *before* I put a bullet in his gun shoulder. Who else?"

"Well, Prosecuter Donovan wanted to know if you were going to be escorting that prisoner on Monday and I said you weren't, because I'd sent you on more important business. He said it was all right to let Wallace watch him, just so *somebody* did. The cuss has made his own war talk about busting loose and killing everybody who's persecuting him. He hasn't figured out yet that we're supposed to persecute land grabbers. Then there was Miss Helga Hansen and—"

"Who in the hell is Helga Hansen?"

"Oh, she's the prisoner's daughter. Not bad looking, but too tall for me, and a furriner besides. She talks funny, but as near as I can figure out, she wanted to jaw with you about her daddy's innocence. Ain't that a bitch? I explained that you wouldn't be on the case, and that it ain't a courtroom escort's business to decide such matters anyway. She left sort of mad, but what the hell."

Longarm rolled some rye on his tongue, swallowed, and said, "Hansen is a Scandinavian name, and you say this gal is tall. Would she be blond, too?"

"Naturally," Vail said, "all them Scandahoovians is big and blond. But if you're headed where I think you're headed, forget it. She ain't *that* tall, and she'd never pass as a man in jeans.

Helga Hansen's one of them full-bodied she-males who'd take up two piano stools when she sets down to play."

Longarm smiled and said, "Sounds tempting. My point is that she could have a brother, even taller and blonder. I've been pondering on this ghost that's stalking me, and his methods are as spooky as his being on this earth at all. Last time I brushed up against Timberline, or Cotton Younger or whoever, he was pretty good at killing folks. Remember how he nailed Deputy Kincaid and too many other folks to mention?"

"Hell, I sent you after him because he was a killer, old son."

"I know. And yet he fluffed three tries on me in less than twenty-four hours. I'll admit that anybody could know where I room and sneak a drink now and again. But I was prowling about on my own and not keeping to any timetable yesterday. He could have staked out the Parthenon. He could have staked out my boardinghouse. But he couldn't have been set up to ambush me in both places at the same time. So he or a sidekick was following me. They had to follow me out to Aurora too. I never even told *you* I was going out there."

"All right," Vail conceded. "You ain't hard to follow, since you walk a head taller than most. Let's say Timberline has these friends in town keeping him informed as to your whereabouts. So what?"

"So why are they doing it the hard way? Why send a circus freak to finalize the contract, when they have me under observation by more normal-looking gents in the same business? I rode alone to Aurora, across that open strip east of town. They could have had me three to one with no cover worth mention. Yet they waited till I was forted up in Kathy's house before they moved in. That made no more sense than robbing the mail from the post office instead of simply catching the delivery wagon on the open prairie and taking what they wanted at less risk."

Vail poured another round with a frown and said, "Try her this way. The not-so-late Timberline wants to kill you personal, so his pals are only allowed to shadow you. By the time they can get word to him, it's too late and you've gotten yourself someplace slick."

"That only works halfway. I might have gotten lucky in the Parthenon, but he missed an easy rifle shot on the Cherry Creek

61

bridge, and daring a man inside a house to come out in the dark for a showdown is just plain stupid. Anybody with a lick of sense would have known I'd just stay put until the neighbors came to see what all the fuss was about. It's starting to look like he ain't trying to kill me, he's trying to haunt me!"

Vail said, "I heard about the incident on the bridge when the coppers dropped by to tell me Soapy Smith was after you, too. Correct me if I'm wrong, but didn't he put a rifle ball through your hat whilst missing you so much?"

Longarm thought and said, "I forgot that. I ducked when some kid yelled a warning, and the round passed through the space my shoulder blades had recently vacated. Unless, of course, he fired after I ducked and—"

"Aimed at your head," Vail cut in. "Buffalo Bill couldn't shoot that fancy at that range if he was only out to *scare* you, old son. That try was for keeps!"

Longarm took another swallow, grimaced, and said, "Dammit, Billy, you just ruined a swell theory. Maybe that play out at Kathy's was just the move of a stupid owlhoot. Thinking back on it, Timberline wasn't all that subtle the last time he walked the earth."

"I read the wanted flyers on him. What sort of subtle stuff were you considering, old son?"

"Getting me out of town, of course. Your first reaction was to send me to Salt Lake, but they were watching and the next move was to kill me or scare me out of town."

Vail pursed his lips and said, "I think they're trying to kill you. Timberline must know by now that you don't scare easy."

"Yeah," Longarm agreed. "He tried that up in Wyoming and he wasn't too subtle there, either. All right, either way, him and his friends want me out of the way. So let's circle in from that direction. What would I be investigating in the near future, Billy?"

"Aside from escorting Gus Hansen to court? Can't think of anything. I said business has been slack."

"Let's study on the Hansen case, then."

"Let's not, and say we did. The Justice Department didn't make the arrest, so it's on Treasury's plate. It's not for us to say or care if he's guilty or not. Had I not assigned Murphy in your place, your only job would have been to make sure he sat still while the judge and jury decided what was to be done with the rascal."

"Yet his daughter wanted to talk to me about it?"

"That's what she said. I told her you'd be neither giving nor receiving evidence, but just sitting there next to her daddy so's we could have a polite trial without leg irons and such. She said she could prove her daddy was innocent, so I told her to get a lawyer and see the judge about it on Monday. Like I said, she's a furriner. I don't think she understood that the marshal's only duty in court is to guard the accused. I said you couldn't let her daddy go even if you disagreed with the jury. But like I said, she went away mad. They say her daddy has an awesome temper too. That's why Donovan requested our help. He says juries tend to feel sorry for a man in irons, and that every time they unchain Hansen he acts crazy."

Longarm picked up his tumbler, swirled the rye around to examine its bead, and said, "This may not sound modest, Billy, but if someone was planning to bust Gus Hansen out of there, they might feel more comfortable if I wasn't the deputy on duty."

"You're right," Vail said, "you're bragging. Wallace ain't as good as you, but he's had his look at the elephant and he's still alive. Aside from having killed four men in the line of duty, Wallace ain't going to be alone in that courtroom. There'll be the armed bailiffs and the federal guards patrolling the halls. The courtroom's on the top floor and the building's made of solid rock. But if you don't think Wallace can handle it, I'll send a couple of extra deputies along. Three trained deputy U.S. marshals ought to add up to at least one of you, don't you reckon?"

Longarm took a sip of rye and said, "It was likely just a straw I was clutching. You're right about this routine court case being a poor tree to bark up. But somebody still wants me out of town, or dead."

"Hell, Longarm, you're making a mountain out of a molehill. Of course somebody's after you. You get shot at more than most folks would find reasonable. It goes with the job. How many men have you gunned or sent to prison in your time?"

"I disremember. After a while it gets like counting how

many gals you've kissed. I know some folks tend to be surly about kith and kin I've had to go after, but generally they act more direct. Maybe I'm just spooked because the man pestering me at the moment is one I already killed."

Vail said, "I'll expect a better job from you the next time you kill him, or better yet, take him alive. Cotton Younger might make a deal to escape the rope, and if he knows where his kin, the James boys, are hiding out—"

"Hell," Longarm cut in, "Timberline couldn't know, even if he was willing. He split off from the James-Younger gang long before they got busted up and scattered in that Northfield raid a couple of years ago. I've hauled in men who've rode with James more recent, and they don't know where he is now. The way I hear it, Cotton Younger's own cousin, Cole Younger, was the one who drummed him out of the corps for being so crazy mean, and nobody ever accused Cole Younger of being sweet and sissy. I'll try to take him alive, though, if only to find out how come he ain't dead. But after that you can hang him high, for he purely deserves it."

"Yeah, he is an ornery son of a bitch," Vail admitted. "I told you about Canada sending us a thank-you note the last time you killed him, didn't I?"

"Yeah, he was wanted up there for murdering a poor little métis squaw, and— Son of a bitch!"

"What did I say wrong, Longarm?"

"You didn't. He did, last night. He threatened the life of Kim Stover, and so of course I mean to wire her. But you just reminded me he does kill women, and kills 'em dirty. He didn't just murder that métis gal for saying no. He tied her to a kitchen table and worked her over with a hot branding iron. And he was jealous as hell about me and old Kim, too."

Before Vail could answer, his wife and Kathy came in. Kathy sat down at the table with them, but Mrs. Vail said, "Custis, there's a lady out front in the sitting room who wants a word with you."

"She's pretty, too," Kathy added with a frown.

Longarm rose with a puzzled smile. "You say she's looking for *me*, ma'am? How could she have known I was here?"

Mrs. Vail said, "Oh, she lives down the block, so she must have seen you ride in. I know her to speak to, and she seems a decent widow woman. She says it's something about her son Larry."

Longarm looked relieved and said, "Oh, Larry Wilson. I was afraid I'd get him in trouble."

He excused himself and walked to the front of the house, where he found young Larry Wilson and his mother sitting in the company-neat room off the hall. As his eyes met those of the woman, they both blinked in surprise, for Mrs. Wilson wasn't only Larry's mother, she was Elanore, from the photography shop.

Elanore said, "Oh, it's you!"

Longarm said, "It's you, too. Howdy, Larry. Did you get that dolly for your kid sister?"

"Yessir, but Mom won't believe me," Larry said.

Longarm took a seat across from the two of them and said, "It's my fault your son fell into a life of folly, Miss Elanore. I rewarded him and his sidekicks yesterday, for aiding and abetting the law. I'll bet you two have been having a financial discussion, right?"

Elanor looked relieved as she said, "Well, Larry seldom lies, but there is always a first time, and when he came home with all the toys and candy, I had a little trouble believing his story."

Larry blurted out, "She thought we stole it, Marshal. I told her about the owlhoot shooting at you down by the creek and all, but you know how moms are."

"Yeah, mine never bought my tale about the dragon in the orchard, either. but he's telling you true, Miss Elanore. He yelled a warning at a fitting moment, and I gave the kids a reward. It's a good thing I didn't give them more, huh?"

Larry said, "That's for sure! She said I wasn't to leave the yard till I told her truly where we found the money. So when I seen you and that lady ride past, I run inside to tell her, and mom drug me down here to make a liar out of me!"

"She was just doing her duty, son," Longarm laughed. "You got to admit, circumstantial evidence was agin you. It's your own fault for being generous to your kid sister. Had you blown it all foolish, like I told you to, we'd have never got caught."

He turned to Elanore and added, "We plead guilty, your honor. What's the punishment to be?"

Elanore laughed and said, "I've told him not to play down in Cherry Creek. But I'm glad he disobeyed me, if the crazy tale is true. Was it that man in the photo you asked me to develop?"

"It would seem so, ma'am, and right now your handiwork's been distributed to every lawman we can think of. I can see you're too polite to ask who that redhead I rode by with was, so I'll tell you he seems to be after her, too. She'll be staying here with the Vails. Uh, how far down the street do you live?"

"Just a couple of houses. Why?"

"I'll have Marshal Vail keep an eye on your place too. I don't see how the other side could know who developed that picture, since they don't know it was took. But it pays to be careful, and this outfit seems more moody than most."

He saw that he'd upset her, so he quickly added, "Look, this is a respectable neighborhood, and somebody will be policing it more than usual for now. I doubt you're in any danger."

She asked, "What about school? Larry goes to the Evans Grammar School, across Lincoln, near the bottom of the hill."

Longarm started to say it was likely safe enough. He knew the red-brick-and-sandstone building she was talking about, and it wasn't far or in rough parts. On the other hand, he owed Larry more than ten dollars, so he said, "Well, it might be a good notion to keep him home for the next few days. How many kids do you have, all told, ma'am?"

"Just Larry and his sister, Iris. She's too young for school."

"She's a pest," added Larry. So Longarm nodded sagely and said, "It won't hurt for them to play at home. Do you have someone watching them while you run the shop across town?"

"I've a live-in colored girl. But I can see she hasn't been keeping an eye on Larry after school, or on Saturdays. Do you think it's safe for me to leave them?"

"Safer for them than for you, maybe. Do you have to open your shop this coming Monday, Miss Elanore?"

She sighed and said, "I do. My late husband left me only the house and his business when he passed away two years ago this summer."

"I'm sorry about that, Miss Elanore. I'll make sure you have a police escort, going and coming, and of course the beat men will be watching your shop, and packing a print of that photograph as they do so." He didn't add that he'd have insisted on her holing up with Kathy if he thought there was a serious chance that Timberline would go for her. Nobody, no matter how vengeful, could be after *everybody*. They hadn't gunned that farm boy who'd spotted them on the prairie, after all, and merely developing a plate taken by someone else couldn't be much worse than seeing them in the flesh and reporting it.

Elanore rose and said, "You're very considerate, and I won't bother you further, Marshal."

He rose too, saying, "It was no bother. You and old Larry are good scouts."

As he escorted them to the front door she asked, in a carefully casual voice, "Will you be dropping by the shop—on business, I mean?" So he said, "Likely, when I get back. I have to do some traveling, up Wyoming way. I'll, uh, look you up when I get back."

They left, and Longarm headed back to the kitchen. Billy Vail was waiting for him in the hall. "What's this about you heading for Wyoming, old son?" the chief marshal asked.

"Why, Billy, have you been listening at door panels again?"

"It's my house, ain't it? Wanted to see this she-male my old woman and the redhead was jawing about. She liked you, Longarm. How come all the gals like you so much?"

"Reckon it's my mustache. I try to keep it neat. As long as we're alone, I'll let you say my good-byes to Kathy and Mrs. Vail. I'm going to Wyoming for two reasons. One: Timberline said that after he got through with the deal out in Aurora, he was figuring on paying a vengeful call on Kim and her man."

"And two?"

"Even if he was only funning, I want him out of town, too. There's too many folks here in Denver that I have to worry about, and I can't be everywhere at once. I figure Timberline or somebody working with him is watching me. So if I hop the UP northbound, somebody's sure to tell him, and he'll likely follow. I got to get the rascals out in more open country if I'm to spot them. And it's open as hell betwixt here and Bitter Creek."

Chapter 5

Longarm was right about the countryside north of Denver being open. The northbound tracks ran over rolling prairie, with the foothills of the Rockies to their left. He'd need a horse when he got to the Bitter Creek country, so his saddle and possibles were riding in the baggage car up front. He kept his Winchester with him as he sat in an end seat of the coach, facing everybody else. He was used to riding backward, since it went with staying alive in his business. He'd hired the most forward seat they had in the coaches. The only reason any other passenger had for moving by him was the dining car, which was the next car forward. The train had pulled out of the yards with the dining car closed, so he'd get to see everyone who meant to dine as they moved toward him the full length of the car. And of course, before taking his position, he'd had a stroll the length of the train just as it left Denver. If anybody standing seven feet tall under a thatch of snow-white hair was aboard, Longarm needed his eyes examined.

He hadn't expected Timberline to be so obvious. There'd be other trains, and any number of the men on board could be a less flamboyant confederate of the man who was stalking him. Longarm had taken his time about boarding, and had made sure the station loafers heard his name by having himself paged in the waiting room a couple of times. But he didn't want to throw Timberline off his trail by accident, so he meant to lay over a few times on the trip north. It saved paying for a pullman bunk if he bedded down for the night in Cheyenne. It would make it easier to check more recent arrivals at the Cheyenne station, too.

He'd wired a warning to Kim Stover too, with some difficulty, since Kim's last name wasn't Stover anymore. He'd had to get her married name from the county clerk in Bitter Creek, and it was Howard. She still owned the Lazy K, though, so by now she'd have gotten his warning. Since she had plenty of hands working for her, and everyone in the Crooked Lance Valley knew Timberline on sight, Kim was likely safe from harm. Some of the cowboys on her payroll had been sort of rugged, as he recalled, so he figured that this Howard gent, whoever he was, had to be one tough hairpin. Aside from poor old Roping Sally, up in the Blackfoot country, Longarm had never met a gal who could wrestle a steer or a man as expertly as Kim could. He recollected how she and he had torn hell out of that bedstead in Cheyenne that time, but then he willed himself to forget it. Roping Sally was dead and Kim was married, which was just as good as dead. Thinking about gals you'd never have again only led to pointless hard-ons.

In the bright sunlight, the prairie rolled by like the rippling muscles of a huge mountain lion. A man could see for miles out here.

A colored gent in white livery came down the aisle, ringing a set of chimes, and folks started getting up to move forward to the open dining car. Longarm was hungry enough, but he stayed put, lighting a smoke as he sized up the passing scene. Most of the passengers looked the way he'd expected them to. A couple of hardcased types wearing serious gun rigs passed him. They weren't looking his way, though, so he just made a mental note of their presence. Lots of folks had good reasons to be packing guns in professional rigs. Aside from other lawmen on a mission, the railroad had its own dicks watching for folks like Timberline's cousins, the James boys. And since that fool, Ned Buntline, had started writing all those yarns about the country out here, even honest cowhands thought they looked spiffier sporting a gunfighter's outfit.

He took a drag of smoke as he thought, and then recalled the name of that dumb young cuss who shot Jim Hickok in the back that time. Jack McCall, that'd been the jasper's handle. Poor old Jim had been written up by Buntline as "Wild Bill," even though his name was Jim. They said that toward the end, Hickok took to acting like he was the wild desperado Buntline had invented, so this Jack McCall had taken a dumb notion that by gunning Wild Bill, he'd be somebody just as famous.

It hadn't worked in real life as it did in a Wild West magazine, though. After gunning Hickok in the back, McCall had gotten off by making up a crazy story about revenge. But then he'd gone to Colorado and bragged openly that it was all a fib and that he'd shot Wild Bill just to see if he could do it. The Colorado trial that resulted was likely unconstitutional; the rascal's lawyers had said it was, anyway. True, it did seem sort of improper to try a man twice for the same crime, and Colorado had no jurisdiction over a shooting in the Dakotas. But it didn't do McCall much good to know he was in the right when they hung him, and he did deserve it.

A big beige hourglass was sailing up the aisle under a picture hat. As it got closer, Longarm saw that it was a right handsome blond lady who ran to considerable size. He wondered how any gal that broad across the hips could have such a skinny waist, even allowing for whalebone and determination. He didn't want to look fresh, so he lowered his eyes politely to let her pass on to the diner. But she didn't. She sat down by Longarm, moving the seat under him alarmingly in the process, for she had to weigh close to one-eighty, wasp waist or no.

He took the cheroot from his mouth and said, "Ma'am?"

"I am Helga Hansen," she announced. "I heard you vas on this train."

He nodded and said, "I know who you are, ma'am. My boss, Marshal Vail, told me about your visit."

"Bah, such an *asna* is your marshal. Forgive me. I meant an ass."

"I didn't think you meant he was a poodle dog, and I savvy you all right. Billy Vail ain't an ass, ma'am. You just didn't listen sharp."

71

"I told him my Papa was innocent and he said there was nothing you could do about it."

"He told you true. Your father's case is betwixt him and the Treasury Department. I work for Justice, so—"

"Be still, it is not polite to butt in like a *get*. I mean a goat."

"Close enough. Have your say, then, ma'am."

"Listen, I have heard of you, Longfellow. Why do they call you Longfellow, by the way?"

"I reckon it's 'cause I'm so poetical. I told you I'd let you have your say, but you ain't making it easy."

"*Ja*, Papa says I talk too much. He did not do the things they say he did. I have heard that you, Longfellow, can prove anything. Is this so?"

"Well, I'm generally paid to prove folks are guilty, but if they ain't, I'm fair-minded. Your father's case is out of my hands, Miss Helga. As a matter of fact, it was never in 'em. As I understand it, he's accused of claiming land under false pretenses, right?"

"No, wrong! My Papa is an honest man. He used to beat me if I stole a *blyerstpenna* from the *skola* as a *flicka*!"

"Well, you have to admit that sounds right serious, ma'am."

"I meant when I was a schoolgirl, if I took another girl's pencil, Papa punished me."

"Even so, it sounds right reasonable. I wasn't allowed to steal much, either. Maybe your father just made a mistake, not knowing the lingo or the laws here all that much."

"Pooey and bah! Papa read about the laws in his own language before he came out here to raise cattle. What he did was not against the law when he did it. How was he to know they would change the Homestead Act so that it was against the law to pay others to file for you?"

Longarm shrugged and started to explain why Washington had plugged up the loopholes in the old law after so many land hogs took advantage of it the way it was first written. Then he frowned thoughtfully and said, "Wait a minute. How long ago did your father go into the land-grabbing business?"

"Over ten years ago, I think. He came to this country right after you had that war over the colored people. He thought it was crazy to give away free land too, but as long as they were willing, he was. You know it takes much prairie to feed one cow. So he tried to get as much land as he could, like all the others were doing."

"Yeah, they call 'em cattle barons now. Are you saying your father ain't grabbed any land *recent*, Miss Helga?"

"Not since they passed the new laws, if that's what you mean."

"That's what I mean. *Post facto* is against the Constitution. What that means is that you can't punish a man for busting a law before the law was passed. I'm sure there's a statute of limitations on homestead claims, too. If your father's held that land for more than five years, it's his under the old law. If it's been more'n seven, I can't see why anybody brung it up. Who pressed the charges against your father, Miss Helga? Some other cattle outfit?"

"No. Those terrible men from the land office. When they said Papa had too much land, he got mad and shot one of them in the leg."

"There you go. Vail had it wrong. It's an assault charge. You're not allowed to shoot federal agents, ma'am, tempting as it may be."

"Papa is sorry he shot that man in the leg, but I don't understand about our ranch."

"I don't either. Unless you left something out, it should stay in the family. I know someone in Prosecutor Donovan's office, so I'll wire them Monday morning and ask about that *post facto* angle."

"Oh, is this person in the prosecutor's office a good friend of yours, Longfellow?"

He smiled and said, "I'd say so. You see, the way your father's been carrying on so wild, he may have caused himself needless trouble. Donovan won't want to hold a trial he's bound to lose, if it's like you say. So—"

And then she grabbed him in a bear hug, kissed him moistly, and gasped, "Oh, they *told* me you were the best, Longfellow! I will do anything to pay you back for helping my poor papa!"

He disengaged himself carefully and said, "Well, what I want you to do for me is get off at the next stop and go back to Denver. If you get a chance to speak to your father before his trial, tell him to simmer down and keep his durned mouth shut. Then tell his lawyer what I said about *post facto*. That's

73

all you have to remember. He'll do the rest. Of course, if you've been stretching the facts, all bets are off."

She came for him again, rolling aboard his lap to kiss him again before she gasped, "I will do as you say. I will save my Papa and the ranch, and then you will come to our house for your reward, *ja*? I am a good cook. My smoked eels are famous!"

He said, "Oh," sort of wistfully, for he'd discovered by now that she wore no whalebone under her traveling dress. It was all Helga, and nobody had a right to curve like that if she was getting off at the next stop.

But she did, so what the hell. It likely would have killed him in any case. Helga was stronger than most men, and that big behind was solid muscle. He hadn't felt her thighs, but each was bigger around than his waist, and it made his eyes water to consider risking his privates in the jaws of such a mighty nutcracker.

Some other folks got on as Helga got off at the next stop. None of them looked like Timberline, either. So the trip got dull and stayed that way until the conductor came down the aisle to announce that they were pulling into Cheyenne.

Longarm got off as the train pulled into the station, and walked forward to get his gear. He'd wired ahead for hotel reservations at a place he remembered fondly. It was still early, and he had some prowling about to do before he even considered how he'd sleep, alone or otherwise.

He slung his saddle and possibles over his left shoulder and started walking toward the hotel across the way. As he stepped off the curb, a buckboard came around a corner a mite too fast, and Longarm moved back to get out of the way, cussing. Suddenly a bullet whipped by, so close he felt the shock wave with his nose. He drew on the way down, twisting to land belly-down with his saddle atop him and his gun aimed back the way he'd come. The gent who'd tried to shoot him in the back was still there and still shooting from the doorway of the station, so Longarm returned the fire and his aim was better. The man yipped like a kicked dog and bounced off the doorjamb, dropping his gun before sliding down the jamb to join his sixgun where it lay on the walk. Longarm saw that he wasn't moving, so he rolled out from under his saddle and eased himself erect, still training the gun on the blackness of the doorway.

He moved out of line from anyone inside, and as he got closer to the downed gunman, a man with a brass star pinned to his vest ran up and yelled, "Drop that gun, mister!"

So Longarm did. It was generally a good idea to do as a man pointing a double-barreled scattergun at you said.

The Cheyenne lawman said flatly, "You're under arrest."

Longarm said, just as flatly, "No I ain't. That rascal in the doorway is, if he's still breathing. I am a deputy U.S. marshal, and he just tried to shoot me in the back."

Another lawman came around the corner, took in the scene, and joined them, saying, "He's all right. I know him, Jake." Then he nodded at Longarm and said, "Might have known it was you, when I heard that .44-40 talking back to a .45. Who made such a dreadful mistake, Longarm?"

Longarm bent over to pick up his pistol and thumbed a fresh round into it as he strolled over to the downed gunman in the doorway. His condition didn't call for gentle treatment, even had he deserved it, so Longarm hooked a boot toe under the gunman's neck and rolled his head for a better look. Then he said, "He was on the train with another gent. Never saw him before today."

The lawman with the scattergun redeemed himself by saying, "I know him. Ran him out of town about a year ago. I disremember his name, but it's on file at the office."

"Do tell? Why'd you run him out of town, constable?"

"Didn't like him. He was a bounty hunter. Said he had a hunting license to shoot folks on my territory. I convinced him he was wrong by shoving Old Widdermaker here up his nose. I told him it would be poor for his health to come back to Cheyenne, and you just made good on my brag, deputy. So you and me is pards, if you need any."

Longarm laughed and said, "I may. I said he was with another gent. I didn't see either one getting off the train, so I can't say whether the other's in town or not."

The lawman who'd recognized him spat and said, "He'd be mighty dumb if he was, right now. But I'll ask around inside."

As he left, the one with the scattergun asked, "You want the body shipped anywhere, or can we put him on ice and find

75

out if he has any papers on him, Longarm?"

"He's all yours," Longarm told the constable, knowing that while a federal lawman couldn't accept rewards, a local lawman could, and did, whenever he got the chance. He added, "You might as well say you gunned him, in case there's a dead-or-alive on him."

The constable smiled and said, "Why, thanks, pard. That's downright neighborly of you."

Longarm knew it was. It also meant he'd avoid a coroner's jury and the fool papers he didn't have time to bother with. He'd find out later who the jasper had been, and whether he was wanted anywhere or not. If he was in truth a professional bounty hunter, he probably wasn't wanted by the law, although most lawmen held a certain contempt for the breed. Bounty hunters skimmed the cream from the labors of hard-working lawmen. Most had private investigator's licenses in one state or another, and that was sort of a hunting permit. But bounty hunters were only allowed to gun wanted men, and Longarm didn't figure there were any dead-or-alives out on him, so the gunfight had been illegal as well as foolish.

Leaving the local lawmen to clean up after him, Longarm picked up his saddle and gear and shoved through the gathering crowd to cross to the hotel. He had to check in and get rid of this load before he sent his wires and paid a courtesy call on the local law boss. He wondered how long it would take to get a line on that pro he'd shot. He knew that some bounty hunters, when business was slack, could be persuaded to hunt out of season as plain old hired killers. That was another reason he looked down on the breed.

The room clerk in the hotel said his room was waiting for him. But when Longarm asked for the key, the clerk said, "Your wife has it, Mr. Long."

"My . . . wife?"

"Yessir. She's up there now. Got in ahead of your train, she said."

These words dismayed Longarm about as much as they would have anybody, but he went up the stairs anyway, his saddle over his shoulder, drawing his .44 as soon as he was alone in the second-story hallway. He counted off the room numbers, and sure enough, the one he'd hired showed light

76

under the door. He was still pondering his next move when the door opened and a woman, outlined by the lamplight behind her, wearing a thin, almost transparent kimono, said, "I was watching from the window as you crossed the street, darling. Don't you ever come to town without announcing it in a blaze of gunfire?"

He blinked and said, "Kim, is it really you? Downstairs that clerk said—"

"I know what he said, you brute. How was I to get the key unless I told them we were married? We told them that the last time we stayed here, don't you remember?"

He followed her inside and dropped the saddle and gear on the floor as he reached for her and said, "I remember it well. But I'm sort of surprised that *you* did, Kim." Then he kissed her. She kissed him back, and it only seemed like old times to start undressing her. But as he fumbled with the sash of her kimono, Kim drew back and said, "Hold on. We have to settle on some new ground rules first. I, uh, got married after you left."

He gazed down at her, drinking in her unbound carrot-colored hair and the way Kim's sometimes conflicting emotions played across her cameo features. They'd first met as enemies and wound up more than friends; Kim tended to have strong feelings, no matter what they might be at the moment. The Lord had likely been a mite mixed up the day he designed her, although he'd made her pretty as hell. Her features were as high-toned as some snotty society gal's, but she was well tanned from range riding in the high country, since she'd been born and raised in the Rockies. The figure inside the thin, pale blue kimono was all woman, yet she had some wire-and-whalebone muscles hidden under her curves.

The French perfume she still wore filled the room and aroused him, but he'd seen her dusty and smeared with cowshit, and she'd looked just as desirable. Aboard a bronc or in a bed, Kim was one hell of a woman. He started to take her in his arms again, and again she pushed him away, saying, "Let's not take too much for granted, cowboy. You said you was coming back to me, remember?"

"Well, I'm back, ain't I?"

"You bastard. You came up here on a job. I got the wire

77

you sent us. Fortunately my husband was away on a business trip, so I didn't have to explain."

He dropped his hands to his sides and frowned down at her, saying, "You're sending 'em over my head this evening, Kim. There was nothing to explain. Nothing a husband shouldn't know about, anyway. I only warned you that Timberline is running around frothing at the mouth and making threats against you and yours."

Kim said, "I was there when you killed Timberline, you fool! Honest to God, Custis, couldn't you have come up with a better excuse to see me again?"

He shook his head and said, "It wasn't an excuse. And I wasn't expecting to see you here in Cheyenne. I told you in the wire I was on my way to Crooked Lance, remember?"

"Oh, great. Those ex in-laws of mine at the Stover General Store would have loved that. As to my husband, he's, ah, possessive."

Longarm nodded and answered, "As well he might be, Kim. But is that why you came down here to head me off? To keep me from fighting your husband for your fair white body?"

"Partly," she admitted. "My fair white body remembers yours and, well, if you mean to demand prior claims on it, I'd rather get it over with where nobody has to know about it."

Longarm frowned and asked, "Is that what you think I am, Kim? A damned old he-brute who has to be serviced lest I might bust up the barn?"

She moved closer again as she replied, "Well, ain't you?"

He knew he was supposed to kiss her some more, but he shook his head like a bull with a fly between its horns and said, "Hold on, Kim. I don't know what this game is supposed to be, but it strikes me as kid stuff, and if I aim to play kid games, I'll get me a kid."

She stiffened and said, "That was dirty. You know I'm not thirty yet, you son of a bitch."

"I wasn't talking about your age, Kim. I was talking about acting grown up. But since you want to bring up Father Time, so be it. Neither one of us just hatched from an egg. We didn't meet as shy virgins under a willow tree. You were married long before I ever bedded you, and now you're married again. I won't comment on what you may or may not have done with other gents and your fair white body, but speaking for myself, if there's any part of you I ain't been to, I'd like to hear about it."

"I told you I was willing to take care of you, dammit. Do we have to talk dirty?"

"Shut up, I ain't finished. You were laying for me here, uninvited, in a see-through kimono and a pint of fancy stink-pretty. You've unbound your hair and turned down the bed-covers. So if anybody hereabouts is talking dirty, it's you! What's this bullshit about me taking things for granted? What in thunder did you expect me to do when I came in here, scalp you? If you're expecting me to roll over and wait for you to tell me I'm a good doggy, forget it. I never rode all this way to steal you from your husband. I'm here to save your pretty ass. So put some clothes on and let's study on it."

Her lower lip trembled and she asked, "Don't you . . . want me, Custis?"

"Oh, stop talking dumb. There ain't a man you ever met who didn't want you, and you know it. But you're married and acting moody, so it's jake with me if you want to keep this encounter formal. I wasn't funning about Timberline, Kim. I know I killed him, but he seems to be up and coming at us again, anyway." He saw that she'd made no move toward the clothes she'd piled on a chair in the corner, so he asked, "Ain't you fixing to put your duds back on, Kim?"

In answer, Kim moved over to the bed, peeled off the kimono, and climbed atop the clean sheets, sighing, "Oh, I'm tired of kid games too. First let's make love and then we can talk."

There wasn't a thing a gent could say to an invitation like that, so Longarm nodded and started shucking his duds as Kim watched, her head propped on one hand as she reclined like one of those oil paintings in the Parthenon Saloon.

She sighed and said, "God, you have a lovely body. I'd forgotten how those shoulders filled a room." And then, as he dropped his pants, her eyes widened and she added, "My God, I'd forgotten that, too. Hurry, you brute!"

So he did, mounting her as she rolled on her back to spread her thighs in welcome. As he entered her, Kim closed her eyes and moaned, "Oh yes, I never forgot what *that* felt like!"

He hadn't either, and it was like coming home after being off to war. He wondered if that was why so many loving husbands went to parlor houses. There was a lot to be said for making love to somebody who knew you well enough to move your way. Yet any pleasure could turn to a chore if you kept at it long enough. Maybe folks needed a change of partners once in a while, just as a man who ate steak and mashed potatoes every night liked a bowl of chili con carne for lunch. It made the steak and potatoes taste more interesting when he went home to supper.

Longarm and Kim shared their first orgasm soon and in time with one another, since their bodies got right down to business like two cowhands cutting a calf from the herd. Then, in unison they rolled sideways to get their breath back without disengaging. He reached out and fumbled a smoke and a match from the shirt he'd draped over the bed table, and when he lit up he knew she wanted the second puff without either of them speaking. He reclined on one elbow, smiling down at Kim as she took a deep drag, opened her eyes, and said, "Howdy, pard," with a roguish thrust of her horsewoman's pelvis.

He gave her a little jab and said, "Howdy yourself," knowing she liked to work back up to full steam this way. It sure was a pleasant position for friendly conversation. As he took the cheroot back she sighed and said, "Jesus, I've missed this. The hell of it is, I think I'm in love with my husband too. Is this love or lust with you, Custis?"

He moved teasingly and said, "Don't know. I've never figured out the difference. Right now I can't think of another gal on earth I'd rather be doing this with. So do we have to bring your husband into bed with us?"

She sighed and contracted on his shaft, enjoying the lazy way they were rutting as she said, "I like to talk man-to-man with you while we do it. And Cyrus just gets mushy when he makes love to me."

"You likely hate that, huh?"

"No. Since we're pards, I won't lie to you. I made sure he was a good lover before I married up with him, but I've often thought back fondly to the last time we stayed here in friendly sin. Do you remember the night we got to talking like this, started to sort of debate, and clean forgot we were fucking until all of a sudden I came?"

He chuckled fondly and said, "Yeah, I noticed you do that a lot."

She moved her hips to swallow him deeper as she shrugged and said, "All right. I'm a warm-natured woman and I've never found anything that feels better. Does it shock you that we're committing cold-blooded adultery?"

"It beats infancy, but I generally avoid married-up gals. It ain't that I'm a prude, but it seems ornery to fight a man after loving up his old woman, and some gents just won't have it any other way."

"Cyrus will never know. He's in Denver, on business. Went down to see about some land they're selling, cheap."

"Do tell? It sure is one small world. What would a spread up near Bitter Creek want with land so far away?"

"Oh, we'll sell the Lazy K and move to Colorado if the deal goes through. You may have noticed that things are slow up in our valley. We're bidding on a much bigger spread, closer to market and close enough to Denver for me to buy my duds from the Denver Dry Goods like a human woman. Uh, would you move a little faster, dear?"

He did, but asked, "Would this land be being auctioned off by the Land Office? I got a reason for asking."

She took the cheroot from his mouth, took a drag on it, and reached past him to snuff it out, pressing her firm breasts and erect nipples against him as she did so, saying, "It is. I think it's being seized by the government for back taxes or something. Let's not talk about it now. I'm ready for some more serious loving."

That sounded reasonable, so he rolled atop her.

The second time was better than the first. He was getting his second wind now, so he let her come, then shifted them both around to where her hips were on the edge of the mattress and his feet were on the floor.

She gasped and warned, "Hey, there are limits to my capacity, cowboy! I don't mind you hitting bottom, in fact I sort of like it, but not quite so hard, huh?"

He laughed and withdrew to roll her over, and Kim knew

what he wanted without being told. She hooked her knees in the seem of the mattress to present her upthrust rump to him as he took one of her hipbones in each hand and entered her like a rutting stallion, feet on the floor and head thrown back in pleasant abandon. He groaned, "Jesus, I'm coming from the toes up!" as he ejaculated in her and just stood there, letting her milk the last drops with her contractions as she sort of purred. He smiled down at the smooth ivory expanse of her back and began to run one hand up and down her spine, the way he knew she liked it.

Kim asked conversationally, "What was all that shooting about just now, dear?"

He started moving gently in and out of her as he answered, "It wasn't just now. It was years ago, before I went to heaven. Some idiot tried to gun me, over to the depot. He lost. When we come down long enough to go out and have some supper, I have to drop by the law and have a talk with them about him. Got to send some wires too. I can see that Timberline ain't about to find you at the Lazy K, so that'll save one. But he may be after other folks, and I'd like to check before we settle down for the night."

She lay with her face on the sheets and arched her back to take him deeper as she mused aloud, "I thought you made that story up to get me down here for this. Are you still trying to convince me a dead man is up and about, pestering folks?"

He said, "Sure looks that way. Since I won't be going up to Crooked Lance after all, I might as well run over the South Pass and have a look-see in Salt Lake. You want to come along?"

"I want to. I can't. There are limits to what even a trusting husband like Cyrus Howard will buy. I told the folks in Crooked Lance I was coming to Cheyenne to buy a new hat. I don't know what in thunder I'd be able to say I was doing in Salt Lake." She moved back against him and added, "And speaking of comings and goings, I ain't going, but I think I'm coming."

So he cupped a hipbone in each hand and rode her to glory. She moaned and fell off him to lie facedown on the bed, sobbing in pleasure and maybe something else. He rolled her over to do it the old-fashioned way as she protested, "Wait, I have to get my breath back!"

82

"No you don't. I'll breathe for both of us," he told her, letting himself really go for the first time, now that he knew the new rules.

He didn't like them too much. She was the old Kim in the flesh, but different-hearted. He knew some of that might be his own fault, for she'd made some demands on him the last time that they'd both known were foolish. The Kim he'd made love to the last time had been a widow woman who'd only had one man before him. This Kim had had three he knew of, and from the way she was going at it, maybe more. For a gal who claimed to be happily married, she sure screwed casually. He wasn't sure it was just because she knew him so well. Teaching a frustrated widow woman to enjoy herself in bed had apparently unleashed a tigress. He figured she likely shopped for hats a lot, lately. He didn't know why that should bother him, but it did. The Good Lord knew he was a casual cuss, himself, but it seemed sort of ornery to cheat on a man she said she was fond of.

Longarm considered marriage about as inviting as that income tax that some fool in Washington had proposed amid considerable laughter. But Longarm knew that if he ever signed on the dotted line with some gal, he'd feel bound to honor the contract. That was why he didn't want to marry up. He hated to tell lies to anybody, and it seemed to him that it would be two-faced as hell to go home to the little woman, grinning like a shit-eating dog after acting like this with another. His moody thoughts slowed down his pending orgasm, to the considerable delight of the adventurous wife he was adulterating.

Kim gasped, "Oh my God, it's here again!" and that woke him up in time to come along with her. It left them both as limp as dishrags, and Longarm could have rolled over and fallen asleep, had he not known it was impolite and that he had other business to attend to.

He dismounted and sat up, wiping himself on a corner of the sheet as he got his breath back and said, "We'd best call a truce and have something to eat whilst we get our strength back. Remember that old Chinese place down the street?"

Kim said, "I don't feel like getting dressed, and I'm not sure I want to risk being seen on the street with you. What if someone from Crooked Lance should be in town?"

83

He was too polite to mention that she should have thought of that sooner. That was another reason not to get married if one wanted to play the field. Married folks who cheated had to be sneaky. Half the fun of a romance was taking the gal to dinner or the theater. Hell, if he wanted to take Elanore Wilson, back in Denver, out to the park for a picnic, there was no reason in the world he couldn't. A man had no business in bed with a female he was ashamed to be seen on the street with.

He grimaced and said, "I'll bring back some Chinese grub in a paper sack, then. It won't take me long, as I only have a few errands, honey."

She said, "Wait. It's early yet and we've been too busy to talk. I don't understand all this about Timberline. How could he be alive after you gunned him in Salt Lake? I don't think I believe in ghosts, Custis."

He said, "I don't believe in them at all. Every one I ever met turned out to be someone else. Closest thing to a ghost I ever met was up on the Blackfoot Reservation. This white crook was scaring the Indians with a Wendigo, a kind of Indian spook. He scared me too, and killed a nice gal I met up there. But in the end he turned out mortal and just as easy to kill as any of us."

"Oh?" Kim frowned, and there was a slight edge to her voice as she asked, "I take it you and this other girl were on friendly terms?"

Longarm shrugged and said, "I reckon you could say that. Her name was Roping Sally, and she sure set a pony nice."

"I'll bet. How was she in bed?"

Roping Sally had been damned fine in bed, but Longarm didn't discuss his friends behind their backs, and Roping Sally was dead. So he said, "It seems to me that jealous tone is a mite dumb, considering."

Kim started an angry retort. Then she sighed and said, "You're right. It's crazy, but I do still love my husband, and he's good in bed too. I'd be lying if I said either of you was better. You're both . . . different."

"Variety is the spice of life, I reckon."

"Were you . . . in love with that other girl, Custis?"

He started to nod, then said, "Don't know. Sometimes I tell myself I was, but maybe that's 'cause it's safe to love a dead

84

woman. You're right about love and lust being hard to sort out. I've felt something sort of downright sentimental about gals I didn't want to trifle with, and I've jumped drooling into bed with gals I didn't like as fellow humans. Have you ever fooled around like this, just for the hell of it, with some man you thought was a skunk?"

She shook her head, then laughed and said, "As a matter of fact, I've often wondered what it would have been like with Timberline. I know I resisted his advances, for he was a bully and I knew somehow he was evil, even before you exposed him. But, well, women daydream too, and I've often wondered what it would be like, just once, to give myself to a man that big."

He grimaced and said, "Jesus. You'd do as well with a pony, and a pony wouldn't murder you afterwards."

Kim smiled enigmatically. Longarm decided to drop the subject. He reached for his duds and started hauling them on, telling Kim he'd be back as soon as he could. He meant it too, for he had no place better to go. But as he kissed her and let himself out, he sort of wished it could be like it was before. The new Kim was too honest for a man to get romantic with, and he sort of missed the white lies that sweetened a good lay, like icing on a cake.

Chapter 6

He went to talk to the local law first. They'd been expecting him for some time, so they had the records ready on the man he'd gunned. The gunslick had indeed been a bounty hunter. He was licensed by the state of Colorado, which surprised Longarm in two ways. He'd expected the rascal to hail from Clay County, Missouri, and he thought he knew most of the gunslicks working out of Denver. The man's name had been Murdoch. The Cheyenne sheriff's office didn't have a copy of his private investigator's license, of course; the wire could only give the serial number. So Longarm wrote it down to check out when he got the chance. Murdoch had no wanted papers on him, so nobody figured to collect. But the Cheyenne law was polite anyway. They'd told the rascal they didn't want him in their fair city, and now he wasn't going to bother them anymore. Longarm asked where the body was, and they told him it was at the undertaker's parlor just down the street. So Longarm moseyed over to study the cadaver at leisure.

The late Gordon Murdoch had been tidied up and looked more peaceable than the last time they'd met. The undertaker seemed concerned as to who was paying for all his trouble, so Longarm said, "If his company won't, I might be able to get Uncle Sam to spring for a cheap burial, if you'll throw in something extra."

"What's that?" the undertaker asked, and Longarm said, "I'd like a photo of this jasper's face to show about. He may or may not have been mixed up in a post office job down Colorado way. A picture is worth a thousand words, like they say, and he's too tedious-looking to describe."

The undertaker said, "Well, I can't do her tonight, but there's a store down the block that sells detective cameras, so in the morning—"

"I'll bite, what's a detective camera?" Longarm cut in.

The undertaker replied, "New kind of camera, invented by a gent back in New York State. It's just coming on the market and it's a humdinger. It takes what this New York jasper calls a snapshot. You just have to point her and thumb a little tin doohicky on the side, and the company does the rest. The camera is sold with the film already in it. You takes a passel of pictures and then send the whole shebang back to the store."

"Sounds easy enough. Maybe I'll just buy one of them things. The law could sure use more pictures, and it's hard as hell to get an owlhoot to come in and set hisself down for a portrait. We'll talk more on it in the morning, for I've some wires to send."

He left and went down to the Western Union office by the depot. He paused in a doorway to see if anybody was following him. After making reasonably sure there wasn't, Longarm went inside and sent a night letter to Marshal Vail, bringing him up to date and suggesting that the Denver office might check out the late Gordon Murdoch with the state license board.

He sent the night letter he'd promised Helga Hansen to Prosecuter Donovan's office, too, knowing they'd get it before Gus Hansen came to the court from the federal lockup. He couldn't order them not to try the cuss; for all Longarm knew, Hansen was guilty. But he suggested they look into the *post facto* angle in case Hansen had been yelling too much to mention it. He failed to see how it could be any skin off Donovan's nose, either way. There were better ways to waste the taxpayers' money than on useless trials.

He paid for the night letters and then showed the Western Union clerk his badge and ID, saying, "I know the comings and goings of other customers are supposed to be private, but this is a federal case and your wires run over federal lands in places, if you follow my drift."

The clerk nodded and said, "I was raised patriotic, Marshal."

Longarm said, "I noticed you in the crowd earlier, when I had that fight over by the depot doorway."

The clerk nodded again. "I got there after it was over, and I was waiting to see if you wanted to jaw about it before I spoke up."

"I admire discreet gents. There was a gent with the man I had it out with. They were together on the train. They weren't twins, but they looked sort of similar in gunbelts, hats, and other habits. You'd have noticed if anyone like that had been here earlier to send a wire, wouldn't you?"

"I would have," the clerk answered, "and they never. You might ask over in the depot waiting room. Some of the old boys hanging out there may have noticed if he's still hereabouts."

"No professional drifter hangs out in waiting rooms," Longarm said. "The law takes too much interest in such public places. He's likely gone somewhere else for his health, as he never backed his sidekick's play. Some old boys are like that, no matter how brave their gunbelts look."

Longarm went outside and sheltered in the shadows to study both ways before crossing back over to the hotel. He could see from here that Kim had left a light in the window for him, but he'd promised her he'd bring some grub, so as soon as he saw that nobody wanted to shoot him, he walked down to the Chinese restaurant and ordered some chop suey and fried rice to go. It took them some time to fix the stuff, so he sat near the counter and lit up a cheroot as he waited. For some reason the smell from the kitchen didn't make his mouth water worth mention. His cheroot tasted stale too. He wondered if he could be coming down with something. But as he got up to pay for the sack of grub and tote it home, he felt as strong as ever, so he knew what was putting him off his feed. It was that stranger waiting for him at the hotel.

He thought about that as he slowly walked back to her. Kim

had changed in a way that disturbed him. His common sense told him such changes as he'd noticed could be considered improvements, for a love-'em-and-leave-'em gent. But, dammit, he'd liked her better the old way.

Somewhere in the night a train whistle called, sad and lonesome and tempting. There was no point now in pushing on up to Crooked Lance in the Bitter Creek country. He knew Kim didn't want him up there where her ex-in-laws, the Stover gals, could talk about them. He knew the Stover gals would, for he'd had them both, and he knew they were jealous of Kim. She'd been warned to take the notion of Timberline seriously and once she was at all on guard, even Timberline would have a chore doing anything ornery enough to matter. There was only one trail in and out of Crooked Lance, and Kim had some experienced hands working for her who'd know Timberline on sight. Longarm had planned to cut across to Salt Lake after seeing that Kim was safe, and so, now that he had fulfilled that obligation, there was nothing stopping him. The north-south and east-west tracks met at Cheyenne, which was why the town was here. They'd trailed him from Denver with the understanding that he was on his way to Crooked Lance. If he was able to hop a night train in the dark, he could be in Salt Lake before anyone cut his trail again. Kim would likely be sore as hell, but 'uty called and she'd just have to put up with it.

He sighed and walked on to the hotel. He'd told her he was coming back with some Chinese food, and it seemed ornery to treat any gal that way after she'd been so friendly. What the hell, it wasn't as if she were fixing to torture him to death. She just wanted to screw hell out of him all night. It sure was funny how a man's desires blew so hot and cold. He could remember many a night when he'd have run barefoot through broken glass to get at something as nice as that redhead upstairs. Hell, he could remember acting silly as hell over stuff that wasn't half as nice. And he knew that once he saw her naked on those sheets up yonder, he'd be just as horny for her as ever.

He went inside and up the stairs, telling himself not to act like such a sissy. They'd sit on the bed naked and eat chop suey till they were both hot again, and he'd worry about the cold gray dawn when it got here.

He noticed the door was ajar, so he didn't give their old signal as he opened it and stepped inside. The room was empty, save for his saddle and gear in the corner. He put down the sack of grub and picked up the note she'd left on the pillow:

"Custis, Dear: I'm sorry, but it isn't working like I thought it would."

She hadn't signed it. Married gals likely knew better. He read it again, then suddenly grinned and said, "Well, Powder River and let her buck! I can eat this grub just as well aboard the Salt Lake train, and who knows who'll be riding it, wearing skirts?"

Longarm ate the Chinese food on the railroad platform, waiting for a mail flyer that was running late. By the time he boarded, the pullman cars had been made up and the passengers were bedded down for the night. Longarm moved back to the coach to sit up with the poorer folks who couldn't afford pullman berths. He made sure nobody suspicious was aboard, then scrunched down in the seat to spend a fitful night, as he'd done so many times before when riding these night coaches. But this time he dropped off to sleep like he'd been clubbed. For some reason he was tired.

He was bright-eyed and bushy-tailed when the train rolled into Salt Lake City Monday morning. He found a beanery open and stuffed some ham and eggs under his belt. Then he went to Temple Square and sat on a bench, watching tourists feeding the pigeons till the federal offices were open. He caught District Judge Hawkins on the granite steps as he was on his way to work. They knew each other from the past, so Judge Hawkins said, "Morning, Longarm. What brings you to the City of the Saints?"

Longarm asked, "Didn't you get the message Marshal Vail sent, Your Honor?"

"Not hardly," Hawkins replied. "I was off for the weekend. But it's likely on my desk inside. What can I do for Denver, Longarm?"

Longarm said, "I need an exhumation order, sir. You remember the time I gunned Cotton Younger just inside?"

"I sure do. The fight started in my chambers and ended up out in the corridors, noisy as hell. Is that who you want to dig up, son? He's been down there long enough to be sort of messy. I've always found it neater to let the dead stay buried."

Longarm said, "I'd like to leave him in his grave, too. But the rascal doesn't seem to want to stay put. I'll explain as we're scouting up the proper forms and all."

Judge Hawkins led Longarm inside and up to his chambers as Longarm filled him in on the corpse who seemed to be stalking him. Hawkins sat down at his desk and opened a drawer as he said, "I'll issue you the order. But it beats me what you're trying to prove, son. We both know who we planted in that grave. It seems obvious to me you're dealing with a double."

"I sure hope so," Longarm said. "But I've wired Missouri, and Clay County has no records of Cotton Younger having a twin."

Hawkins found the form he was looking for and started filling it out as he said, "Doesn't have to be a twin. Just somebody that looks like old Timberline."

"That would take some doing, sir. Things like giantism and albinism run in families. I'll buy another giant albino, but this cuss has the selfsame features."

He took out the photograph and handed it to the older man as Hawkins signed the exhumation order. Hawkins looked at it and said, "Damn, that sure as hell looks like Timberline. Didn't you say you had a picture of a sidekick of his you shot last night?"

Longarm said, "Not yet. I didn't want to waste time waiting about for it, so I left a message to send it to my Denver office. I ain't worried about the one in Cheyenne. I know who he was, and this is the first time he's been killed."

"You say he worked for a Denver agency?"

"Yep, and I mean to discuss this in detail with them as soon as I get back there. Bounty hunting's bad enough, but assassination is illegal. I mean to point that out to them when I discuss the bond they posted with the state of Colorado."

Hawkins handed Longarm the court order, but said, "If it's all the same to you, I'd just as soon not go with you to the

92

burial grounds. Who's to pay the workmen there for the nasty job?"

"I reckon I'll have to, sir. You reckon they'll want extra for the deed?"

Hawkins grimaced and said, "I would. Wouldn't you?"

Judge Hawkins was right. When Longarm took a hired hack out to the burial grounds, the gravediggers raised unholy hell with him. The leader of the three-man crew said, "Look here, we're only paid to bury 'em, not dig 'em up, Deputy."

"Come on, boys, surely you've exhumed a few in your time out here, ain't you?"

"We have, and that's why we don't like to. You ever smell an overripe cadaver, Deputy?"

"I was at Shiloh, long before I took up this line of work. What the hell, how bad can *one* dead man smell?"

"Bad enough, We'll lend you a shovel for six bits."

Longarm swore and said, "I ain't got time. How much do you boys get to dig?"

"Dollar an hour. Hard to find gravediggers when there's coal mines in the neighborhood."

Longarm knew they were lying; nobody made a dollar an hour at manual labor, anywhere. But he said, "All right. I'll pay two. How about it?"

They knew they were lying, too. So, after some more dickering, they led him out to the plot and fell to work. It was funny how quiet and spooky a graveyard felt, even in bright sunshine. It didn't seem polite to sit on one of the other headstones, so he paced up and down, puffing a smoke, as the gravediggers worked. They'd taken advantage of him, but they were honest enough workmen, so it only seemed like a million years before one of them, standing neck-deep in the hole, said, "Oh shit, it's a cheap pine box. The rains and worms will have played pure Ned with what's in here, Deputy."

Longarm walked over, saying, "He didn't have any friends interested in a fancy coffin." Then he looked down at the muddy planks that the workman's brogans were on and said, "Let's pop her open, boys."

The man in the hole swung his pick skillfully into a corner and heaved. A long strip of pine came off with a gasp of pained

93

rusty nails. The gravedigger held his breath as he pulled more splintered wood away. Then he frowned down and said, "What the hell . . . ?"

Longarm felt sort of funny too. The coffin was empty!

Another gravedigger asked, "Have you been funning us, mister?"

Longarm said, "Nope. Somebody has been funning the law. A funeral was bought and paid for here. But as you can all see, nobody seems to be buried."

He blew out a lungful of smoke and added, "You boys would likely recall any other exhumation orders, right?"

"Of course, Deputy. You're the first gent who's ever asked to peek in this particular grave."

"You mean you do get some such requests from time to time?"

"Sure, we already told you that. We had to take an infernal Mormon up from over there by that birdbath at few weeks ago, as a matter of fact. He died alone on the desert, and it took some time before his kin in Ogden found out about it and asked to have him shipped home."

Longarm stared past the birdbath and saw the place they meant. The grass hadn't come back to full green yet. He said, "I'm talking about *this* neck of the woods."

The gravedigger said, "No. There hasn't been anyone buried or dug up around here recent."

"Could somebody maybe sneak in here at night and do her without a proper exhumation order?"

The three gravediggers exchanged uneasy glances. Then the foreman shook his head and said, "They'd have to be mighty sneaky. There's a night watchman with a dog, and them street-lights, yonder, shine all night on these headstones. Makes 'em look spooky as hell."

Another man asked Longarm who Timberline had been. He didn't have time to tell the whole tale, so he just said, "Wanted outlaw. Looks like he's still wanted. You boys may as well fill the hole. He sure as hell ain't where he's supposed to be."

94

Chapter 7

The train back to Denver wouldn't leave until late afternoon, so Longarm faced a few hours to kill in one of the tamest places west of the Big Muddy. He'd left his saddle and possibles checked at the depot. He hoped Marshal Vail would understand the travel expenses he was piling up; he would have needed that saddle if he'd gone up to the Bitter Creek country as planned. Now it was just something else to lug around.

He considered paying a visit to his friend Quincy Boggs, a rather free-thinking pillar of the Mormon community—and the father of three even more free-thinking, insatiable daughters—but decided that since only Judge Hawkins and the grave-diggers knew he was in town, it might be better to keep it that way.

As he strode along Main Street, Longarm passed a photography shop with a number of what appeared to be a smaller-than-usual type of folding cameras in the window, arrayed around a large hand-lettered sign. As he continued on down the street, the words on the sign sank slowly into his mind. He stopped abruptly, frowned, and walked back.

The sign touted a new kind of camera, one that could be

used by anyone; its main feature seemed to be that it used a new kind of film that came on a roll with paper backing. The kind of pictures it took were called "snapshots."

"Hell, old son," Longarm muttered to himself, "you're an old hand at snapshooting. Let's take a look-see."

Inside the store, he asked the clerk about those snapshot doohickies, and the clerk put an album of pictures on the counter between them.

The clerk said, "Folks have been taking pictures of one another, at home and at play, with this amazing new invention. See this one? It was taken out by the lake by a man who'd never used a camera before!"

Longarm stared morosely down at the little snapshot of three fat gals wading in the Great Salt Lake with their skirts hiked up. He couldn't see why anyone would care to immortalize the occasion, but he noticed that the picture was clear and you could see all three of their silly, smirking faces.

"I don't know," he said. "I've seen some photographers taking tintypes and such, and they seem to spend all kinds of time fooling around with the lenses. Afraid it'd be a mite scientific for me."

The clerk leaned forward and said conspiratorially, with a wide smile, "That's the secret of this great invention. There's no lens setting. Let me show you."

He took one of the devices from under the counter and placed it between them, clicking the shutter as he said, "That's all there is to it. You just aim it with this gunsight notion here, and click her once. This little wheel on the side cranks the roll of film forward to the next shot. You look through this red peephole on the back, and when you see the next number printed on the roll—"

"Did you just take my picture?" Longarm asked.

"No," the clerk replied, "this is just a demonstration model."

"Hell," Longarm said, "show me one that works."

"They all work," the clerk protested. "The ones on sale have the film already in them. You just shoot your pictures and bring back the camera, and we develop them for you."

Longarm was skeptical. "It needs more work if you mean to sell many of these contraptions. It's like buying a pig in a poke. How am I to know the gadget you sold me is any good or not, if I can't try her out? There ought to be some way a body could put his own film in that thing and take it out again his own self."

The clerk looked shocked. "Oh, sir, the general public is not intelligent enough to load and unload its own camera film, and it has to be loaded and unloaded in a darkroom."

Longarm pushed his Stetson back on his head and rested an elbow on the counter. "We load and unload our own guns, don't we? How many guns do you reckon Sam Colt would sell if they had to be loaded and unloaded by a gunsmith?"

"A lot of people have been buying them, sir," the clerk said smugly.

"A lot of people go to spirit rappings and rub snake oil on their bald heads too," Longarm said. "The folks that make these things have got some bugs to work out if they ever expect 'em to catch on with sensible folks."

The clerk looked resigned. Longarm took out his wallet and said, "Here, give me one of the infernal contraptions and make sure it's set to fire."

"But, sir, you said—"

"I know what I just said. It so happens that I am after a spirit, and this makes a mite more sense than listening for raps. I'll take one of those shoulder straps for the critter too. If I take off my frock coat and hang it over my shoulder, it ought to ride sort of to one side of my Ingersoll watch. But I'm sure going to look dumb."

He paid in cash, not daring to put such a notion on his expense account, and as the clerk made his change, Longarm removed his coat and fiddled the loaded camera into position, riding above his .44 and half hidden by the coat when he put it back on. He saw that it bulged even worse if he buttoned up, so he left his coat open as he took his change and said, "I have to go to Denver. Can they unload and develop this notion there?"

"Of course, sir. Any distributor anywhere will be pleased to assist you."

"Suppose I took it to some other lab? I have a friend in Denver who develops photographs."

The clerk shook his head and said, "I don't think that's a good idea, sir. We only guarantee the results if we do it ourselves."

"But it could be done?"

"In a darkroom, by someone who knew what they were doing and used our chemicals? I suppose so. But I don't advise it."

Longarm grumped out and went back to Temple Square to watch the pigeons. Pigeons were tedious just to look at, and not much more fun to shoot at, but a nice-looking young mother was encouraging her two kids to waste breadcrumbs on the feathered vermin. So Longarm watched *her*. She was maybe in her late twenties, and nursing those little rascals hadn't hurt her bust worth mention. She was likely Mormon, but you couldn't tell. Mormons were more sensible than some of the odd little sects out here. They dressed as nicely as anyone else and kept themselves clean. The young mother looked like she could handle kids and housework without forgetting that a man expected a woman in bed with him at night. He wondered what it would be like to come home every night to a nice-looking wife and some cute little rascals. He wasn't planning for it to happen soon, but a man had to think on his retirement years, and most of the older men he knew were married up. He didn't think it would be all that painful to find that Mormon gal waiting for him at home with her long dark hair unpinned and hanging softly in the lamplight, and hell, she wasn't half as good-looking as Elanore Wilson.

He warned himself that he was thinking silly thoughts, but nobody was looking. The nice thing about getting a gal who already had her own litter was the savings in time and expectation. Young Larry was already a decent little cuss. So even if later ones turned out mean and ugly, they'd be ahead of the game. But hell, he was a long way from retirement, and he doubted that Elanore would be running loose when he got ready to surrender.

The young mother shot a wary glance his way, aware of his eyes on her. Longarm leaned back on the bench and looked innocent; he meant her no harm, and it never hurt a pretty gal to admire her at a polite distance. It was a public park, and if he was bothering her by being there, she could always move

98

down to the other end. There were pigeons all over the place.

She might have done so, too. But then the little gal she was with decided she'd fed enough birds and decided to catch 'em by the tails. She ran his way, yelling at the pigeons as they exploded from the walk to flutter over Longarm, trying to hit his hat with pigeon shit in passing. The young mother trotted wearily after her, calling out to the child as her eye caught Longarm's and quickly looked away, to his left rear, where there was nothing fresher-looking than bushes. Then her eyes widened and she screamed, "Oh no! Malvinia!"

Malvinia wasn't his name, but he rolled sideways as he saw the look of total terror in her eyes, for he somehow doubted that she was all that scared of *him*. A bullet thunked into the backrest of the bench and showered him with splinters as it tore on through the wood his back had been leaning against!

Longarm spun on his knee to face the echoing gunshot as he yelled out, "Hit the ground with them young'uns ma'am!" and reached for his own gun in its cross-draw rig. The fool camera he'd just bought was hung up in the way as he hunkered to make as small a target as he knew how. He swore, then had a better idea and pulled the camera instead of the gun.

He raised it as high as he could, aimed it in the direction he thought the gunshot had come from, and clicked the shutter. The gun fired again, ticking the sleeve of his upraised arm, so Longarm figured the cuss just didn't want his picture taken.

He put the camera on the seat of the bench, moved sideways, and risked a look behind him. The young mother had scooped up a kid under each arm and was running like hell. But nobody was shooting at her, so they were all right. He drew his more serious weapon, took a deep breath, and crabbed sideways before rising to face the shooter, man to man.

There was nobody there. Blue gunsmoke hung between Longarm and the line of ornamental shrubbery blocking his view. He vaulted the line of benches and tore through the bushes to find himself staring at a wide-open avenue. A uniformed policeman was crossing against the traffic, so Longarm holstered his revolver and wearily took out his ID.

The copper came over to him and said, "I heard gunshots."

Longarm said, "I know. They were meant for me." He didn't mention that he might have a picture of the rascal.

Longarm told the Salt Lake copper the little he knew, and they parted amicably.

Since Longarm still had some time to kill, he found a library where a man could kill some time in peace and quiet, with his back against a solid wall. Longarm didn't want it to get around Larimer Street, but his secret vice was reading. Like most self-educated men, he read like he played the typewriter, hunt-and-peck. There was no end to the odd facts a man could find in books, and you never knew when it might come in handy to know the yearly rainfall in Venezuela, or that roses were the cash crop of Bulgaria. Since he'd just taken up snapshooting, Longarm got a book on photography and cracked it open, wishing he was allowed to smoke in the reading room. There was nothing in the book about these newfangled cameras, since the book was four or five years old. Longarm had to move his lips as he read off all the chemicals you had to know about. It was small wonder it had taken until 1839 to figure out picture-taking. A body had to know about halides, bromides, cyanides, and all sort of other *ides*. The book said they used silver to make photograph plates. No wonder it was expensive. He found himself admiring Elanore Wilson even more as he read about how tricky the art was. The people back East who made these new cameras figured to lose their shirts. There was no way the average gent was likely to take up photography as a hobby. It was too durned complicated.

He found a chapter on special effects, and read it carefully. The part about double exposure was right interesting and not nearly as hard to grasp as all those *ides*. The book said you could get two things in the same picture by opening the shutter twice. But there'd only been one face in the picture Flash Stubbs had taken in front of the Parthenon. Longarm took the print out and studied it. A double exposure could account for nothing he could see. There was just old Timberline against the sky, with that corniced building behind him, and what the hell, they'd both been there. Longarm had taken the plate directly to another photographer and watched as she developed it in all those *ides*. The book said that if you opened the shutter twice on the same plate, you had to use less developer than usual, and Elanore had run it through the regular way. He read on and came to a passage on backdrops. It said that sometimes

100

when you saw a couple standing in front of Niagara Falls, or Buffalo Bill smiling from amid a herd of buffalo, they were fooling. The picture could be taken in a studio with a big fake scene behind them. But he didn't see where that trail led. If Cotton Younger had ever stood in front of a Denver backdrop, it made no more sense than anything else about the spooky rascal. If he was really dead, this picture had to have been taken while he was alive, a while back. Supposing it had been taken in front of a real or fake Denver, how in the hell was Cotton Younger or anybody else to know that someday he'd be sneaking up on folks in the Parthenon Saloon? The picture the street photographer had taken was likely the real McCoy. The one he'd just taken over in the park was real for sure, if he hadn't missed and taken a snapshot of a shitting pigeon. So if the face of the man who'd tried for him just now matched the one in the first photograph, it would be proof that old Timberline or his ghost . . .

Longarm looked in the index, and sure enough, there was a chapter on "spirit photography." The author didn't believe in it and said those spooky pictures some lady in England had taken in a haunted house were likely double exposures. But it seemed some folks thought the camera could see things the human eye might miss, like floating ectoplasm in a dimly lit room. Longarm had an open mind on such scientific notions, but the spook he kept meeting up with wasn't made of wispy ectoplasm. It would take something more solid to fire a gun. Timberline was running around solid, in broad-ass daylight. Ghosts that substantial were against common sense.

Longarm had been raised Christian, and while he took some parts of the Good Book with a grain of salt, he figured some-body logical had started the universe and had to be running it along rational lines. He wasn't sure about life after death, but if there was, it had to be someplace less substantial than Denver or Salt Lake City. There'd be no damned point to having folks die in the first damned place if they could just get up and go about their business. Besides, all those other folks in the burial ground he'd just come from had been staying put. Who would want to lie in a grave forever if it was at all possible to get out?

He gazed down at the photograph of Timberline and said,

"You're alive, you son of a bitch. I don't know how you done it. But you're still flesh and blood, like me. So we're still even as to the odds, as you likely know, or you wouldn't be so shy about letting me get a clear shot at you!"

He put the picture back in his pocket and took the book back to the shelf. He still had a little time to kill, so he moseyed back to the Salt Lake City Federal Building and picked up a few new flyers and government notices to read on the train. He went to the depot, booked a bunk on the night train to Denver, and while he was at it, he stocked up on smokes and a copy of Ned Buntline's latest Wild West magazine. He needed a few good chuckles.

The most direct way back to Denver was via the Denver & Rio Grande Western. But even that wasn't very direct; it was well over five hundred miles on a twisting mountain track. He tipped a porter to put his saddle and possibles aboard the baggage car, and took up a position on a platform bench before the train started letting passengers get on. He watched over the top of the Wild West magazine as folks boarded in groups or alone. He saw all sorts of folks getting on, pretty, ugly, and in between. He didn't see any giant albinos who seemed interested in riding with him. He waited until the train crew hauled up the loading steps and then he waited longer till the train was moving, before he got up, stepped to the edge of the platform, and caught the grab-irons of the rear platform on the fly to haul himself aboard. There were some folks in the observation car, and they looked at him funny when he got on that way, but none of them said anything and none of them was Timberline, so what the hell.

He nodded politely and made his way forward to the car he'd booked a berth on, looking over the other passengers along the way. He met the conductor and let him punch his ticket. Then he found the colored porter and handed him a silver dollar, saying, "I know they call you George, but if you'd rather have me call you something else, speak up."

The porter looked at the coin in his palm and said, "Suh, you can call me George if it suits your fancy. What is I supposed to do for this?"

Longarm said, "I'll give you the usual two bits for making up my bunk when we get to Denver. I want you to tell me if anybody on this train asks any questions about me. To satisfy your curiosity, I am the U.S. law and somebody may be interested. Are you following my drift?"

"Yessuh. I don't know who you is, and if somebody axes, I'll tell you."

"I took you for another professional. Uh, I noticed there is more than one attractive she-male riding in the coach back there. How strict is the D&RGW about such matters, George?"

The porter grinned and said, "What we don't see, we don't mess with. It's supposed to be agin the rules for more than one passenger to occupy a single bunk, but who's gonna look?"

Longarm grinned back and said, "I'll take care of you some more if I get lucky. When do you start making up the bunks?"

"Oh, not till nine or so, suh. You'll have plenty of time to sashay back and forth to the club car. You want a tip on a certain lady I'd say don't look like she likes to ride sitting up, suh?"

"No thanks, George. I like to do my own hunting."

So he did, walking slowly back to the club and observation car. There was more than one pretty gal to choose from, even after eliminating the obviously prim ones. Longarm had two things going for him: There weren't too many gents riding solo, and he wasn't desperate. He hardly cared if he picked up anyone or not, since he had other things to worry about. He knew the sensible thing would be to skip the whole notion, since it had been a while since he'd had a night's sleep alone, and if the gal got attached to him it could be a pain in the ass when the train got to Denver.

He hooked a boot over the brass rail in the club car and ordered a beer as the train rolled eastward across irrigated Mormon farmlands in the sunset. Naturally, since he wasn't trying, his eye caught that of a nice-looking brunette as soon as he turned to lean his back on the bar, beer glass in hand. She was sitting at a table by the window across from him, nursing a tall gin and tonic. He didn't care if he blew it or not, so he smiled.

She smiled back and then looked away, as if all that celery growing out there was more interesting. But he'd read her smoke signals.

He moved over casually, and asked her if the seat across

from her was taken. She shrugged and didn't say one way or the other, so he sat down and introduced himself. "I'm Custis Long and I am going to Denver. I got me a pullman bunk reserved, up forward."

She said, "I'm Sally DuVal and I'm going as far as Chicago. I'm riding pullman too, but I thank you for the invitation. Do you always come on so directly, cowboy?"

He smiled sheepishly and said, "Not always, Miss Sally. But when time is of the essence, it pays to put one's cards on the table. I knew a gal named Sally one time. They called her Roping Sally. She was a cowboy too."

The other Sally dimpled and said, "I imagine you've known a lot of girls named Sally and everything else. Are those shoulders padded, or is that you in there?"

"I grew up working for a living, ma'am. I could comment nice about how you fill your own duds, but I wouldn't want to give you the impression I was forward."

Sally DuVal laughed and said, "Heaven forfend! I can see you're one of those shy boys a girl has to lead by the hand."

"Where would you like to lead me, Miss Sally?"

"Down, boy," she said. "I haven't decided yet if I want to have dinner with you or not. They did say this train takes all night to get to Denver, didn't they?"

"Yes, ma'am. It has to stop at tedious places like Grand Junction, and it's mostly an uphill grade. If you'll have dinner with me, I'd sure admire paying for the both of us."

She laughed a trifle wildly, and said, "You're cute, in a crazy way. But we'd better get a few things straight before we carry this conversation any further. If I let you buy me dinner, it's with the understanding that dinner is all you're buying, agreed?"

He grinned and said, "Sure." He knew they all said that up front. He knew that she knew he was onto her, too. But, like him, she likely found it more fun to spar around some in the opening stages.

So they had a few more drinks back in the club car to sort of break the ice, and by the time the dining car chimes sounded, he was calling her Sally and she was calling him Custis. He rose and took her arm to steer her the length of the train to the dining car. As they passed through the coaches, a couple of other gals who hadn't had sense enough to go back and drink alone looked up at them sort of wistfully, and Sally looked sort of smug about that, too.

From there on, the details would have been tedious to brag on in a saloon, although Longarm found each move interesting enough at the time, because she looked even nicer by lamplight as it got dark outside. It was Sally who started playing footsies under the table in the dining car. He reached across and took her hand as they were having coffee and dessert.

After that, as she'd said she might, Sally took to leading him around by the hand, and where she led him was to her compartment at the end of the car where he'd booked a bunk. It was mighty fancy, next to a fold-down bunk. The door locked on the inside, and they were all to themselves when Sally unpinned her hat, put it on the rack above the bunk, and turned to kiss him as though they were old pals coming home from a night on the town.

He responded in kind, and things were pretty hot from the neck up. But between her whalebone corset and the camera and gunbelt under his frock coat, rubbing their bodies against each other was a sheer waste of motion.

They came up for air and Sally said, "That was nice. But slow down, it's early yet, and what on earth have you got under your coat?"

He let go of her to peel the coat off, hanging it on a hook as he held the camera up and said, "I have taken up a new hobby, if this thing works. And it ain't all that early, considering I'll have to get off in Denver in the wee small hours."

Not asking for permission, Longarm took his gun rig and hat off too, and hung them over the coat and camera strap. He didn't think he'd better take off his vest until he had her out of something besides her hat. But the gold-plated chain draped across between his vest pockets was attached to a watch at one end and a brass derringer at the other. So he whipped them out and tucked them in his pants pocket, not wanting to leave bruises as he hauled her in for another exploratory kiss. They could get a lot closer now. But as he held her to him with one palm in the small of her back and the other cupping her derriere, he was painfully aware that she was encased in more of Jonah's whale than the Good Lord had intended. There was no way in hell a man could shuck a lady out of a laced-up corset without her cooperation. He took advantage of a sudden sway of the car to sort of fall with her to the made-up bunk and work his leg between her thighs to open them a mite before he eased up in the kissing enough to let her have her say.

"You're mixing me up, cowboy. It's true we don't have as much time as I'd like, but I don't want you to think I do this sort of thing with every man I meet aboard a train!"

He said, "I don't either. There's a whole mess of gals aboard this night train, but as you can see, I only have eyes for you."

She giggled and asked, "Don't you mean hands? I swear, you must have been sired by an octopus! How on earth are you doing what you're doing with my dress and underpinnings between us? Stop that, you fool!"

He didn't. He kissed her some more as he went on fingering her through the folds of her skirt and drawers. It took some ingenuity, but he had long fingers and the lower edge of her formidable corset ended just below her bellybutton. She opened her thighs wider as she moaned and braced her high-button shoes against the floor boards to thrust her pelvis up at a better angle of attack. Longarm had a better grasp on the situation now, and while he couldn't get his fingers deep with all that infernal cloth in the way, he was able to massage her Gates of Paradise tolerably, and she seemed to like it, from the way she began to move.

She rolled her lips off his and gasped, "My God, what are you doing to me? I haven't done this with my clothes on since I was a schoolgirl!"

"You want me to stop?"

"You know I don't, you bastard! But you ought to be horse-whipped just the same! A girl's not safe around you, even fully dressed, and . . . Oh . . . Custis!"

He kissed her hard and held her tight as he felt her coming. She reached down to grasp his erection, still inside his pants. She opened her thighs wider and moaned, "Oh, finish right, darling! You're driving me out of my mind with this teasing!"

So he let go of his advantage to hoist her skirts quickly as she unbuttoned his fly and gripped him tightly. He rolled atop her, with her hips on the edge of the bunk and her legs braced wide, feet on the decking. She had on thigh-length stockings, held by lacy elastic garters, and of course she still wore her loose silk underpants. He couldn't figure out a way to haul them down that wouldn't give her a chance to change her mind as her legs and thoughts came together, so he reached down between them to move one of the elastic leg openings aside and worked the tip of his erection into place as she said, "You idiot, you can't get in that way."

And then her eyes opened wide as she gasped, "Oh, I see you *can*!"

It was awkward as hell, but she was too hot to care as she moved her hips to meet his thrusts, the silk of her drawers crackling sparks as it rubbed against the wool tweed surrounding the base of his naked shaft. He got his booted feet well-braced and tried to work deeper, excited in his own right by the way she felt somehow more naked with everything covered up. He put a hand on one of her breasts as he nuzzled her neck. And while the neck was downright indecent against his lips, the breast was just a sort of bump in her armor. She closed her eyes and hissed as he felt her warm, moist vagina contract in orgasm. So he joined her, coming harder than a man had any right to in such a ridiculous position. He stayed put as they throbbed down together from the clouds, and when she opened her eyes and smiled radiantly up at him, he said, "Howdy. I don't know where you've just been, but I just brushed wings with the angels."

She laughed, face flushed, and said, "You big fool. We're going to ruin our clothes."

"I know," he said. "Why don't we take 'em off, seeing we ain't strangers anymore?"

She said, "You're going to have to help me with my corset. I was so worried about that. You see, I had a maid at the hotel in Salt Lake lace me into it, and I meant to sleep with it on until I got off the train. I was wondering how to get around that all the time we were dining. I know you won't believe me, but I really don't usually make friends so quickly."

He withdrew gingerly and helped her to a sitting position, one arm still around her, as he said, "That's why I figured we'd best do it the first time without bothering. Let's shuck you right, and in the morning I'll lace you back up proper."

Sally nodded as she unbuttoned her bodice, then flinched

and said, "Oh my God, that window shade was up all the time!"

Longarm glanced at their reflection in the dark glass and said, "Hell, we're passing through open country, going fifty miles an hour."

"Maybe, but what if somebody saw us just now?"

"Likely left some sheepherder frustrated as hell. We're rolling through the foothills now, and there's nobody else out there. Besides, we had our faces buried in each other's, so what could anyone have seen that they'll ever be able to rawhide us about?"

"You're awful. I'll bet you'd do it in broad daylight in the middle of a crossroads, wouldn't you?"

"Don't know. Never had the opportunity. Here, I'll yank the curtain down and we'll say no more about it."

Sally stood and peeled her dress off, standing in her stockings and unmentionables. The corset damned near cut her in two, and she looked saucy as hell with her patches of bare flesh playing peek-a-boo with all that frilly black lace and pink silk. She unpinned her hair and let it cascade down her back in soft waves of lamplit sepia. He stood to move behind her and part it to unlace her corset. She asked, "Is that really a camera hanging over there? Don't tell me you take dirty pictures too."

He said, "I never have, so far. I've only exposed one picture on the roll, and I'll be switched if anyone's on it at all. But if he is, it's a sort of ugly man."

The brunette sighed with relief as she started popping out of the corset he was unlacing for her. She said, "I've posed for lots of pictures. With my clothes on, of course. I'm a concert singer, if you're curious at all about anything else I do."

"I noticed you had a nice voice. Not that there's a thing wrong with the rest of you, of course."

He finished unlacing her, and she gripped the edges of the corset to take it off by lowering and stepping out of it. She cast it aside and turned to face him, asking, "Well?"

His mouth went damned near dry as he nodded and said, "Well, indeed!"

She'd shucked the pants in the process and stood facing him, hands on hips, in nothing but her garters and silk stockings. Sally didn't need that fool corset to look good. He liked her natural curves as the lamplight shaded them and made her look like a Greek statue of Aphrodite. The parts that were generally covered by a fig leaf were smooth-shaven. He'd suspected as much before, but couldn't be sure with all the duds between them. He didn't comment on her shaving down there. It was her own business why she did it. But she said, "I suppose you wonder why I shave under my arms and all."

He said, "I had to do that once, in the army. But I don't suspicion you of nits, for anyone can see you bathe regular."

He started to unbutton his own shirt as he added, "I'd better join you in the altogether."

But Sally sat on the bunk with a coy smile and said, "Take my picture first."

"Take your *what*? You're *naked*, honey."

"I know. I'll give you my forwarding address and you can send me some prints. You may think I'm vain about my body, but—"

"Honey, you got a body to be vain about! But are you sure it would be proper?"

"For God's sake, Custis, you just laid me."

"As I aim to some more, Lord willing and the creeks don't rise. But I wasn't talking about us. I was talking about taking pictures of you in the altogether."

"Don't you think nude studies are artistic?" she asked, raising her elbows to strike a pose. It made her firm breasts look even better, as she likely knew. "Well," he said, "I've seen some interesting paintings of naked ladies over many a bar, but most of the photographs along those lines that I've seen were shown to me by a feller in an alley who said 'psst.'"

"I'm not talking about dirty pictures, Custis. I'd like some prints of me looking Grecian. Come on, let's photograph my flesh. Why should you be bashful?"

Longarm didn't want to say another gal would be developing the film, if Elanore in Denver knew how to unload the new-fangled camera. He hadn't told Sally he was a lawman or what was on the first frame; he'd learned not to leave his own forwarding address with strangers on a train.

He said, "I don't think the light in here is bright enough. You have to use flash powder indoors at night, don't you?"

"How should I know? Let's just take a couple for fun and see how they turn out."

He shrugged and took the camera from its hanging case. What the hell, it wasn't as if he and Elanore had exchanged vows. He raised the camera, sighted on her, and said, "Uh, you don't look very Grecian with those socks on. Anybody seeing a picture of a naked lady in bed like that is likely to think I took this in a bawdy house."

She laughed and said, "I know. I may as well confess, this is making me feel hot and sort of naughty."

That was a nice way to make any pretty gal feel, so Longarm snapped the shutter and said, "Well, now you're took. Can I take my clothes off now?"

Sally rolled over and struck another pose, with her elbows on the bunk and her smooth, rounded rump raised teasingly as she said, "Let's get me this way." So he did. Elanore was going to ask some mighty interesting questions in any case, damn it.

Sally giggled, rolled into another pose, and said, "One more. Let's make it a good one."

He stared through the sight, frowned, and said, "Hold on, now you're getting downright dirty."

The curvy brunette had her thighs apart and was fingering herself as she stuck out her tongue at the camera. She said, "Do it, and then mount me. I don't suppose there's a way for us both to be in the picture, is there?"

He said, "Not hardly," and snapped the shutter before he'd had time to consider how he was going to explain this shot to Elanore. He sighed and decided there was no way. Maybe he'd just have to find another lab in Denver. A gent couldn't ask a lady to look at photographs like this.

Sally asked, "Is there any more film in the camera?"

"Yeah," he said, "and I'll likely get arrested trying to have it developed."

He turned to put the camera away in the case hanging on the door hook. As he did so, the clicking of the wheels under them was drowned out by the roar of a sixgun—*two* sixguns!—going off right outside.

"Hit the floor and stay there, gal!" Longarm snapped as he snuffed the lamp and drew the derringer from his pants pocket.

A woman was screaming outside as he cracked the door for a look-see. The narrow corridor between the compartments and the far windows was empty, so Longarm stepped out, smelling gunsmoke and hearing boot heels. A man packing two smoking sixguns came around the angle from the canvas-draped pullman bunks to the rear. As he saw Longarm he gasped and said, "Oh no!"

"Freeze! I'm law!" Longarm barked.

Some folks just never listen. The two-gun man fired from the hip, wildly, and Longarm returned his fire with the deadly little derringer as the other's round tore a divot of paneling from the wall, too near for comfort. Longarm's .44 slug took the mysterious stranger higher than he'd aimed, but since he'd aimed at his fly, it folded the fellow around his belt buckle like a jackknife, and the second round from the derringer slammed through the top of his Stetson to part his hair and skull in the middle. As the man and his guns scattered on the floor, Longarm reached one arm inside Sally's compartment and fished his double-action Colt out of its hanging holster.

But the next man who came up the aisle was wearing a conductor's uniform and an ashen expression, so Longarm didn't shoot him.

The conductor said, "What happened? I heard gunshots!" Then, as the smoke cleared and he looked down, he croaked, "Oh my God!"

Longarm said, "I'm law. Don't know who the hell he was, but I asked him polite to freeze and he never. Anybody hurt back there?"

The conductor said, "I don't know! I was in the car behind when all hell busted loose up here!"

The pullman porter came to join them, looking sort of ashen too, which took some doing. He spotted Longarm and looked even more surprised. He said, "Lord of mercy, suh! I thought he'd killed you! Your pullman curtains back there has been shot up awesome! A passenger across the aisle said he saw it. That rascal on the floor stopped when he read the number on your berth, whupped out both guns, and fired through them curtains at you. Or, what I means is—"

"I follow your meaning," Longarm cut in, rolling the dead man over with his boot. The face was sort of messed up, but

Longarm could make out enough. "One of you block off this passage," he said. "I'll see what his pockets have to say about him."

He knelt, patting for bulges until he found a wallet and took it out with his free hand. He flipped it open and read, "'Rocky Mountain Detective Agency. Operative Will McSorley.' Looks like what we have here is another bounty hunter. Only there was no price on my head, so the gent was working as a hired assassin."

The conductor had moved back to block curiosity-seekers. The porter said, "He sure assassinated the hell out of your berth, suh! I'll get some fresh linen for you when you is ready to really occupy it."

Longarm shook his head and said, "I'll take care of you good before I get off in Denver. But right now I have more important chores for you than fluffing up my pillow, George. I mean to have a serious discussion about their state bond with the folks at that detective agency in Denver, but we ain't fixing to get there for a spell. Do you think you could find a place to store this gent for me?"

The porter nodded. "Yessuh, it's cool up in the baggage car. But where will you sleep?" And then he noticed the door ajar nearby and wisely said, "Yessuh, you just leave him to me. I'll 'splain to the conductor that you is conducting an investigation and don't want folks pestering you."

Longarm smiled at the porter. "I don't know if there's a reward on this hombre, but if there is, you boys on the train crew will be let in on it. I, uh, have to get back to my investigating."

He ducked inside the darkened compartment and Sally whispered from the berth, "What on earth was all that about? Did I hear you say you were a lawman, Custis?"

He locked the door and started to peel as he said, "Yeah, but I ain't on duty at the moment, and what I have in mind ain't no federal crime."

Chapter 8

Longarm got off the train in Denver feeling sort of stiff, partly because it was a cold, clammy morning and partly because he hadn't gotten much sleep. The body of the man he'd shot was wrapped in a tarp and even stiffer. It lay on a baggage cart as the train pulled out. Sally waved from the observation platform and Longarm waved wearily back. She'd left her address with him, but he didn't mean to send her any dirty snapshots. He knew that by the time she'd had breakfast, she'd be having cooled-off second thoughts.

A uniformed Denver copper joined Longarm by the baggage cart on which his saddle and possibles were stacked along with the corpse. The copper said, "Morning, Longarm. Railroad wired ahead that you had some trouble on the night train."

Longarm pointed at the canvas-wrapped cadaver with his chin and said, "I didn't have the trouble. He did. His ID says he works for a detective agency here in town. His name was McSorley."

"Will McSorley? I know him. He works for that Rocky Mountain agency up on Colfax. Or he did. I'm surprised you had trouble with him. Old Will wasn't a bad cuss, considering."

Longarm frowned and said, "You may save me a tedious discussion with his boss, then. Let me show the rascal to you."

He unwrapped the upper folds of the tarp and the copper shook his head and said, "That ain't Will McSorley. McSorley's got a red beard."

"Hmm. That's sort of interesting. You know another bounty hunter called Murdoch, works for the same outfit?"

The copper said, "Sure. Saw him maybe an hour ago, having ham and eggs at the Greek's on Larimer. Why?"

Longarm rewrapped the dead man's face as he said, "Why, indeed? I gunned a man in Cheyenne the other night who said he was Murdoch. They're sending me his morgue portrait by mail. If this ain't McSorley and he wasn't Murdoch, what we have here is a couple of other folk pretending to be private detectives. I'll have my office send photos of both faces and maybe find out who and why. Could you see about putting this one on ice for me? I have a busy day ahead, and I'll send you the proper forms for the coroner and such."

The copper nodded and said, "Sure, Longarm. Always glad to help out Uncle Sam. But the Denver Morgue's sure getting crowded. Two cowboys committed mutual suicide last night by slapping leather, drunk, at five paces. Somebody gunned a street photographer too. We ain't found out who did it yet."

Longarm frowned and asked, "Was the victim by any chance named Stubbs?"

"Yeah. How did you know? Happened yesterday. Poor old Flash had his camera set up over by the opera house, and the way we put her together, he never saw it coming. He was drilled in the back of the head with a .30-30 rifle, likely from a window or rooftop. No witnesses saw the gunman. Old Flash just sort of fell forward, camera and all. Busted it all to hell."

"Shit. That means any glass plates he might have took was likely busted too?"

"You know it. We ain't as dumb as we look. Our detectives had his plates developed. Most were fogged and the rest were just yokels who wanted their pictures took in the big city. He wouldn't have been photographing a sniper behind him in any case."

Longarm thanked the copper for his assistance and grabbed a hired hack to go uptown. He got out, packing his saddle and

114

possibles, in front of Elanore Wilson's studio. The door was locked, but as he stood there cussing, the brown-haired widow came down the street, saying, "Marshal, what are you doing here so early?"

He said, "I was afraid I might be too late. I ain't even been to the office yet, for I just found out somebody gunned that photographer and you could be next!"

"Photographer? Gunned?"

"Inside, pronto."

She unlocked her door with a key from her purse. As he followed her in, he explained the little he knew and dumped his belongings behind her counter for the time being. He said, "I'm putting you and your kids under protective custody, Miss Elanore. At least until I can figure out why they're so mad about having their pictures took."

She said, "I sent the children to my in-laws on their ranch, northwest of town. Larry loves it out there at his grandfather's, and school's almost out in any case, so—"

"I admire a woman who thinks on her feet, Miss Elanore. But that still leaves your pretty face to hide. I reckon you'd be safe at Marshal Vail's."

"Aren't they already sheltering that little postmistress?"

"I hope so. But they have plenty of spare rooms. Unless you'd rather stay someplace else. What about this ranch you just mentioned?"

She looked uncertain and said, "Oh, I don't think so. My late husband's father and I always got along, and his mother likes the children, but—"

"I follow your drift. This old Chinaman I know once told me the Chinese picture-writing for the word 'trouble' was two women under a single roof. If you don't want to hole up with in-laws, what about a hotel? I know a decent one on Stout. It's got hot and cold running water and if you yell out the window, someone in the Federal Building would likely hear you."

"Mr. Long, I can't afford a hotel."

"Sure you can. It's on Uncle Sam. Let's just give the streets time to crowd up a mite, and I'll run you over there."

"What about this studio? I have pictures to develop and customers to serve."

"You haven't been paying attention, ma'am. There's a killer

115

out there with a rifle who shoots folks in your line of work. I'll tell you what let's do. You go ahead and develop your pictures. Then we'll leave a sign in your window telling folks they can pick them up at my office. It might be sort of interesting to see who turns up there."

"All right," she said. "It will only take a few minutes. Let's go back to the darkroom."

As she led the way, she asked, "Is that one of those new snapshot cameras you're wearing under your coat.?"

He said, "Yeah. I understand you have to send it to the folks who sold it to you to have the pictures developed, right?"

She said, "Heavens, I know how to take the back off, and the chemistry is the same. What have you been photographing, Custis?"

"Oh, a little of this and a little of that. I'd best have it done somewhere else. You got enough on your plate with your regular custom."

She locked the door behind them and lit the little ruby lamp before she said, "Come on, it will only take a minute. I assume you shot them all in full sunlight?"

"Not all, ma'am. Why?"

"You have to. Unless you use flash powder indoors, the film will be underexposed."

He swallowed a sigh of relief and said, "Well, I have got one sunlit frame I'm anxious to see. The ones that don't come out won't matter."

Elanore started pouring chemicals as he took the camera off and placed it on her workbench. "How long is all this likely to take, ma'am?" he asked.

"Only half an hour or so. Why?"

"I ought to let my boss know I'm back. Can I get out of here without ruining anything?"

"Of course. I haven't exposed any plates or film yet."

"All right. I want you to lock up after me, with that 'closed' sign in the window. Don't let anybody in until I get back. Better yet, stay back here out of sight." He knocked a signal on the workbench and said, "Come out and let me in when you hear this. Don't open up for anybody else."

She smiled uncertainly, and said, "You're frightening me. What's so important about these pictures you need developed?"

116

He said, "Only need the first one on the roll, if it pans out. You may only wind up with some bushes. I took it fast and on the fly in Temple Square in Salt Lake City, yesterday. If I'm lucky, there's a gent on it pointing a gun my way. If I ain't, we'll say no more about it."

He left her there and legged it over to the Federal Building, beating Marshal Vail to work for a change. As he stood fuming in the hallway, a portly, silver-haired man in a snuff-colored suit came down the hall and stopped, saying, "There you are, Longarm. I got the night letter you sent us from Cheyenne. You certainly get around, don't you?"

Longarm nodded and replied, "Morning, Prosecutor Donovan. I hope I wasn't stepping on another department's toes when I suggested that *post facto* angle on the Hansen case?"

Donovan said, "You may have done us a favor. I've asked for a postponement until I can look into whether we have a case or not."

"Does that mean Gus Hansen's out of the lockup? His daughter is sort of anxious."

Donovan took Longarm by the arm and steered him toward his chambers as he said, "Let's talk about that and other things, son. I know the lady you mean. She's sort of excitable, like her father, but a lot prettier. I still have a wounded Treasury agent to discuss with that crazy Swede. So he's going to have to stay put until we see if Treasury wants to pursue it further. The big case, as you know, was his alleged land grab. If it turns out we don't have a case, I'll be in your debt. I'd rather drop a dozen cases than lose one in court."

Donovan led him into his chambers, and Longarm didn't look at the big leather davenport he'd had Nan aboard. Donovan went to a sideboard and poured them both drinks from a cut-glass decanter. He handed one to Longarm and said, "Here's mud in your eye. There's something else I wanted to have a private talk with you about, Longarm."

Longarm took a sip and answered innocently, "Ask away, then."

Donovan looked down at the rug as though he'd suddenly noticed something interesting about it. "I hope you won't take this wrong, son, but the girls who work in the building have been gossiping about you and my secretary, Nancy."

"Do tell? Well, that's the trouble with hiring she-males. I'll go along with Miss Virginia Woodhull on letting women vote, since they pay taxes too. But offices were a lot more peaceable when all we had was he-clerks."

Donovan shrugged and said, "Washington says we got to set an example. The First Lady hired some gals to work in the White House too. But let's not discuss the suffrage issue. I'll put it to you straight, son. Some of the she-clerks have been saying you and Nancy have been playing slap-and-tickle."

Longarm pasted a look of innocent horror across his tanned face as he said, "You see what I mean? It just ain't possible to have men and women working together under the same roof, Mr. Donovan. Have you asked poor Nancy about all this bullshit?"

"Hell, you know no gent can ask any lady a thing like that, Longarm! What would the poor child think of me if I was to ask her that right out?"

"I can see you have a problem. How do you mean to deal with it?"

"Well, it might help if you sort of steered clear of the girl for a time, Longarm. *I* know you're not dumb enough to shit where you eat, but we got to consider poor Nan's reputation. Agreed?"

"Hell, it's your secretary and your office. But how am I to get in touch with you if I ain't allowed to come in here anymore?"

Donovan said, "I never said you couldn't come on official business, son. But it might be best if you made sure it was when I was in, if you follow my meaning."

Longarm nodded and said, "I have yet to come when I knew you were out. But what do you aim to do about that, hang a sign on your door or something? Suppose Billy Vail sends me, or I want to ask questions about that Hansen case?"

Donovan looked up with a frown and said, "I told you the Hansen case may be dropped, and Vail's assigned other deputies to it in any case. Did you make any foolish promises to that Helga Hansen?"

"Nope. I had my say on the matter when I wired you. But as long as we're jawing about that family, would you know if Helga has a brother? Maybe a big blond Swede?"

"No, she's an only child. Why?"

"Just covering all bets. I forgot to ask her when she blubbered up all over me. I was sort of anxious to get rid of her."

Donovan laughed. "I know the feeling. I swear, I think that big blond would even seduce *me* to get her father off! The two of them are sort of excitable. That's why I can't let her father out until we settle it one way or the other. He doesn't know a peace bond from a Swedish meatball, and if he were to take it in his head to run off—"

"He'd be leaving the disputed land behind, wouldn't he?" Longarm said, adding, "Seems to me you're being a mite harsh, even if he did shoot a man he didn't understand in the leg. The poor old furriner only tried to defend what he thinks is his, right or wrong. Why in thunder are we holding him without bail? If he ain't there for the hearings, he'll lose everything automatic, right?"

Donovan thought for a moment, then said, "You may be right. I'll talk to the judge about it in a few minutes when we ask for the postponement. Speaking of which, I have to be on my way, so if we have an understanding about what I was talking about before..."

"Old Nan's all yours," said Longarm, downing the last of his drink. Donovan looked sort of wistful as Longarm left him. Longarm could have told him Nan wasn't all that hard to get to know, but he figured if Donovan needed another gent to lead the way, he didn't deserve to get there.

As he returned to his own office down the hall, he almost bumped into Billy Vail. The marshal said, "There you are, you crazy bastard. What's this I hear about you digging up empty graves in Salt Lake City? Come on inside."

Longarm followed him and lit a smoke as he filled Vail in. When he got done, Vail said, "That's what I mean. You're crazy. I swear to God, I've never met a man who can get in more spooky fixes. I send you up to the Blackfoot Agency and you meet evil spirits. Send you down to the Four Corners and you run up against a road agent in Old Spanish armor. I swear to God, I don't know what gets into you, Longarm. None of my other deputies meet up with anybody as crazy as you do."

"I noticed. Who do the other deps bring in, Billy?"

"Hardly anybody. That's why I send you after the crazy-sounding outlaws. It takes one to know one. But this time you seem to be getting chased as well as chasing. Don't it make you a mite nervous to have a corpse stalking you, old son?"

"Hell, I whipped Timberline the last time he went up against me, and I still don't believe in ghosts."

"I don't either, but what in thunder is he if he ain't a ghost?"

"Don't know. If I did, I'd have him by now. The two he had with him out at that Aurora post office job were likely the two rascals I just finished off. So now it's me and him."

Vail frowned, nodded, and said, "Yeah, I can count too. You don't know who those jaspers really were yet, do you?"

"Nope, but I'll be surprised as hell and sort of disappointed in the Colt Arms Company if I run into them again. I reckon they must have wants out on them. They were using forged or stolen papers to account for themselves when curious lawmen asked about the serious-looking gun rigs they wore. It worked once, on the Cheyenne law. Might have worked on me, had they been more polite. How's that little redhead, Kathy Mahoney, getting along with your wife, Billy?"

Vail shrugged and said, "Thick as thieves and talking about you, of course. You know my old woman don't think it's right for any man to run about single. I've had a time convincing her I can't order a deputy to marry up and settle down."

Longarm grimaced and said, "There's much to be said for the U.S. Constitution. I ought to have Kathy off your hands and sorting mail in a day or so, assuming I'm allowed to work free of this infernal office. I just talked to Donovan and they're fixing to let Gus Hansen go, so you'll get back the deps you assigned court duty to."

Vail nodded. "Take a week, if you like. But ain't you being sort of optimistic, old son? You have no idea where that Timberline is right now, do you?"

"I figure he never left Denver. I'll know as soon as I get back to the photograph studio. The way it works best is that Timberline stayed here, knowing he'd stand out on a train, and had his two sidekicks tail me. I got one in Cheyenne and the other coming back from Salt Lake. That leaves him somewhere here, alone."

*   *   *

Elanore Wilson made a liar out of him. When she let him in, the first words out of her mouth were, "It was the same man as in the picture poor Flash Stubbs took. The prints are drying now. Come on. Let me show you."

He followed her to the darkroom, which was now sky-lighted, and Elanore unclipped a snapshot from a drying wire and handed it to him, saying, "Be careful, it's still damp."

He looked down and swore softly under his breath. The snapshot was mostly the tower of the Mormon Temple. The tower rose above a treeline, with the statue of the Angel Moroni atop it shining in the sunlight. But though he'd centered on the temple, a close-up face occupied one edge, like a man peering into a porthole. One ear and part of the jaw was missing, but the rest of it looked like Timberline, or Cotton Younger, grinning at him like a maniac.

Longarm shook his head and said, "Damn! Sorry, ma'am. This rascal had no call to be in Salt Lake City. I had it figured that he sent those other men after me to avoid being seen on the train!"

Elanore said, "He might not have been on your train, Mr. Long."

"No might about it. He wasn't. But he could have taken others. It would be just as mysterious when you get right down to it, though. I never told anyone I was cutting over to Salt Lake from Cheyenne instead of forging on to the Bitter Creek country."

She took the print and hung it up again to dry some more as she mused, "He obviously knew where to find you, near the Temple, because you took his picture there. Maybe he wanted to kill you himself for personal reasons."

"He sure tried. But if he's feeling that personal about it, why were the others allowed to tangle with me, and what's he got to get so personal about?"

Elanore blinked and said, "Mr. Long, you told me you once *shot* this Timberline person!"

"I did. But study on that. Let's say there are such things as ghosts. It seems to me that if somebody killed me, and then I found out it didn't count and I could just get up and walk away, I'd be too happy to go after anybody! It would be a

121

mighty relief to discover there was life after death. And what's the point of killing anyone if you knew for certain that nobody had to stay dead?"

"But I've heard lots of tales of revengeful ghosts, Mr. Long."

"So have I. And tales is all they are. I just got done explaining that a revengeful ghosts makes no sense, even if such things were possible. Timberline, or somebody that looks like him, is alive and well. Which gets us to the next dumb question. Why? I killed Timberline, not somebody that only looked like him. And before you ask, he didn't have a twin brother. So why would a gent who only looked like a dead outlaw want to spook us all like this?"

"Maybe he's trying to cover something up?"

"What? A resemblence to a dead man? The original case was closed, Miss Elanore. Nobody has been looking for any big albino that looked like Timberline. So he ain't wanted and we weren't bothering him. Why did he find it so infernal needful to bother us? This stuff ain't covering up his looking like Timberline. It's advertising it!"

She shrugged and said, "Maybe he's just some sort of lunatic. I have your other pictures here. They were badly underexposed and I had some time bringing up the images, but where there's a will there's always a way."

Longarm felt the back of his neck getting warm as she met his gaze and said, with a Mona Lisa smile, "I didn't know you were interested in art photography, Custis."

She reached out and unclipped a picture of Sally fingering herself and sticking her tongue out at the camera. The picture was dark, but you could make out what she was doing. Longarm knew he was expected to say something, but he was damned if he could figure out what.

Longarm swallowed and said, "Those pictures are connected with another case, ma'am."

"I can see she was committing crimes against nature. How did you ever aim that camera through that keyhole?"

"Uh, it wasn't easy. How'd you know about that keyhole, Miss Elanore?"

"Well, she obviously wouldn't have been, well, abusing

herself like that with a man in the same room. Who is she, some outlaw's doxie?"

Longarm frowned soberly and said, "She's known as Nebraska Nan. I'm sorry you had to see such shocking pictures, ma'am. I wouldn't have asked you to develop the roll, had I known they showed more than her face. You see, she was sort of moving about on the far side of that keyhole and—"

"For God's sake, Custis, why don't you quit when you're ahead?" she cut in with a laugh.

So he laughed back and said, "Right. We'd best run you over to the hotel and get you hid. Uncle Sam can afford you a front room with a connecting bath, so you can look out the window and don't have to go out alone."

She grimaced and said, "I'm not sure I like the idea of being cooped up like I was in jail, Custis."

"A hotel room with hot and cold running water ain't at all like being in jail, as anybody who's ever been in jail can tell you. I ain't confining you for a life sentence, Miss Elanore. Just till it's safe for you to show your pretty face on the streets of Denver again." He pointed with his chin at the racks of chemicals over her workbench and added, "You'd be stuck here fooling with those fuming bottles and such all day in any case, wouldn't you? Seems to me it would be a nice change for you."

"Well, it would be nice to treat myself to a long hot soak with a magazine in a tub I didn't have to heat myself. But with the children away and nobody to talk to in the evening—"

"I'll come by after hours, if Timberline don't kill me, Miss Elanore. I know how it feels to be alone in a strange hotel with the sun going down. We could maybe go out for dinner someplace. I know a couple of decent restaurants in the neighborhood where a freak like Timberline couldn't get past the velvet rope without making a mess of noise. Going to a show afterwards could be risky, but—"

"Why, Deputy Long, are you asking me for a date?"

He looked abashed and said, "Just being neighborly, ma'am. I hardly ever get forward with government witnesses."

She glanced at the prints drying on the line and quickly dropped her eyes, saying, "One should certainly hope so. We'll talk about our plans for this evening later. You've about convinced me the hotel is safer than my empty house. But I wasn't expecting this. I don't have anything to take with me to the hotel."

"They don't care if you check in without luggage, as long as they get paid in advance, ma'am. I'll be proud to spring for a toothbrush and such. You can order anything you need along those lines from the hotel drugstore."

"I don't have a change of clothes, or anything to sleep in."

"Well, if you can't sleep natural, there's a ladies' notion shop just off the lobby, too. I told you it was a first-class hotel, Miss Elanore."

"You sound like you must have checked a lot of ladies into hotels, Custis."

He shook his head and grinned as he said, "Not in any other than a proper manner, ma'am. Not in any hotel like that. I'd never be able to afford it on my salary."

She suppressed a laugh and said, "All right, just let me gather my few things and close up. I have to empty these trays before we leave."

"I'll help you, ma'am."

"I wish you wouldn't. Some of these chemicals are dangerous, and I know what I'm doing. If you want to smoke while I finish up here, do it outside."

He hesitated, nodded, and walked out to the front, fishing out a smoke and thumbing a sulfur match to light it. He considered the saddle, rifle, and possibles he'd left behind her counter and decided to leave well enough alone. They weren't bothering anybody where they were, and if he needed them he'd just ask Elanore for the key.

She came out, smoothing the front of her skirt after taking off the apron she wore when she was working, and picked up her big handbag from the counter, saying, "There, shall we go?"

So they went. It was only a few blocks to the hotel, but Longarm hailed a passing hack anyway. It was a lot harder to snipe at folks inside a hired hack. As they settled into the leather cusions, Longarm put his arm across the seat behind her.

Elanore looked sort of warily at him, so he quickly said,

"I ain't getting forward, ma'am. I'm watching out this bitty back window."

"Heavens, do you think we're being followed?"

"Don't know. That's why I'm looking in back of us."

The hack was weaving in and out of heavy traffic, and as they cut in front of a streetcar, Longarm said, "I don't think we're being trailed. But since you keep reminding me that you're a proper gal, I'd best tell you in advance, so you won't go all fluttery in the hotel lobby. You see, I'll have to check us in as, well, man and wife. We won't use our right names, of course. No telling who might read a hotel register."

She blanched and said, "Oh no, I couldn't! What would people say?"

"Ma'am you don't listen good. People can't say anything if they don't know about it. That's why we're checking in as Mr. and Mrs. Dillingwater."

"Dillingwater? That's an awfully strange name, Custis."

"I know. That's why I just made her up. Hardly anybody ever uses a silly name unless it's their own. You'd be surprised how suspicious hotel clerks can be about Smith and Jones."

She laughed, lashes lowered, and said, "I'm sure you'd know that better than me. But why do we have to check in as man and wife in the first place?"

"Because it's a proper hotel, Miss Elanore. The reason I've picked it, aside from it being close to my office, is that they don't allow strange men to visit ladies upstairs. If a gent comes to call on a gal staying there, they ring her room and she has to come down to the lobby. There's a house dick hiding in the potted ferns to make sure. Since I don't want to be hung up explaining if I need to get to your room in a hurry—"

"It's all right. I understand. But for some reason I still feel sort of, well, wicked about all this."

The hack pulled up in front of the hotel and he helped her out. The room clerk never batted an eye as Longarm signed them in, with Elanore standing off a ways and staring hard at a potted plant, as though she'd never seen one before. The clerk handed their key to the bellhop and murmured, "Nice," as Longarm turned away from the registry desk. Longarm had told a white lie about the hotel to his pretty material witness, and the clerk likely remembered him from the last time he'd been here with another "wife" that looked nothing like this one. But it really was about the most respectable hotel he knew of, and no matter what that detective over there behind the newspaper thought of the names they'd seen fit to check in under, he wouldn't let anybody else up the stairs at Elanore.

They followed the bellhop up to the second floor and the tall deputy paid him for the key. The bellhop sort of smirked, too. Elanore was a nice-looking gal, and it was a shame a man had to have the name without the game. Longarm closed the door as she looked the room and adjoining bath over. The room was clean and had fancy wallpaper, with real-looking orange flowers on a field of mustard. There was a big framed picture of Custer's Last Stand over the double bed. A new Bell Telephone sat on the table next to it. Longarm didn't follow the girl into the bath, but from what he could see, it was a pretty fancy layout. He sure hoped Billy Vail was going to understand when it came time to settle up on this month's expenses. He'd paid with his own money, downstairs, and since it was such a fancy hotel, he'd had to give the fool bellhop a whole two bits.

Elanore came out of the bath, smiling, and said, "Well, I must say it's the nicest hotel I've ever stayed in. But I don't know how to use that telephone thing and I would like to order some, uh, unmentionables."

Longarm thought for a moment before he said, "Well, I can't hardly translate for you, if it's gal talk. But I think I see a way out. I got to get going in any case."

He picked up the telephone, asked the switchboard downstairs to hook him up to the notions shop, and when a gal's voice came on, he handed the works to Elanore and said, "There you go. Just tell this lady what you need sent up and charge it to this room number. Here's the key. Number is on the tag."

"Wait, Custis. When will you be back?"

"Let's shoot for six, if I ain't been shot. Lock up after me and don't let anybody in until you have a look-see through that little peephole on yonder door panel. Talk to the store lady."

She nodded, and, as he let himself out, he heard her confiding that she needed a peignoir, whatever that was. He got to the steps, realized he hadn't taken a leak for some time, and cut down the cross-hall toward a sign that said GENTLEMEN.

He knew the folks who couldn't afford the dollar-a-day room had to use the toilets provided by the management off the hallways. He went in and relieved himself, then buttoned up and headed out again, wondering why his old tool was at half mast. Elanore hadn't said or done a thing to encourage such hard feelings.

As he strolled toward the stairwell, pondering his next moves, a door opened and a big blond gal came out, pinning her hat on. She and Longarm recognized one another at the same time and she said, "Oh, how will I ever thank you, you nice good friend?"

He touched the brim of his Stetson and said, "Morning, Miss Helga."

Helga Hansen grabbed him by the sleeve to sort of keelhaul him inside as she gasped, "They are going to let my Papa go! They said this afternoon, when the judge can get back from his lunch to give Papa a good scolding, and we owe it all to you!"

They were inside now, and she'd closed the door with one ample hip without letting go of his sleeve. In fact, she had hold of the other one now, and though she stood at what might have been a proper distance for dancing, there was a lot of her bulging out front and rubbing against his chest. He said, "I didn't do all that much, Miss Helga. Just pointed out some angles that likely would have come out in court in any case. Your father never would have gotten in such a fix if he'd been a mite more polite to process-servers."

She pulled him closer as she smiled up at him and said, "I know. They are making us post what they call a peace bond, and Papa will lose it if he shoots any more people in the leg."

"That sounds fair. Were you, uh, going out, Miss Helga?"

"Just for a walk. I am so excited I can't sit still. This afternoon I will take my Papa back to our ranch and hide all his shotgun shells. Oh, I am so glad I ran into you before we left Denver."

Running into him was what she seemed intent on doing. she kept moving nervously below the waistline, and as she bumped against him he was uncomfortably aware that if she couldn't feel the bulge in his pants, she was wearing one thick pair of drawers under that calico summer skirt. She must have been

127

embarrassed too, for she suddenly lowered her pale lashes, sighed, "Oh, Custis!" and hauled him even closer. So he kissed her, not knowing what else to do with a blond lady rubbing against him like that.

He could tell right off that he might have made a mistake. Helga wrapped her big strong arms around him and proceeded to swallow his tongue as she ground her pelvis against his. She was nearly as tall as he was and had long legs, so they met just right below the belt buckle. Her rumpled bed was across the room, and while sweeping her up and carrying her might have struck her as romantic, it struck him as a real chore. He had other fish to fry, in any case. Officially, he was supposed to be out looking for Timberline, and wherever Timberline was, he wasn't here in Helga's hotel room. He tried to stop kissing her, but she was stuck to his front like glue, and the embrace was shifting from polite to cruel and unusual punishment. He had a full erection, and she was gripping it between her thighs as she moved her hips like they were old friends indeed. He was having trouble keeping his balance, so he sort of rolled around until he had her back against the door instead of his. She leaned back against it from the waist up, thrusting her pubic region out even more as she went on kissing him.

He managed to come up for air long enough to gasp, "Helga, we'd sure better stop this. I'm on duty and you have to get back to your ranch, remember?"

She smiled adoringly at him and said, "We would have no ranch if it wasn't for you, and I'll never be able to thank you enough. Don't you want me to thank you properly, my sweet bashful *kalv*?"

He said, "I sure do, as you likely must have noticed by now. But you don't owe me a thing for just doing my job, Helga."

She told him to shut up and started kissing him some more, reaching down to fumble with his fly. As she did so, he hoisted her calico skirts and discovered that she was wearing nothing under them. As she hauled his shaft out, she sort of flinched. Gals could be like that at the last minute. He took it from her to guide it into position as Helga giggled with her lips on him and murmured, "Standing up? Is it possible?"

"Let's find out," he said.

He'd never met a gal who had legs exactly the same length as his before, and it was worth the waiting. Helga was built big all over, but when she got aboard and clamped down, legs together, it was a perfect fit. So they screwed hell out of each other, leaning against the door, and he knew he wasn't taking advantage of any innocent farm gal, no matter how she talked. No woman moved like that without a lot of practice. She likely had a lot of cowhands anxious for her to get back to the ranch.

They got the introductory orgasm out of the way fast, for she was a natural, earthy gal who apparently just liked to enjoy life. But as they leaned against the door, panting, he said, "This would be a lot nicer in a bed, with our duds off, don't you reckon?"

Helga laughed and said, "I too was thinking this. But I warn you, I am sort of fat, and it is so daylight in here."

"Hell, little darling, you ain't fat, you're just built solid. I'll close my eyes if you want, but let's shuck our duds and do her right."

So he let her off the door and she moved over to the bed, tossing her hat aside and peeling her one-piece summer dress off over her head with her back to him as she said, "You must not laugh at Helga, please."

He didn't, but she did look sort of amusing as she dropped her dress on the floor to climb aboard the bed on her hands and knees. She'd have been grotesquely fat if it hadn't been for her narrow waist, which made her more of an hourglass than a big pink piggy. The position she was in didn't help. She was on the sheets on elbows and knees, her big rump raised like some she-critter waiting to be served by a he-critter. Long-arm got his own things out of the way as quickly as possible and strode over to her, naked and erect, to take advantage of her dog-style offering. As he hooked a hand in the small of her waist and entered her again, it looked more wild than romantic. But if that was the way she liked it, it was jake with him.

Apparently she did, for she moaned and said, "Oh, it's better than I thought it would be. I have never done it standing up, and so I thought that was why it felt so different. But even this way, a man is better."

He was enjoying himself too much to stop. But he frowned

down at the astounding view as he asked, "What do you mean, a *man* is better? Who else have you ever done this with, a gal?"

She giggled, her face against the sheets, and arched her spine to take him deeper as she answered, "Of course not, silly. *Flickas* can't do this to each other. I have been wanting to try it with a man since I was a child, and yes, I like it."

Icewater ran down Longarm's naked spine as he held his fire and said, "Hold on, are you saying you're an infernal virgin, girl?"

She moved in a way that told him this was impossible and said, "Of course not. I have loved to do this since I was maybe ten. Papa was out riding the range when I did it first, with Gunnar. Do we have to talk about it? I am getting excited some more."

He was too, despite the weird conversation, so he rolled her over and mounted her the old-fashioned way, enjoying that view more as he did so. Her eyes opened wide as he reentered her and she gasped, "Oh God, this way is even nicer!"

He kissed her and settled down to enjoy the ride, and it was a nice one. She came twice to his once, for Helga was uncomplicated physically, no matter how crazily she talked. When he collapsed, sated for the moment, she stroked his back with her big pink hands and said, "Oh, that was lovely. Can we ever do it again?"

He said, "Won't have to wait forever. I just need to get my wind back."

He saw that she was crying for some fool reason, so he stayed where he was and kissed her wet eyelids, saying, "Hell, let's not blubber up, pard. What's the matter? Am I too heavy for you?"

"No, you feel wonderful and I never want to stop. But this afternoon I must get my Papa out of jail and take him back to the ranch. Then I will have nobody like you to make love with."

He didn't like the way this conversation was drifting. Gals could be unfair that way. He could understand a shy little schoolmarm acting all mushy when it came time to say adios, but you'd think a bawdy old gal who just up and did it like this would have more sense. He'd never figured out that Border Mex gal who'd tried to knife him just for looking down the front of another cantina gal's dress. What the hell, he'd picked her up in an infernal taproom and she'd started undressing before he even asked. Yet once they'd played some slap-and-tickle, old Conchita had acted like she owned him.

Longarm kissed another tear off Helga and soothed, "Hush, now. You got old Gunnar out to the ranch, ain't you?"

She sniffed and said, "It's not the same. None of them will be the same."

"Them? Plural? How many of the hands have you been messing with when your dad's out riding fence, Helga?"

She sighed and said, "Oh, none of them are hands. I was talking about my pets. Gunnar is a Great Dane. I make love to him the most. Our cart pony, Stal, has a nicer thing, but it's very complicated to make love to a pony."

He grimaced and said, "I'd have said it was impossible. Jesus H. Christ, girl, I've heard of animal lovers, but that's overdoing it! Why in thunder would a pretty thing like you want to mess about with he-brutes, anyway?"

"Who else is there? My Papa chases all the boys away with his shotgun, and a girl has feelings."

He felt her contraction and said, "I noticed. This ain't any of my business, but your old man's jealousy ain't, uh, personal, is it?"

"Heavens, Custis, do you think I would commit an incest with my own Papa?"

"Well, according to Colorado law, you could get twenty years either way. You're too pretty to make love to the livestock, Helga. There's got to be a better way."

She started moving as she said, "I know. I like this way better."

He did too, so they said no more about it until they'd finished again. But Longarm was still thinking about her tale as he rolled off for a smoke and some pillow talk. He said, "As I see it, you and your dad have an unnatural relationship, whether you've been at each other or not. How far are you from the nearest town?"

"A few hours' ride in the pony cart. Why?"

"Ain't sure. It seems to me you ought to spend more time off that ranch, though. I'm almost sorry I got your old man off. Seems to me that if he was to spend a few months in jail, a pretty gal like you could be married up with a human being by the time he got out. You want me to have another word with Prosecuter Donovan?"

"Oh no, I love my Papa. As a daughter, I mean."

"All right. But I want you to listen sharp. Are you listening, Helga?"

"Yes. I will do anything you say, dear."

"In a minute. This situation out at your place ain't healthy, girl. I reckon there's no real harm done to the livestock, for they don't know it's a mortal sin and likely enjoy it. But sooner or later somebody is bound to catch you rutting like a critter with a critter, and there's no telling what will happen. I heard a sad, pathetic story one time that sounds like a dirty joke until you study on it. This one old sheepherder gunned another sheepherder for stealing his girl, who was a ewe. People get mixed up enough about natural sex. It's best to stick to just petting, riding, or eating lower animals."

"Oh, but Custis, Gunnar does it so good to me, and the time I got under the cart and managed to mate with Stal—"

"Variety appeals to me, too. But within limits. I ain't finished. This next part's likely to upset you, so get a firm grip and . . . not on *me*, dammit!"

She fondled him teasingly and said, "I love to feel these things."

"Yeah. But leave ponies alone. It sounds dangerous as well as dirty. Getting to more delicate matters, I have had to make some sort of grim arrests at lonesome spreads where a father or grandfather lived alone with a growing young gal. I'll take your word that your dad has been a gent about such matters, but that business of his running off suitors don't bode well for the future. You'd be doing both of you a favor if you got out more, whether he cottons to it or not. How much range does your father own?"

"Oh, about two hundred sections, why?"

Longarm whistled and said, "Kee-rist, that ain't a cow spread, it's fixing to be a quarter of a county! I know Indian reserves smaller than that, and it's no wonder they accused him of being a land hog. How in thunder does he work a spread that big with no hired hands, Helga?"

"Oh, Papa says the land will be valuable as just land in a

132

few more years. So close to Denver, with water and timber on it, somebody will want it, no?"

"Hmm, I suspicion somebody already does, and that's why they disputed his untidy claim. But since that's over, let's get back to his other odd notions. it ain't natural for a father to hog a single daughter, Helga. Or, what I mean is, it might be too natural to be lawful. I don't want to see his name on the court dockets anymore. So once you get him home you'd better start acting more independent."

Longarm didn't think she was paying much attention to his brotherly advice, since she'd rolled over to commit another serious breach of state law upon his person. But her lips felt too good to argue about it, and he didn't really want to know if she'd ever tried *that* on her dog, or, God forbid, old Stal! He was sure glad he knew she'd been in town and staying in a room with a bath for a spell, for as she started sucking harder, he suspected she had some experience at that, too.

He stared down bemused at her center-parted blond hair as her head bobbed up and down. He knew he ought to feel sort of disgusted, for she was ignorant as hell, besides being inclined to bestiality. But there was something so innocent about Helga's dirtiness that he couldn't feel she was bad.

He didn't get out of there until noon, and when the two of them came down the stairs together to go over to the courthouse, the house detective in the corner stared at them funny as hell.

Longarm couldn't see why. They were both fully dressed as they passed him in the lobby.

Chapter 9

Considering how interestingly the day had started, the rest of it was downright tedious. After leaving Helga at the Federal Building, he found a lunchroom and filled his gut with chili con carne and Arbuckle. Then he started making the rounds. Denver was a big town and there were a lot of rounds to make. But nobody answering Timberline's description had been seen anywhere he checked.

Longarm ambled down toward the Burlington yards, figuring to stop in Henry's to see if his old pal Soapy Smith was still looking for him. Word was that Soapy had last been seen boarding a train for parts unknown. So Longarm figured the sullen con man had taken his well-meant advice. He asked Henry if Soapy had many friends in town, and Henry said nobody who knew him was likely to take his personal quarrels seriously enough to take on a U.S. deputy with Longarm's rep. So Longarm left Soapy Smith on a back burner and moseyed over to the morgue to see if they could tell him anything about the body he'd delivered to them.

The chief attendant said, "He's on ice if you want another look at him."

"I know what he looks like," Longarm said. "What I want

to know is who he might be."

"He could be a lot of folk," the attendant said. "He wasn't a very distinguished-looking gent, and his description matches a dozen yellow sheets or so."

"Any from Clay County, Missouri?"

"Not as I remember, Longarm. You want us to make up copies of the wants we have that might fit him?"

Longarm nodded, told him to send them to the office, and caught an eastbound streetcar. He got off near Colfax and peered about until he saw a sign in an upstairs window. When he got inside the Rocky Mountain Detective Agency, a pretty gal was playing the typewriter alone. She had wispy brown hair with a pencil stuck in it, and must have known Longarm was too worn out to ravish her across her desk, for she smiled as flirty as hell and batted her eyes like a Spanish fan as she asked what she could do for him.

He told her, and she seemed surprised to hear he'd shot it out with Murdoch and McSorley, for the two of them were out on a divorce case at the moment, alive and well.

He described the two gunslicks and she said she had no more idea than he did who they might have been. Folks in her line didn't always tell the truth, but she seemed sincerely shocked when he suggested hired guns. She said, "You've come to the wrong agency, Deputy Long. We have a fifty-thousand-dollar bond posted with the state against such goings-on. Our operatives aren't lawmen or even armed guards. We're private investigators, specializing in domestic cases. We generally work with lawyers and insurance firms. You can check us out with the court clerks if you want."

He nodded and said, "I didn't think they'd been assigned to gun me by your outfit, ma'am. But they were pretending to be on your payroll. How would I go about getting such identification, assuming none of your boys have been rolled in an alley of late?"

The girl pursed her lips and said, "I have no idea. I suppose some crook could forge our printed-up cards, or perhaps steal one from our printer. We have them printed, you see."

"I'm beginning to. Where's this print shop?"

She opened a drawer and handed him a business card from

it, saying, "It's just down the street. They do all our letterheads and so forth."

He thanked her, let himself out, and went to the small print shop down Colfax to see what they had to say.

It was a hole-in-the-wall outfit with a hand press. They printed up small batches of bills, letterheads, business cards, and such for the surrounding businessmen. The journeyman who talked to Longarm heard him out before he shook his head and said, "We haven't printed any ID cards for Rocky Mountain in a year or more. It's not like they need a lot, you know."

"What about the plates? You still have 'em somewhere around?"

"Hell no, we're strictly hand-set. We never made a plate for those IDs, Deputy. Just set the type, ran off a few dozen, and busted up the type to use on other jobs."

Longarm didn't look too pleased to hear this, so, wanting to be more helpful, the journeyman said, "Anyone with some standard type could run one off, you know."

Longarm fumbled around in a pocket for the two IDs and handed them over, asking, "Look 'em over anyway and tell me if there's anything I missed."

The journeyman stared down, shrugged, and said, "Looks like the ones we printed. But like I said, any printer in town could have done 'em as well."

Longarm tucked them away, growling, "I was afraid you were about to say something like that. But why, if they had blank IDs made up, would they use the names of real private detectives?"

The journeyman shrugged again and said, "You're the lawman. I just work here. Maybe they used real names in case anybody checked them out with the agency?"

"Hmm, could be. But it could backfire too. The office might say, sure, they knew of such a gent on their payroll. On the other hand, they could ask what in thunder he was doing there when they had him somewhere else. I got it from the horse's mouth that the names on these cards are working a case right here in Denver. So neither ID was worth much in Cheyenne or Salt Lake."

He took out the photos of Timberline and said, "As long

as I'm here, have you ever done any work for this rascal?"

"No. Who is he? He looks sort of wild."

"He is. Name's Cotton Younger, nicknamed Timberline, and if he should ever come in here for some letterheads, I'd sure like to hear about it."

The journeyman said they had a deal and Longarm left, wondering where the hell to go now. He'd done all the easy stuff and hadn't cut the big bastard's trail. Of course, Timberline was looking for him too, so if the two of them kept wandering around long enough, they might bump noses someday. But it was a big town, he didn't have till someday, and he was purely stumped.

He consulted his Ingersoll and saw that he'd chewed up most of the afternoon doing nothing much. He went back to the Federal Building and had a smoke with Marshal Vail as he brought him up to date.

"It's my considered opinion that we're wasting time on this ghost, old son," Vail said. "What if Timberline's lit out for good? It might make any man nervous to have his two sidekicks gunned out from under him, you know. If he had a loco longhorn's common sense, he'd be making for the border about now."

Longarm blew smoke out his nose like a loco longhorn and replied, "If he'd had any sense to begin with, he'd have stayed the hell in his grave or wherever. It was a dare, to get us feds on the case. Timberline might have figured you'd assign me to chase him, since you're so fond of me."

Vail nodded and said, "I did, and you've chased him all over. But what's the point to all this chasing, old son?"

"I'll be damned if I know! It don't work no matter how you study it." Then he paused and said, "Wait a minute. Let's back over that bump. Have we any other important wants out on anybody who just might be in this neck of the woods, Billy?"

Vail thought and shook his head, saying, "No. None I was fixing to send you after, if you're hinting at diversionary tactics."

"I ain't hinting, Billy, I'm just asking. As you can see, all this shilly-shally with long-dead owlhoots got me out of town for a spell and set me up more than once for an ambush. Some slicker who knew how friendly old Timberline and me used to be couldn't come up with a better way to make me tear-ass all over creation instead of minding the store, could he?"

Vail nodded. "Yeah, you are one curious cuss, and a ghost would get most anyone's undivided interest. But there's nothing heavy enough on my yellow sheets to justify such fun and games, and if there was, how do you account for the fact that you keep meeting up with this here ghost?"

Longarm took out the pictures again and said, "I've been wondering about that too. A pretty picture is one thing. Seeing a man in the flesh long enough to matter is another. What if some tall galoot was wearing, well, some kind of mask?"

"You mean like a Halloween false face? That's mighty wild, Longarm."

"Not as wild as climbing out of a grave. Try her this way. Some ornery cuss dug the body of Cotton Younger up, holding his nose. They told me over yonder it couldn't be done, but who in hell watches graveyards all the time?"

"I thought there was a night watchman with a dog."

"I sure wish you wouldn't bring up tedious details, Billy. I never said it would be easy. But it still beats Timberline climbing out of that grave without help. I'll study on how they got his coffin empty. Meanwhile, as further spookiness, they had this mask made up, see?"

"No, I don't see. You're forgetting the two expressions in those photos. In one his mouth is shut. in the other he's grinning crazy, and neither looks like a man wearing a mask to me."

Longarm frowned uncertainly and said, "Spoilsport. All right, make it two masks. Or maybe one made out of india rubber or something, so he can move his features natural. Timberline must have set for his picture at one time or another. Everybody does. I've seen two of Billy the Kid, and even though they're two different fellows, one of them might be him. Let's say somebody used an old picture of Timberline, taken while he was alive, and had this mask and wig made up. The rascal hasn't stood still long enough for me to see exactly how tall he is, or if that cotton top is real, and—"

"Dammit, Longarm, you jawed with him out at Kathy Mahoney's place, remember?"

"Sure I remember. A voice is as easy to fake as a face. Hell, it's easier. One old Missouri boy don't sound that different from any other, and let's face it, I was sort of nervous at the time. I could have been tricked."

Vail shook his head in exasperation. "It's too damned much trouble, no matter what! There's no motive to all this spooky stuff, no matter how it's been working. Who the hell would go to so much effort, and why?"

"Don't know," Longarm said. "But they've done it. Alive or a haunt, they've tried to kill me more than once. So there has to be a reason."

"Maybe the jasper is just crazy, no matter who he might be."

"It's crossed my mind, Billy. And a lunatic who works so hard at it ain't much more cheerful to think about than a stalking corpse."

The shadows on the walk were getting longer as Longarm left his office. As usual, Marshal Vail had overstayed his work day and they'd talked themselves into the evening as well as blue in the face. He remembered that he'd promised Elanore he'd come back by six, and it was getting there. But he didn't head directly for her hotel, nearby as it might be. He studied his reflection, and everything else behind him, in the plate-glass window of a storefront. Then he cut west as if he meant to go to Larimer Street and belly up with the boys for the night. His real intent was to move along some side streets until he was sure nobody who knew he worked at the Federal Building had staked him out. This time of the summer, it would still be light for a spell, and he didn't want to risk taking the girl out for dinner before dark. So she'd just have to fret if she was worried about him being a mite late. He was sure nobody but Vail and he knew where Elanore was. So she was safe, and he aimed to keep her that way. He strode down the deserted side street, cut around a corner, and ducked into a doorway. Nothing happened. That was the trouble with ghosts. You never seemed to see them when you looked carefully about.

He decided the coast was clear and took another side street back to the rear of the hotel. Guests were supposed to enter by the front entrance, but guests, and folks tailing them, didn't know everything. He remembered the service entrance he'd noticed the last time he'd stayed there with a less refined "wife."

Nobody was using the unguarded service entrance, so Longarm mounted the steps to Elanore's floor, glad that Helga, down the hall, had checked out that afternoon. He sure hoped old Helga was going to take his advice. He'd never know unless her dad went crazy again.

He swung around the corner into the corridor leading to Elanore's door. Then he crabbed to one side, slapping leather, as the man lying in wait there fired both barrels of the shotgun in his hands, blowing one hell of a hole out of the wallpaper as Longarm in turn fired into the smoke cloud, aiming for the shadowy form on the far side. The man yelled like a woman with a mouse up her skirt and Longarm heard the shotgun hit the rug. But since the barely visible enemy could always have a gunbelt on, he fired again, and this time the son of a bitch didn't yell, he went down.

Elanore's door opened, spilling light on the figure sprawled on her doorstep, so she screamed too, and Longarm yelled, "Get back inside, goddammit!" Then he added, "That goes for all of you!" as other fools came to their doors to see what was going on.

Longarm wasn't sure what was going on, either. But as the man who'd tried to blow him in two wasn't moving, Longarm moved forward, thumbing fresh rounds into his .44 as he saw that Elanore had obeyed his impolite command. The house dick called down the hall, "All right! You're all under arrest! I'm the law!"

Longarm didn't turn as he called back, "No you're not. I am. Come down here and see if you can tell me how come you have such unruly guests."

The house dick joined Longarm as he rolled the dead man over with his booted toe. It wasn't Timberline or anyone else Longarm knew. He was just a middle-aged man in a shabby suit, with a brace of S&Ws around his hips. None of Longarm's rounds had hit him in the face, but it didn't ring a bell with the house dick, either. He said, "He ain't no guest here. But I know who *you* are, now. You're that federal man they calls Longarm, right?"

"Yeah. It's injurious to the health to be so famous. How

did this gent get past you in the lobby?"

"Beats me. How did *you* do it? I don't remember seeing you come in just now."

"Never mind. I think you just answered my question. Do you want to go down and call the coppers?"

The detective said he would. So as he left, Longarm knocked on Elanore's door and she came out, wrapped herself around him, and sobbed, "Oh, darling, I thought they'd killed you!"

Since other folks were sticking their heads out again, he moved her inside, saying, "Well, so much for my great notion about hiding you out in a hotel. We have to stay put until the local law takes my statement and all, but since I see you're dressed, we'll just get out of here as soon afterwards as we can."

He'd left the door ajar. Elanore stared past him and whispered, "Oh God, is he . . . ?"

He said, "Yeah. Don't look at it. The way his eyelids are twitching don't mean anything. They all do that for a spell, after."

She buried her face in his chest and sobbed, "Oh, if that had been you out there when I opened the door . . ."

"I *was* out there. But I was the one on his feet. He must have been about to pay you a call when I came around the corner and surprised him."

"Oh no, you can't mean that! I thought he was following *you*!"

Longarm shook his head and said, "I don't follow easy. I made sure I was alone before I came back. So they knew you were here. That's why we have to get you someplace else. They'd know your house, if they're that interested in you."

"Oh, thank God I sent the children away! But where can I hide if not here or my own place?"

"I'll study on it. My place ain't respectable. Even if it was, they likely have my address too. Hold on, I hear the coppers coming. Why don't you go wash your face and such while I sort it out with them?"

"All right. Can I trust you to take me to a place where we'll both be safe, dear?"

Longarm didn't answer. He never intentionally took a lady anyplace she figured to get shot, but how safe she'd be depended on how she meant it.

Chapter 10

It was well after sundown by the time Longarm was able to take Elanore out to get something to eat. They went to Romano's, a family-owned-and-operated Italian walk-down restaurant in a part of Denver that ladies like Elanore weren't supposed to visit. Romano's was small and intimate, but, more important, had only one narrow doorway that a man could keep his eye on while he ate.

"I like this little place, Custis," Elanore said, looking around with a smile. "But I didn't know there were Italian restaurants in Denver."

"Well," Longarm said, "I only know about this one. I don't eat Eye-talian food regular. Old Mr. Romano, the owner, came out here with the forty-niners. He just retired from a hard-rock mine and I guess he must have been feeling nostalgic, so he opened up a place that served home cooking. It ain't fancy, but nobody unfriendly is likely to show up with our dessert."

"That's a comfort," Elanore said, "but I'm afraid you'll have to order for me. I don't know a thing about Italian cooking."

"Then you know as much as I do," Longarm said. He turned around in his chair and caught the eye of one of the dark, shy Romano daughters, who came over with a menu.

"Evening, Gina," he said. "Me and this lady will have to trust you to provide for us, for I don't remember what you call the dish I like, and she knows even less."

Their young waitress said she'd rustle up some manicotti, whatever that was, and he said that meanwhile they'd like some of her dad's homemade wine. As he poured, Longarm told Elanore, "This red moonshine ain't exactly lawful, but me and Mr. Romano have an understanding. He dug me out of a caved-in mine one time and I've never arrested him since."

She dimpled and said, "You have a flexible way of enforcing the law, I see. How do people go about corrupting you to look the other way?"

He thought and said, "They don't, if it's serious. I've never been a man to get excited about a decent Indian having a drink or maybe an unemployed Mexican crossing the border, quiet, to find honest work. But I disremember looking the other way on anything serious."

"I thought drunken Indians and illegal immigrants were frowned on by the government, Custis. Just where do you draw the line?"

He said, "Hurting folks. I know the First Lady thinks Demon Rum will destroy us all, but Lemonade Lucy Hayes wouldn't know a decent Indian from a bad one if she woke up in bed with him. There's lots of fool regulations some paper-pusher back East made up just to feel needed. But some of the law makes sense. Anybody who knows the Golden Rule knows all the sensible law there is. I'm a peace officer, not a lawyer or a judge, so I figure my job is to keep things peaceable and not let anyone get hurt. I'd pistolwhip a man mistreating his horse before I'd arrest some poor old Paiute for nipping at the jug and not bothering nobody."

He reached for a breadstick, bit off the end, and added, "I'd be a hypocrite if I bothered folks for having harmless fun, for I've always been partial to the same myself."

She stared at him archly over the rim of her wineglass, then lowered it and asked demurely, "Are you only partial to good clean fun, Custis?"

He said, "What's clean and what's not goes with the Golden Rule, too. I've always figured a man who works little kids in a cotton mill back East is dirtier than any gent I ever met playing piano in a house of ill repute."

Gina brought their orders, and as she left, Elanore said, "Speaking of housing, have you decided where the two of us are going after we leave here?"

"I have. I want you to sit still and not throw that dish of whatever in my face until you hear me out. The notion sounds more shocking than it really is."

"Heavens! Where were you planning on hiding me, Custis?"

"The last place anyone would expect to find a respected widow woman from the hill. I'm on what you might call good platonic terms with a lady who, uh, rents by the hour."

"Are you serious? You mean to introduce me to a woman of the town?"

"You won't have to shake hands with old Tiger Lil, Miss Elanore. I have a key to her flat, and she ain't going to be there tonight in any case. She works the night shift at the Silver Dollar."

"Oh? And you expect me to believe you and she are platonic friends?"

"Don't matter if you believe it or not, Miss Elanore. The point is that you'll be safe there. It ain't like Tiger Lil, uh, *worked* in her flat. She just uses it on her days off and hardly anybody knows the address, so . . ."

Elanore suddenly laughed and said, "Well, I always said I wanted to see the world. But where do *you* intend to spend the night, Custis?"

"Same place. It's a four-room flat and you can lock the bedroom door on the inside, if that's what you're worried about."

She chewed some pasta, swallowed some wine after it, and said, "I'll have to think about that. You realize, of course, that if anyone I know ever suspected I'd spent the night with a man in such a place, it really wouldn't matter whether I said the door between us was locked or not?"

"We'd best not ever tell anybody, then. Anything that happens between us at Tiger Lil's will be strictly between the two of us, no matter what, right?"

She sort of choked, then looked down at her plate and said, "This takes some getting used to."

"Yeah, that sauce is sort of spicy, when you ain't used to it."

"I'm not talking about our food, you goose! I've just agreed to spend the night with a man in a prostitute's flat on the wrong side of Larimer Street! Can a lady trust you, Custis?"

He shrugged and said, "A gent can be trusted to act toward a lady the way she's expecting him to act. I told you there was a door lock, but I wouldn't want you to think I was a sissy."

"Are you trying to reassure me or proposition me, dear?"

"Neither one. Just answering questions with my cards face-up. I want to keep you from harm, not harm you. You don't have to stay with me if you don't want to. You ain't under arrest."

She sighed and said, "I know, Lord give me strength. You must have guessed I find you attractive, right?"

"Well, neither of us is deformed. I find you a handsome woman, too."

"That's what I'm worried about. I'm not sure I can trust either one of us. I know this may seem shocking, but I was happily married for some time and, uh, it's been some time since I was happy that way."

"Yeah," he said. "Queen Victoria and Lemonade Lucy have a lot to answer for. But look, if this notion of mine upsets you so, I'll be proud to run you out to that family spread of yours. I know you said you don't get along with your mother-in-law, but she'd hardly get forward with you."

She looked wistful and said, "I'd like to see my children again. But to say she doesn't like me would be putting it mildly. I suppose I'll just have to take my chances with you, but I've seldom felt so wicked."

He grinned across the checkered tablecloth at her. "Yeah, ain't it fun?" Then he changed the subject to give her time to reconsider. They listened to the story of each other's lives through coffee and dessert. And then, as little Gina was taking away the dishes, Elanore asked if they could take along a bottle of Romano's red wine, adding, "I don't know if it's affecting my judgment or not, but it seems so, well, cold-blooded to run off with you dead sober!"

146

So he bought the bottle and they left. The street outside was dark. He took her elbow and guided her to the left, saying, "It ain't far, Miss Elanore."

"Somehow I didn't think it would be," she said dryly.

They came to a side door in a brick wall, and he took out his borrowed key to unlock it. Elanore was as silent as a sphinx until he led her up the dark, narrow steps, opened another door, and struck a match, saying, "Well, this is it."

"This is it, indeed! Where do you suppose she ever found that red and black wallpaper?" Elanore asked.

"Mail order, most likely. It does take getting used to. This here's the setting room. Yonder is the bedroom and that other doorway leads to the kitchen and water closet. It ain't fancy, but it's safe."

"I hope so. Are you sure nobody knows we're here, Custis?"

"Yep. I didn't even get a chance to tell Billy Vail I planned to bring you here. The gal who owns it won't know, neither, till I tell her. She won't be back until that Shriner's convention they're having breaks up."

He tossed his hat on an overstuffed brown velvet sofa and put the bottle on the table in front of it. Elanore said, "Maybe I'll feel more at home after I freshen up and put something on more comfortable. I'll be right back."

She went into the bedroom and shut the door. Longarm took off his gun rig and draped it over a nearby chair. Then he went out to the kitchen and rustled up two glass tumblers. He came back, sat them empty by the wine bottle, and sat down to light a smoke, feeling sort of dry-mouthed even though he'd just had coffee. Romano's served this coffee called Express Train, and he knew it would keep him awake half the night. He'd sort of planned on not getting much sleep.

Elanore came back in, still packing her big handbag, but not much else, as she said, "You're not going to believe this. Tiger Lil has tiger-striped satin sheets on that bed in there."

"That's likely why they call her Tiger Lil, Miss Elanore. Uh, is that thing you got on what they call a . . . pen-war?"

She put down her handbag and twirled girlishly, saying, "Yes. I got it at the hotel. How do you like it?"

He liked it fine, but he sure hoped Uncle Sam hadn't paid much for it. It was a sort of skimpy nightgown made out of dark cobwebs with lace edgings. He could see by the lamplight that she wasn't wearing a stitch under it, and she was built better than he'd dared to dream. But the black lace was strategically placed, and so, while he could see her rosy nipples under the filmy folds, the more private parts played peek-a-boo and you couldn't be sure if what you were looking at was pubic hair or lace. She sat down beside him and said, "This is all I had to wear. I'd have ordered something more modest, had I known I'd be alone with you like this."

He said, "I like it fine," and placed a casual arm on the backrest behind her.

She said, "Wait, let's have some wine, a lot of wine. Please don't think I'm teasing, dear. But it's been some time and I'm, well, confused."

He nodded and leaned forward to pour the wine. She held her tumbler up and her eyes glowed in the lamplight as she toasted, "Well, here goes all my mother taught me."

He clinked his glass against hers and said, "Mud in your eye."

For some reason that made her laugh hysterically as she put the glass to her lips. He took a sip. Then he put the glass down and murmured, "Quiet. I'll be back directly," as he rose, slipped the .44 from its nearby holster, and eased out to the kitchen. There was nobody there, of course. He went to the water closet beyond and sneaked a quick leak, telling his tool to simmer down as he shook it off and put it back where it belonged. He went back inside, and when Elanore asked what he'd heard, he said, "Mouse, most likely."

He sat down again, sniffing, and asked, "Did you put more perfume on?"

She took a sip of wine and asked, "What if I did? Don't you like it?"

He saw the perfume bottle by her open handbag and said, "I like you any old way and you know it."

He raised his glass, put it down untasted, and said, "Hell, a man needs a clear head at a time like this." Then he took her in his arms. Her lips met his, and it was nothing at all like kissing a raunchy bawd like Helga Hanson. Elanore was a properly raised lady, and her body seemed to be fighting another part of her that said good clean fun was dirty. He ran a hand up to cup one thinly clad breast.

She protested, "Wait, darling. I need more time. Can't we just sit and, well, talk? You haven't had your wine yet."

He said, "Don't want it. Want you." This time, when he reeled her in, she sighed in soft surrender and allowed him to unfasten her peignoir. He ran his hand teasingly down her smooth belly, and as his fingertips touched soft hair above her tightly pressed naked thighs, she stiffened, sighed, and relaxed in surrender, allowing him to finger her. He did so with considerable confusion on his own part. While one part of him was feeling aroused and raring to go, a dry, cold part of him was saying no. He knew he'd seldom gotten this far, still soft between his own legs, but he was glad, in a way, even though he knew he'd cuss himself some day in a lonesome place. He fingered her some more to make sure. Then he sighed and said, "Hell, there's no sense in both of us faking, Miss Elanore. I reckon it's time we had a serious discussion on photography."

She looked dismayed and asked, "Have you gone mad? I was about to give in, you fool!"

His face was sad as he said, "I know you were, ma'am, and a lot of gents less experienced in the feelings of women would have took you up on it, dry and frigid as you feel right now."

"What are you talking about? I just let you . . . *touch* me, dear!"

"I know. You started out a little hot, enjoying the game you were playing on an ignorant lawman who wasn't going to get too far. But I put you off your feed when I didn't drink that wine just now, didn't I?"

"Custis, stop this foolishness and *take* me, damn it! I don't care if you drink your wine or not!"

His eyes were sad but cold as he said, "You know that ain't true, ma'am. You've been lying to me since that first moment I walked in your shop like a fool, the way it was planned. It was the closest lab to where you set me up with that street photographer your boyfriend duped and later murdered."

"Are you suggesting I played some kind of trick on you, darling?"

"I ain't suggesting it, I'm saying it right out. Flash Stubbs never took any photograph of Timberline. How could he, with Timberline dead and buried? Stubbs already had the exposed plate you'd given him loaded in his camera as a backup ploy, when the gunslick they sent after me turned tail and ran out on that fight in the Parthenon Saloon."

"You're mad! You were standing there as I developed it for you, remember?"

"Sure I do. You were wearing that same perfume. The plate in Stubbs's box camera was real. You'd made a double exposure of an old photograph of Cotton Younger and that street scene. After I had that fight with him, his picture was in a lot of papers, so getting your hands on some old photos was no big deal. You had that one with him grinning as a backup when I came in with another undeveloped snapshot. That's why he looks so crazy in the snapshot you whipped up with a stock shot of the Salt Lake City Temple. Timberline never grinned at me like that in Temple Square. He was smiling at the birdy in some photograph studio, long ago and far away."

She sniffed and said, "That's ridiculous. You brought the undeveloped roll to me in the first place, and you'll never prove the picture I developed wasn't on that roll, fake or otherwise!"

He said, "You're wrong. I have a Salt Lake police officer as a witness. The bushes the shots were fired from faced Main Street, and we were both there, smelling the smoke. So he'd likely be able to say in court that as long as any Mormon can remember their temple ain't in that direction! It's dead across Temple Square, the way I'd just come. The temple was over *my* shoulder, not the gunslicks, as he fired at me!"

Elanore began to peel her peignoir off as she pleaded, "Please believe me, darling, I had nothing to do with any tricks someone may have tried to play on you. I can see now how someone may have tried to trick you with double exposures, but I swear it wasn't me. Do I look like a gunfighter?"

As she sat there naked, with the soft folds falling around her firm, rounded hips, he sighed and said, "You look more like Delilah must have looked to Sampson. You're as deadly, too. That was the part I had to be sure about before I made my play. You see, Miss Elanore, we can still play this more than one way. I explained that I'm allowed some leeway. So if you saw fit to switch sides, we might be able to work something out."

She reached out to take one of his hands and place it in her lap, opening her thighs to him as she sobbed, "I don't know what you're talking about! Don't you . . . want me, Custis?"

"I'd be a liar if I said I didn't. But we both know how it would look in court if I trifled with you in the middle of an arrest. So who put you up to all this crazy photography, and more important, why?"

She shoved his hand away, humiliated at his rejection, and covered her face with her own hands, sobbing, "You're crazy, crazy, crazy! I came here and offered myself to you because I loved you, you bastard!"

He glanced at his untasted wine and said, "I sure wish I could believe that, ma'am. But that cyanide you slipped in my drink sort of makes me tend to doubt your good intentions."

"Cyanide? What on earth are you talking about?"

"Aw, let's cut the bullshit, girl. That trick with the perfume didn't work, either. We both know cyanide smells like bitter almonds and that you use it in your line of work. I saw the jar on your shelf. Knowing we'd likely wind up in this ridiculous position if that gunslick waiting for me outside your room didn't make it, you brought some from your lab when I took you to the hotel. And please don't hand me a line about that cuss with the shotgun following me there. I know he didn't. Nobody could have, and nobody knew you were there, either, until you told them."

"Custis, I swear—"

"Hush, I know what you're fixing to swear, and I ain't finished. Let's say I was willing enough to buy it that you were just a poor, innocent photograph lady. Let's say I believed that somehow the men who were after me found out I had you in that hotel room. How in thunder do you get around the fact that we're the only folks here in Tiger Lil's, and that my glass of Romero's wine is laced with enough potassium cyanide to smell from here where I'm sitting?"

She fell away from him, giving him an interesting view as she lay there bawling, with her naked rump aimed at him. He nodded and said, "I never heard no mouse. I went out to take a leak and give you the rope you just hung yourself with."

She rolled over and spread her legs, sobbing, "Please don't arrest me! I'll do anything you want. Anything at all! I'll be your slave! Just don't let me face arrest with two children to think of!"

He didn't like the idea of explaining to young Larry Wilson about arresting his mother, either. But he made his voice hard as he said, "I don't need any slave, ma'am. I need some *facts*, or by thunder, I'll take you in wearing irons! You're in this up to your pretty neck, and what you're twitching at me will hang too, if you don't tell me who put you up to funning me with those fake pictures!"

"I'm frightened," she sobbed. "I'm a woman alone and they said it was all a joke. I need a man to protect and cherish me, darling. Maybe if you'd make love to me and I could feel you cared . . ."

He snorted in disbelief and said, "Oh, hell, girl, you make gals like poor Tiger Lil look like schoolgirls when it comes to that act. You want me to make love to you about as much as you want me to saw you in half."

"Prove it, Custis. Take me. Then tell me I have no feelings!"

He said, "It's tempting. I know you'd be good, as scared as you are. But somehow gals who try to murder me just don't put me in a romantic mood. You likely never heard the old dodge that a female suspect has been known to play in court on an arresting officer who took advantage of her, right?"

She was moving her hips in a mockery of wild desire, so he said, "All right. I can see you don't aim to tell me. So you'd best put your street clothes on before I cuff you and take you over to the lockup."

She suddenly sat up, wearing a wild expression as she said, "Wait, I'll tell you. It was Cotton Younger's kinsmen, the James boys!"

He curled his lip and said, "Not hardly. Not one member of that gang is that known or wanted where Timberline and his kin come from. I don't know how Cousin Jesse feels about the first time I killed Timberline, but it was a spell back and a fair fight, so I won't buy revenge from the James-Younger gang. The folks you're working with are after something. I'm in the way for some reason. You want to tell me about it? It's the last time I'll offer."

She moved closer to him, kicking the discarded peignoir to the floor as she asked, "What can you do for me if I tell you? Will you let me go, no further strings?"

He said, "I could lie to you, but I won't. The very least

you'll get is five years for aiding and abetting. But don't that beat life, or maybe even the rope?"

"Oh no, I never killed anyone, Custis!"

"I know. It's lucky I know the smell of cyanide. I'll allow that three of your friends went down trying. But let's not forget Flash Stubbs, gunned down from behind by a friend of yours that you're still covering for. I suspect that when we get to the bottom of this mess, we may find more folks dead, robbed, or whatever. But I'll tell you what. I'll ask the judge to consider your sex, and I'll even forget the cyanide in that glass if you'll make a clean breast of it."

She laughed, defeated, and cupped one of her breasts up to the light for him as she said, "Clean breast indeed. I was ready to give my whole body to you, you cold-blooded son of a bitch." Then she flinched and gasped, "Oh! There *is* a mouse!"

As Longarm turned his head without thinking, Elanore reached for the poisoned wine and swallowed one big gulp before he could slap it from her hand to send it flying, spilling wine all over Tiger Lil's rug.

"You little fool!" he swore, and leaped up to run for the kitchen, grabbing his gun along the way, just in case. He shoved the .44 in his waistband as he rummaged for mustard powder and poured it with condensed milk in a kitchen glass. But when he dashed back inside, Elanore lay smiling up serenely, naked on the sofa, her body glowing a faint cherry red. He moved over, felt the side of her throat, and muttered, "Damn. That stuff sure works sudden!"

Elanore didn't answer. She couldn't. He sighed down at her still-lovely nude form and said, "I sure wish you hadn't done that, ma'am. How in thunder am I ever going to explain this to my old pard, Larry?"

Then he nodded to himself and got to work. He had to work fast, before she stiffened. He ran in the other room and got her clothes. Then he started dressing her. It wasn't easy. He'd had more experience disrobing gals than dressing them, and she was as limp as a dishrag and was no help. He knew undertakers cheated by cutting the backs out of dead folks' duds, but he had to make it look like she'd died fully dressed. So he did. Then he went out to the kitchen and washed his hands. The dead woman's relaxing innards had betrayed her and he'd had to slip her drawers over a real mess. He'd felt funny as hell, feeling up her still-warm body like that, but he'd satisfied any curiosity he may ever have had about necrophilia. It was a crying shame that all that sweet-looking stuff had to go to waste, but as pretty as she still was, it wasn't his cup of tea. He was disgusted with himself for even thinking about it.

He stole a sheet from Lil's linen closet and rolled the pretty cadaver in it, along with her bag.

He put on his gun rig, coat, and hat, picked up the body, and snuffed the lamp as he let himself out. There was nobody on the narrow, dark street. It was only a couple of blocks to the South Platte River, so he carried her there, walked out on the railroad trestle with her balanced on his shoulder, and then, after making sure they were unobserved, he said, "Your kin are going to be upset by your drowning like this, Miss Elanore. But it's the best I can do."

Then he dropped her in and took off, wondering why he was crying all of a sudden.

Chapter 11

Leaving Elanore to the stark mercies of the sluggish, shallow Platte, Longarm headed for Marshal Vail's place. It was almost ten, but the boss was a night owl who seldom packed it in before eleven. Mrs. Vail and Kathy Mahoney were long gone to bed, of course. But sure enough, Billy Vail was in his study, reading Sir Walter Scott. He led Longarm in there after opening the back door to him. He picked up the book he'd been reading, hefted it, and put it aside with a sigh, saying, "I was just getting to the part where this Jewish gal's about to throw herself off the castle tower because this wicked knight won't stop pestering her. Can I just finish the chapter and find out if she made it or not?"

Longarm said, "Later. I just committed a crime and I thought you ought to know about it."

Vail asked, "Federal or state?"

Longarm said, "State."

Billy Vail said, "Hell, let's find out how that Jewish gal got away from the wicked knight. You see, she's a high-born Jewish lady, like in the Good Book, and this rascal is all hot for her, even though he's swore a vow not to mess with gals,

155

Jewish or not. How do you figure a man would trifle with a gal in a suit of armor, Longarm?"

"Very gently. Listen, Billy, I just faked a suicide to look like a suicide."

"You what? Why would anybody want to do a fool thing like that, old son?"

"To save some innocent kids from having to grow up knowing their ma was no good. That Elanore Wilson was trying to pull the wool over my new snapshot camera, and when I confronted her with it, she took cyanide."

Vail whistled softly, and said, "She must have been serious about dying. But you said you faked something."

"I did. I throwed her in the Platte so it'll look like she was drowned, by accident or whatever. Do you reckon you pull enough weight with the county coroner to keep them from performing an autopsy?"

"Sure. I'll tell him we know how she died and want to keep it to ourselves. Sometimes telling the truth works best. But you've whetted my interest more than Sir Walter, Longarm. Let's get back to what she was trying to pull on you."

So Longarm sat down and explained about the photographs until Vail held up a hand and said, "I get the idea. It's sure good to hear that Timberline is likely still dead. But he ain't in his grave, and some son of a bitch is after you, trying to make you think it's a dead man."

Longarm said, "I noticed. The razzle-dazzle with the fake pictures was a ruse to throw us off the scent if they didn't manage to gun me right."

Vail said, "Giving the devil his due, it's working! I still don't have the first notion what we're up against. Do you?"

"No. But I'm getting it whittled down. That fake robbery was meant to have everybody up in arms about a dead man back from the grave and up to his old tricks. You did try to send me straight to Salt Lake to check it out, remember?"

"I do, and when you got there in your own casual time, you found the cupboard was bare. Wasn't digging up a stinky corpse a lot of work to go to, just to fun the law?"

Longarm said, "Birdbath," and when Billy Vail looked at him as though he thought he was drunk, he added, "Birdbath in the burial ground in Salt Lake. They told me some Mormon was dug up and moved, but I was too dumb to see it right off. They never dug Timberline up. They didn't have to. They just had to switch his headstone and a small cement birdbath. Then they peeled the sod off Timberline's real grave, or maybe just salted the sod to kill it. Anyway, they moved Timberline's headstone to the empty grave so that when I had the grave dug up, we'd find an empty charity box."

"How come they never lifted the dead Mormon out, box and all?"

"That was shithouse luck they couldn't have planned on. The box was rotted and stuck in the subsoil, so the men who were hired to take the Mormon out and put him in a nicer one saw no reason to go to all that trouble. They just took the poor gent out, nailed the lid back down, and said no more about it."

Vail suppressed a shudder and said, "Remind me never to get buried. It would have given me a hell of a turn to dig up any coffin, empty or not."

Longarm nodded and said, "I'll confess I was too spooked and braced for ugly sights to think straight at the time. That's the whole point of this nonsense, to spook us out of thinking straight. I don't mind telling you that having a lady die in front of you can upset your digestion too. But like I said, I've started to whittle her down. I know who held up the Aurora post office, or tried to. I shot the last one earlier tonight."

Vail said, "I heard about the shootout at the hotel. But hold on, old son. None of them three hired guns looked anything much like the late Timberline."

Longarm nodded and said, "I know. But I can count, and three would-be holdup artists add up to three hired guns. The one at the hotel was tall and could have had a white wig on. That's all it would take, you know, since the description given by rattled witnesses was three men, one tall and white-headed, period."

Vail thought, nodded, and said, "Well, hell, it's over and I can get back to *Ivanhoe*. Don't you wish you could live in the olden times, Longarm? Being a lawman must have been more interesting back then."

"It's kind of interesting here and now in the modern world, Billy. You ain't been paying attention."

"Hell, sure I have. Those three foxy rascals and the photograph gal worked together to mix you up. Only you saw through it and now all four of 'em's dead. So what's left?"

"Whoever is behind it all, of course. Elanore was a dupe, like poor little Stubbs. I couldn't get her to talk, so they must have had some hold on her."

"Hell, she might have been afraid they'd kill her for talking. Wait a minute. She did see you gun the last of the three, didn't she?"

"She did. And the three hired guns didn't have the brains to play so many cruel jokes on their Uncle Sam. I ain't given to maidenly modesty, but when you get three cracks at a man and lose three times, you have no business calling yourself a killer. All three were pretending to be private detectives, but I doubt they could hold a steady job as railroad bulls. They were just three dumb thugs, outfitted and sicked on yours truly by the mastermind."

Vail said, "He must not be feeling all that masterful right now. If I was him I'd be scared shitless."

Longarm nodded and said, "I sure hope not. Either he takes another crack at me, or we'll never catch him unless we can figure out his motive. Are you sure there's nothing important coming up, like another Indian Ring swindle, or somebody selling Pike's Peak again?"

Vail shook his head and said, "Dammit, I told you business was slow."

Longarm frowned and asked, "Did they let Gus Hansen off like they said?"

"I'm ahead of you there. I could see as well as anybody that if that dumb Swede was innocent of that land grab, somebody had to have framed him. So while you were out chasing wild men and women, I went down the hall and looked over the case with Prosecuter Donovan. Say, did you know that little gal he has working with him is flirty as hell? It may have been an accident, but when she moved against my hand where it was braced on Donovan's desk, I could have sworn she was advertising with a free feel."

Longarm grimaced and said, "Never mind about oversexed secretaries. Who charged Gus Hansen with obtaining U.S. land by fraud?"

"The U.S. did. What really happened was they asked him

to come in for a review of his claim when somebody at the land office noticed how much one ignorant immigrant had added to an original quarter-section grant. Like you figured out, it was legal under the old sloppy laws before this reform administration, and it would have been cleared up with a simple hearing if Hansen had been sensible instead of ornery. Donovan showed me his brief. He agreed he'd have been murdered in court by any decent lawyer, and he says he owes us a favor."

Longarm chuckled in fond recollection and said, "He's already paid off, but I hope he never finds out. Back up and tell me who would have gotten the Hansen holdings if they'd been repossessed by the land office."

Vail frowned and said, "The land office, of course. And before you start arresting folks for just doing their jobs like you and me, there's no way anyone working for the government could have made a plugged nickel on that land hog's big spread. I asked Donovan, and when he didn't know, I went direct to the land office and asked them. I don't always sit behind my desk, you know."

"That's likely why you're so skinny. Tell me what they told you, dammit."

"I thought I just did. If Hansen's claims had been set aside, the land would have reverted to public domain. The land office would have resold it. But such holdings are auctioned off to the highest bidder, and the money goes direct to the U.S. Treasury. Do you reckon our master crook is the U.S. Treasury?"

"It wouldn't surprise me as much as you might think. But I can't see them playing foolish games with dead men and fake photographs. Generally, when the bastards in Washington want something, they just take it, as my old friend Sitting Bull can tell you."

He pondered and added, "Shit. I had a grand notion about the Hansen land being grabbed by some sneaky cusses, and you just tore it up on me."

Vail said, "I can do better than that. That last try on your life was made this evening, long after the Hansens went home, still owning the land, remember? Let's say you throwed your boot in the works by suggesting that Uncle Sam drop the case. Let's say that was what they were out to prevent by gunning

159

you or getting you out of town. It still don't work. Anybody after Hansen's land would have dropped the fight as soon as they saw it was over. Hell, even Hansen himself would have dropped it, if he'd been behind wanting you killed, and I'll be damned if I can see why."

"He'd have sent somebody to gun Donovan, not the low-ranking deputy that was just there to keep him company," Longarm pointed out. "Besides, Hansen was in jail as well as stupid. He had no son, and if his daughter has the brains to mastermind her way to a church social, I'm too dumb to be packing my badge. But dammit, Billy, that don't leave us *anybody*!"

"I noticed. Where are you figuring on bunking tonight?" Vail asked.

"I dunno. Tiger Lil's, or my own digs over the creek, I reckon."

"I wouldn't go back to your roominghouse until we know who's after you, and Lil's is a far piece. Why don't you use one of our spare rooms upstairs? That way I'd know why you were late to work in the morning for a change."

Longarm started to object. Then he nodded and replied, "Makes sense. I might as well see Miss Kathy back out to Aurora in the morning. I doubt like hell anyone could actually be after her, since they were only using her to convince me there were ghosts."

Vail agreed and led the way up with a candle, saying Longarm should make himself at home and that he was going back down to find out how that Jewish gal got away from the wicked knight.

Longarm could have told him, since he'd read the book, but it seemd a shame to spoil it. The poor armored cuss had stopped when Rebecca threatened to jump off the tower unless he stopped pawing her, and since he'd loved her true despite being a rascal, he'd eased up on her.

Longarm undressed by candlelight as he foresaw poor Billy's disgust with the ending. He'd never figured out why the book was called *Ivanhoe*, since all that the one called Ivanhoe did was mope about, nursing a wound, through most of the yarn. That Jewish gal, Rebecca, had more spunk than almost anybody else in the infernal book, and if Ivanhoe had

160

had a lick of sense he'd have married up with her, for she'd saved his life a hundred times and was crazy in love with him. But no, the poor simp had passed up old Rebecca for a stuck-up society gal named Rowena, who just moaned and sobbed a lot. That wicked knight who loved Rebecca had more hair on his chest, even though he was supposed to be the villain. He'd loved that spunky dark-haired gal so much it killed him in the end. So Longarm had always wondered who the hell wound up with Rebecca, the only decent gal in the whole book. Some men just didn't have a lick of sense when it came to women.

He got in bed naked, luxuriating between the clean lavender-scented sheets. There was a lot to be said for living permanent with a gal, even if she looked like old Mrs. Vail. She cooked good and kept old Billy's house neat as a pin. He wondered what she was like in bed. Then he wondered why he wondered that and told himself to cut it out.

He knew his latest erection was occasioned by the sensuous sheets and the wild scene with poor Elanore at Tiger Lil's. Hell, right now he could have used Tiger Lil, and that was thinking desperate!

But it had been a long day and he was tired. So he finally drifted off to sleep, perchance to dream, and dream he did. He was surprised as hell to find himself in bed with Elanore Wilson, naked as a jaybird and playing with his tool. He asked her, "How did you get out of the Platte, ma'am?" and she said, "Where there's a will, there's a way. We never got to screw before I killed myself, remember?"

He felt horny as hell, but he said, "I remember, and, no disrespect, I don't think I want to screw a dead lady, ma'am."

Elanore squeezed so hard it would have hurt if it hadn't felt so good as she said, "I may be dead, but I'm not just lying there, you fool. Come on, I'm hot as a two-dollar pistol, and you're a liar if you say that's only a piss-hard-on!"

She sure talked dirtier than he remembered, and her face was as red as a beet from the cyanide she'd drunk. But she was stroking him mighty sensuously for a dead gal, and as he stared down at her bright red breasts, it looked like she was panting in heat, dead or whatever. He said, "Well, I'll likely hate myself for this in the morning, but if we become good friends I'll expect you to tell me who the mastermind is, hear?"

She wrapped her other arm around him to haul him into the saddle as she said, "Anything. I'll do anything for you, darling, just screw me."

So he did. Or at least he started to. As he entered her she gasped, "Oh my, that does feel nice!" in a funny little-girl voice. She moved sort of shyly and awkwardly too, considering how anxious she'd been acting up to now.

But now he was enveloped in the moist warmth of a totally dedicated seductress, and he decided to question the suspect later, so he buckled down to attend to business and she bit her lip and hissed, "Not so loud! They'll hear us!"

He wondered who she meant. He hadn't wondered, up to now, where they were and how they'd gotten there. But as he looked back over his shoulder he saw they were back at Tiger Lil's, making love on striped satin sheets. In the doorway, Timberline pointed the gun he was holding at them and said, "Hurry up and finish, Longarm. For I aim to kill you with a smile on your face."

"This is ridiculous," Longarm said. "Both of you are dead."

Timberline asked, "Don't you believe in ghosts, old son?"

Longarm said, "No. I must be dreaming." So he woke up.

At least he thought he was waking up. He opened his eyes and found himself in bed in the Vail's spare bedroom. But there was somebody in bed with him, and he was in her, still going at it hot and heavy!

He didn't stop. He couldn't. Judging from the way she was moving, she didn't want him to. But natural curiosity made him blurt out, "Who the hell might you be, ma'am?"

"Not so loud!" she whispered. "The Vails will hear you!"

"Kathy? Is that you?"

"Yes. Don't stop! I had no idea this here screwing felt so good!"

She was right, and Longarm couldn't have stopped this late in the game at anything less than gunpoint. But even as he felt himself coming, he had serious reservations about his strength of character and common sense. He knew the only thing worse than breaking in a virgin was leaving her hanging, so he forced himself to keep moving, and from the way *she* was moving, it seemed he was making a noble sacrifice indeed. Kathy bit her lip again to keep from crying out in joy as she contracted, went limp, and sighed, "Oh my, that sure beats fingers any day of the week!"

He stopped, staying in her, as he nuzzled her neck and whispered, "Did you come, honey?"

"I must have," she said. "Nothing else could have felt so wonderful. Lord of mercy, do it some more!"

So he did, but he moved slow and easy, as curious as he was aroused with the first blush off the rose. He asked, "Are you sure you're a virgin, or were you just funning me the other night because you didn't want to do this?"

She giggled and said, "I used to be a virgin, but I ain't anymore, and I thank you from the bottom of my heart."

"How did we wind up like this? I must have missed something."

She giggled again and said, "I was having trouble falling asleep even before I heard Marshal Vail light your way to bed. I waited forever till the house was quiet and then I crept in here to shuck my social disadvantages."

"That was mighty brassy, considering. I thought you young gals set great store by being virgins, Kathy."

She moved her hips experimentally and said, "Oh, I'll still tell folks I'm a virgin. But while you menfolk were out gadding about, I've been going over the facts of life with Mrs. Vail."

"Jesus. She told a pretty young gal like you that Queen Victoria was wrong?"

"Not in so many words. I told her how shy I was around men, even though I bluster and show my red-headed temper more than I feel it. I asked her how come some of the other gals at the church socials manage to be so bold and forward whilst me and the other wallflowers just watch, all mortified and goosebumped. There's this one mean old girl named Mary Lou who jokes back at the boys and never flinches when one holds her close to two-step across the dance floor. You know the kind I mean? Anyway, mean old Mary Lou is about to be married and she had her pick of a dozen, while I'm just stuck sorting that infernal mail, too shy to catch a man."

Longarm chuckled softly and said, "I think I met up with Mary Lou's intended the other day. She's not getting much. But I can see how things like that could vex a small-town gal."

"I want to try something," Kathy said.

She raised her thighs, locked her ankles across Longarm's rump, and sighed, "Oh, nice. Anyway, Mrs. Vail explained about sassy gals like Mary Lou. She said a lot of sweet young things who still act like virgins ain't, and that's why they can handle men so easy. You ever met any sneaky gals like that, Custis?"

"They're my favorite kind. And now that you seem intent on joining their ranks, all I can say for the men of Aurora is heaven help 'em. You're going to be lethal."

"I hope so. I don't feel half as shy now as I did only a little while ago. I'll confess I was afraid to creep in here like this, Custis. For though I'd made my mind up to get rid of that infernal burden with you, I don't mind telling you I was scared as hell when I snuck in here."

He said, "That sounds reasonable. But why me? Seems to me you could have done as well or better with any number of young gents offering better odds on permanence. You see, honey, a tumbleweed cuss like me ain't much of a bet for any woman, virgin or otherwise."

She said, "I know. You ain't looking to get all mushy and moo-cow with me, right?"

"Well, I'll moo-cow you all you want, but you have to understand it has to be good clean fun between, uh, pals."

She laughed and hugged him with her wiry little legs as she replied, "That's why I figured you of all he-brutes was the best a gal could choose to lose her cherry scientific. I ain't about to settle down till I've had some fun, and I figured a man who's had as many gals as you could show me the ropes. I mean, everybody knows what's supposed to go where, but I want to learn it right!"

He suppressed a roar of laughter and kissed her before he said, "As you can see, it ain't all that complicated. Almost any two willing folk can manage to enjoy it, once they get over the shyness."

She sighed and said, "I know. I was shaking like a leaf and I thought I'd wet myself when I first crept in here and under the covers with you. When you rolled over and took me in your arms, I thought I'd scream. But I couldn't, because of the Vails down the hall. And then you just started making love

164

to me, so sweet and natural, and all of a sudden you were in me and I thought, My God, I'm doing it! And it was even easier than learning to dance, after that!"

He could tell it was time to cut the idle chatter and treat her right. So he started moving faster as she unlocked her ankles and opened wider in sweet welcome. She came, sobbing with happiness, so he put both hands under her little firm buttocks and pounded her for his own enjoyment. But she beat him to heaven a second time and then they just lay still, feeling each other's hearts beating in the darkness.

After a time, Kathy sighed contentedly, then giggled like a naughty kid. She said, "Lordy, I almost missed out on this. I was just down the hall, knowing you were in here. I wanted to learn how to do it right, but I was afraid. Then I heard the Vails in the next room. I heard what they were doing, for their bedspring creaks. It made me feel so left out to know that even old folks do it every night. And so I started picturing you and even Marshal Vail, acting just awful with me, and I just couldn't stand it so I came down here and slipped in bed with you and . . . oh, great day in the morning! I think I'm coming again!"

She was, too. So he helped her out by hooking his toes under the footboard for purchase as he drove deep and hard. For a beginner, Kathy sure was something else. After years of spinsterhood she seemed intent on making up for lost opportunities. They enjoyed one another again, and then he said, "We'd better get you back to your own bed, honey. I ain't sure Mrs. Vail intended her guest rooms for double occupancy."

She protested, "I want you to teach me all the tricks, Custis. I've heard stories about all sorts of positions and things that sound sort of wicked but must feel good."

"Let's save some of the wild stuff for soft lights and more privacy. When do you have to be back in Aurora?"

"Never, if I don't want to! If I do go back to that infernal post office job, it'll be after I'm a woman of the world."

That meant they had maybe a month before she started nagging him about changing the little habits women never seemed to notice about a man at first. He said, "Well, I hired a nice hotel room near my office, and I'm still paid up till high noon tomorrow. I can likely sneak another day on the bill by calling you a material witness. We've yet to wrap up the attempted robbery of your post office."

"Oh Lordy, I get to learn the facts of life in a real hotel, smack in the big city?"

He chuckled fondly and said, "Yeah, they got hot and cold running water and a mirror across the room for us to admire ourselves in while I teach you how to be an acrobat in bed. You ought to be safe there, and after work I'll show you the big-city lights and teach you how to eat Eye-talian noodles too. We'll have all sorts of fun. But meanwhile, if you don't creep back where you belong, you'll get me fired."

So she went. But not until he'd made her come again for luck.

Chapter 12

The three of them drove downtown in the morning in Vail's surrey. Marshal Vail made no objection to Longarm's dropping Kathy off at the nearby hotel. But the room clerk looked at them sort of curiously as Longarm and his "wife" picked up the key. Longarm said, "All right, she had her hair dyed. Want to make something of it?"

The room clerk just shrugged and turned away.

When they got upstairs, Kathy clapped her hands and ran to the window to look out, crying, "Lordy, we're on the second floor and I can see all sorts of things. Look, darling, here comes a big brewery wagon with a matched team of eight!"

He said, "Yeah. I'll show you how to use the flush toilet and the room-service telephone. But go easy on the room service unless you really need something. There's no reason for you to stay holed up, as far as I can see, so you can go down and walk about to window-shop or whatever. I'll try to get back early, but now I have to go."

"Can we, you know, first?"

"I'd like to, but I can't, Kathy. I'm on duty."

"Oh. I suppose you had your way with that other gal in that very same bed, huh?"

He shook his head and said, "No. Those sheets are more virgin than either one of us. You ain't jealous, are you?"

"I'm trying not to be. But I'm glad you never did it with nobody else here."

He kissed her good-bye and left her to her own devices. He cornered the house dick down in the lobby and said, "As you may have noticed, I have another material witness upstairs. I see they fixed the wallpaper and I'd take it neighborly if you sort of kept an eye on her."

The detective grinned and said, "Keeping an eye on anything that nice will be a pleasure, Longarm. How come you find so many pretty material witnesses?"

"Friends in high places. Got to go see one now."

The man Longarm had in mind was One-Name Fred, the fixer. He'd told Marshal Vail on the way in that he meant to pay an early call on One-Name Fred, and Vail had said it was all right, as long as it wasn't official.

One-Name Fred was not as big a fixer as some folks said these days, with the Republicans in power. But if the Democrats ever won again, watch out! Longarm found One-Name Fred in his second-story office near the Denver Dry Goods Store on California Street. One-Name Fred was a beefy one-time lawyer who'd been drummed out of the Bar Association a while back for some minor error in jurisprudence that nobody had managed to jail him for. He sat at his desk behind a bank of telephones, for while no city was yet hooked up the way Professor Bell kept promising, many advanced thinkers had strung private lines, and so One-Name Fred was hooked up to his stockbroker, his bookmaker, and many Denver public officials who never spoke to him in public.

One-Name Fred waved Longarm to a chair and produced a humidor of four-bit cigars, saying, "It's been a long time, Longarm. What do you need fixed this time?"

Longarm bit the end off the expensive smoke and waited until One-Name Fred reseated himself before he leaned forward to light them both up and said, "I don't need anything fixed, exactly. Officially, I ain't even here."

"Naturally. Let's hear your tale, son."

So Longarm told him most of the story, leaving out the dirty parts. When he'd finished, One-Name Fred stared at the tip of his own cigar and said, "All of this is as interesting as hell, Longarm. But I fail to see why you came to me. Are you accusing me of being this mastermind you're after?"

Longarm shook his head and said, "I'd be wasting my time if you were, for we both know no lawman born of mortal woman could hang a conviction on you in front of the judges who owe you. I thought, since you have so many fingers in the pie, you might be able to offer some suggestions."

One-Name Fred said, "Well, I agree with you that somebody sure has gone to a lot of trouble if they don't mean to get something out of it. I'll ask about, but at the moment I'll be switched if I can see any way to make money out of all them Halloween pranks. That land-grab angle's sort of interesting, but I agree with Donovan and Vail that it's a blind alley. That piggy Swede had no motive to spook you, since the only thing you could do, and did, was help him. The other side's off the hook because there's just no way anybody working for Uncle Sam could have made a dime on the deal, either way."

Longarm said, "I know. Maybe I was meant to think my way up a blind alley. Just like I was meant to think dead men could get up and stalk me. What other action's going on in Denver that Billy Vail don't know about?"

One-Name Fred thought and said, "Can't think of anything calling for such high table stakes, Longarm. It's an election year under a reform administration, so most of the boys are standing pat with the cards they hold. There's a bond issue that someone who ought to be ashamed of hisself is saving for next year. But I fail to see any connection between a little local graft and you federal men."

"Tell me about it anyway. What goldbrick civic improvement are the boys in the smoke-filled rooms planning for the suckers next year?"

One-Name Fred hesitated, then shrugged and said, "Hell, I can tell Republican secrets. Some asshole says he can make a streetcar run on electricity. Ain't that a bitch?"

"Sounds mighty wild. Don't see how it could be connected with the case I'm on, though. But get to the crooked parts. I don't see anything illegal about an electric streetcar, whether it works or not. Just how *do* you crooks make money every time you put up a new office building or finance a county road?"

One-Name Fred frowned and said, "Crook's a harsh word, son. I peddle influence. I don't bust any laws worth mention."

"So I hear. Just what in thunder is this influence stuff you hawk to the highest bidder, One-Name Fred?"

"Oh, hell, you know how it works. One hand washes the other. A man with lots of friends is in a position to put a good word in for some old boy with money and no political pull. Only greenhorns take bribes, since Grant got caught. But everyone savvies an unspoken gentleman's agreement. Let's say you had some cash and needed a franchise to build some eyesore or other. You'd come to me, and the next time I shot pool with the official who could issue it to you pronto, saving paperwork and tedious hearings—"

"I follow your drift, and I thought that was what you sold," Longarm cut in, sort of bored. He thanked One-Name Fred for the cigar, and the fixer told him he'd ask questions around town as he ushered Longarm out.

Longarm went next to police headquarters and was shown in to the detectives' squad room. Longarm wasn't the only lawman in Denver, or even the only good one. The Denver P.D. had been doing their homework on the two bodies in the morgue, and Cheyenne had identified theirs too. A burly dick in a derby told Longarm, "Their names were Casey, Lipton, and Floyd. Casey was the one you got in Cheyenne. You nailed Lipton on the train, so naturally the one who tried to shotgun you last night was Floyd. He was six-foot-four in his socks, and taller in his boots. So he was likely the one who wore the white wig above his face mask out Aurora way."

Longarm nodded and asked, "What did they do for a living when they wasn't scaring folks? None of them were worth shit as gunfighters."

The Denver dick nodded and said, "That's 'cause all three was stockmen."

"Cowboys?"

"Not exactly. They had been. But all three have, or had, small spreads of their own. All within a day's ride of Denver, but spread out in different directions. That's why it took us a while to figure out who they were. All three have sold cows in the local stockyards at one time or another, but as small operators, none of them were famous. Couple of old boys down to the yards recognized Floyd from his morgue shot, as the beat men showed it around this morning. Once we saw we weren't looking for your usual High Plains drifter, it was easy enough to tie Lipton to Floyd, and Cheyenne already had Casey made. Before he went into business as a small holder, he got arrested a couple of times for being too familiar with other folks' beef. No solid convictions, but he had a modest record as a shady stockman, and you can see how it goes from there."

Longarm nodded as if he knew something. The Denver dick said, "You feds had been questioning a gal named Elanore Wilson, hadn't you?"

Longarm swallowed and said, "Yeah. Just routine. Why?"

"She's dead. Found on the banks of the Platte this morning. Looks like she drowned, but we don't know if it's suicide, accident, or something ugly. Thought you ought to know, in case you want an autopsy report. They'll be slicing her up sometime this afternoon."

Not if I can help it, Longarm thought, but he didn't say it aloud. He thanked the Denver dick and left for the Denver land office.

A nice-looking brunette there said she'd be proud to let him see the charts on Arapaho, Adams, and Jefferson Counties. It was making him uneasy, the way they had so many women working in offices the last few years. The pretty land office gal didn't get forward with him as they bent over the spread-out charts together, but he'd have found it easier to concentrate if she'd been a man, or at least an ugly gal who didn't wear perfume. He believed business was business and that a person's private parts shouldn't matter one way or the other during office hours, but it complicated work. He wondered if she'd feel easier in her mind if he assured her it didn't matter to him that she was a pretty gal. But if he said that, it might be sort of insulting. So how in hell was a man supposed to act at a time like this?

He decided the best way was to just pretend she was a sweet-smelling boy and say no more about it. She asked what he was looking for, and when he told her, she went to a filing cabinet to look up the chart numbers that went with the names of the dead men, just like a regular gent would have. He asked her to dig the Hansen claims out while she was at it, and she did. They read off the benchmarks and she said, "Oh, here's Mr. Casey's spread, southeast of Denver."

"Yeah," he said, "and here's Floyd's, tucked between the Diamond K and the foothills to the west. I know the folks at the Diamond K, and they don't act crazy. So that's two small holders with a bigger outfit between 'em and, up here near Golden is where Lipton raised cows when he wasn't acting silly. It's, let's see, a good forty miles from the Hansen spread."

"That's the ranch our office was disputing claim to, wasn't it?"

"Yeah. You lost. I might have too. It had occurred to me that someone might have duped those three land-hungry rascals into misbehaving themselves by offering them a chance to expand their holdings. But I see that all the lands we're jawing about are boxed in between innocent bystanders. I already know where the Wilson spread is, and that don't fit either, so they must have had some other hold on her."

"*Her*, Deputy Long?" the pretty land office gal asked, interested at the mention of things co-workers weren't supposed to notice.

He nodded and said, "She-male suspect. Eliminated by drowning. I sure thank you for being so helpful, ma'am. If there's anything Justice can ever do for you . . ."

She dimpled and said, "Well, I get off for lunch at noon."

She sounded like she meant it. He smiled down at her and said gallantly, "I wish I did, ma'am. But I have to get on down the road."

She looked sort of wistful as he left. He chuckled and felt a mite wistful too, as he headed for his own office. She'd been a nice-looking little gal, and if he hadn't had Kathy waiting for him, and if he hadn't learned his lesson about fooling with other federal employees, he'd have been sorely tempted.

He spied his own grinning reflection in a window he was passing and told himself to stop feeling so smug. Better-looking gents than him had to pass on the opportunities offered by nubile secretaries, and a lot of them had more willpower.

He was climbing the marble steps to Billy Vail's office when he suddenly stopped dead in his tracks and snapped his fingers. He went on up and saw that Vail's clerk had left for lunch too. So he yelled, "Hey, Billy? You'd better come out here! I have to make an arrest and I may not have the rank!"

Vail popped out of his office and snapped, "Stop yelling like that. Were you birthed in a barn? What's all this about?"

Longarm said, "Come on, I have to arrest Donovan down the hall."

"You mean Prosecutor Donovan?" Vail replied. "I thought he was on our side!"

"He's the mastermind. I'll explain it all as we cuff him and carry him to the lockup. Let's hurry, I'm hoping he ain't gone to lunch yet."

Vail tagged after Longarm, warning, "If you're wrong, we'll both be in a hell of a mess, old son!"

As they approached the prosecutor's office, suddenly the door exploded open and the silvery-haired man burst out toward them, screaming in rage and waving a big Navy Colt .36!

"I hate you, you son of a bitch!" Donovan yelled as he fired at Longarm—or, more accurately, where Longarm had just been, for Longarm had crabbed to one side, going for his own gun.

Billy Vail was slapping leather too, as he yelled, "Simmer down, Donovan!"

Donovan fired his way too, and missed a second time as Vail showed him how he'd learned to move in the Texas Rangers as a boy. Longarm fired less wildly, and Donovan staggered as the .44 slug slammed into him and shoved him against the wall. He stared down owlishly at the smoking muzzle of Longarm's gun, looking sort of green, and the pistol Donovan was holding slipped from his grasp to clatter on the hard stone floor.

"Christ, I hate you," Donovan murmured, and stood straighter, like a dignified drunk. He started walking, stary-eyed, and when Vail raised his own gun, Longarm said, "Don't shoot him anymore, Billy. He's gutshot."

So the two of them followed as the prosecutor walked gravely down the hall toward the stairwell, like a drunk walking to some important appointment. Vail said, "You'd better sit down, Donovan. Let me help you."

But when Vail put a hand on the wounded man's sleeve, Donovan shook it off, staggered wildly forward, and pitched

173

headfirst down the marble steps of the federal building to fetch up on the landing like a broken doll, eyes staring blankly.

Longarm holstered his gun and went down to him as one of the uniformed guards from below came up gingerly. Longarm felt for Donovan's pulse. There wasn't any. As Billy Vail joined him on the landing, Longarm said, "This must be what the French call 'D.J. view.' The last time it was the Salt Lake Federal Building, and the man laying on the landing was Timberline. Ain't that spooky? This poor old lovesick rascal went to all that trouble pretending to be Timberline's ghost, and now he's dead in the same way and the very same position, on the same sort of marble steps! Sometimes it do seem the Good Lord has a sardonic sense of humor."

Chapter 13

There were things you couldn't talk about in front of people, and the killing had drawn a modest crowd, once it seemed safe to come out in the gunsmoke-filled hallway. So Longarm waited until Donovan had been carried off and they were alone in the chief marshal's office before he explained:

"Prosecutor Donovan had more than one motive. That's why I wasted so much time looking for one. He'd been given a weak case to prosecute, but he was a proud man and wanted to look good in an election year. So he figured he'd try and take Hansen's land away from him. That bullshit about him not knowing there was a *post facto* angle was just not true. Any kid fresh out of law school would have known you can't convict a fellow on any law enacted after the alleged offense. So Donovan must have shit his britches when you said you were assigning me to sit through the trial with Hansen."

Vail nodded and said, "You do have a rep for noticing things. But hell, anyone in court might have stood up for the Swede."

"Yeah, but he hated me for other reasons already. He was a jealous older man that the gals around the building thought of as a fatherly cuss."

"Which you ain't," said Vail, adding, "Sometimes I'm jealous of you myself. I'm a happily married man, but it can be annoying to see a randy young stud like you attracting all the admiring glances from gals that just look through anybody old enough to be their father. Tell me, did you ever trifle with that sassy little secretary of his?"

Longarm lit a smoke before he said, "I hadn't, at the time Donovan conceived his crazy hate for me. But there'd been gossip and he likely thought she was meeting me on the sly. You see, he loved her, Billy. Loved her pure, as only an old fool can love a pretty young gal he knows he just can't have."

"You mean like that wicked knight in *Ivanhoe* loved that Rebecca gal?"

"Yeah, I know it sounds dumb, but as a lawman you know how many men act dumb enough to kill over women. The hell of it is, he likely could have had old Nan any time he wanted. Don't ask me how I know, but it's true. He had her sassy little behind on a pedestal. And like most of us, he wanted to show off for her. He wanted her sitting there in court, watching with admiration as he showed his stuff. It was a tough case, a case it would take a damned good man to win. They must have talked about it in their office alone, while she was taking dictation and typing up the briefs."

Vail nodded and said, "I can see it. Him sitting there behind a big cigar with the little blond gal asking him how he figured to win, and him spinning tales of all the wonders and cucumbers he'd et in his time. So that's why he wanted you away from the courtroom and why he set up spooky reasons for me to send you off to Salt Lake. But how did he get the others to go along with it? What were they getting out of the deal?"

"Influence. That's all a bigshot has to promise little folks. Casey, Lipton, and Floyd wanted land. but with the way the country around Denver is growing, land is getting hard to find and expensive when you find it. He told the three small stockmen he could see that they were allowed to bid on Hansen's land if they'd help him rob the Swede."

"But hell, he couldn't have done that, Longarm. Even had he won his case, it wasn't his land to sell anybody!"

Longarm nodded and said, "You know that and I know that. But a man too stupid to aim at a man he has the drop on don't

176

know much about anything. He was duping them. He played bigshot with them, just like he liked to do with Nan. That nonsense with the fake detective agency ID wouldn't have meant anything to professionals, but it impressed them, and a highly placed public official had no trouble getting copies of real bonded detectives' papers, so what the hell. He likely just paid Flash Stubbs off to fool me with that fake photo plate. Stubbs was a hardscrabble street character who was probably flattered to be working undercover for a public prosecutor, and Donovan could have told Stubbs anything, since he meant to kill him once he'd done the deed."

Vail lit a smoke for himself and said, "I can see how easy that was, and I know you can make a camera lie if you know how. But how did he get that poor Elanore Wilson in on it, Longarm?"

Longarm said, "Blackmail, most likely. From some words of hers, I know she didn't enjoy her married life as much as she let on. Her mother-in-law hated her so bad that Elanore was afraid of her. Or did she have a guilty conscience?"

"You mean you suspicion Miss Elanore became a widow on purpose?"

"Well, she tried to poison *me*, and I never saddled her with two kids and a boring life she didn't fancy. With him dead, she owned the business and got to meet more folks. I don't see how anyone could ever prove it at this late date, since cyanide ain't like arsenic when you look for traces of it in dead bodies. But if you were a murderess and a prosecuting gent asked you for a few favors, wouldn't you be inclined to go along with him? He might have offered her land or money too. We'll never know now. But since she was working with them, the details don't matter."

Vail grimaced and said, "She must have been one cold cookie. She even used her little boy to trick you, right?"

"No, Larry Wilson's a good kid and that's why he must never know his mother didn't just fall in the Platte. His being there that time to warn me when one of those jaspers took a shot at me was pure good fortune. She'd told him not to play in Cherry Creek, but show me a Denver boy who don't, and I'll show you a sissy. She must have damned near wet her pants when she found out what he'd done for the modest reward

177

I gave him. But she saw a way to use it to get in thicker with me, so she used it. I ain't sure but what Larry and his little sister won't be better off with their grandparents. She wasn't as good a mother as she let on."

Vail said, "I agree. But no matter how you slice it, the whole mess was too complicated. Why in hell did Donovan go to so much trouble scaring you when he had four folks willing to kill you?"

"It might not have started out as a killing matter. Even if he wanted me dead, it would have been better to dupe you into sending me someplace else for my execution, and you would have wasted a heap of time and trouble looking for the dead owlhoot you'd have blamed it on. It's more likely he only wanted me scared at first. But his hate was gnawing at him and, well, I made a foolish move and gave him something he could hate me more about."

"Hot damn! You *was* the one in there with Nancy when the wastebasket caught on fire, right?"

"I ain't saying. But if the watchman told you about her being in there with somebody, he must have told Donovan. Hell, for all I know, Nancy told him. She ain't bashful and might have thought she was confiding in a fatherly old gent. Anyway, somewhere along the line they got orders to play rough. By that time I was sending wires all over creation, so he had to pull in his horns on the Hansen case with a two-faced smile, throwing us off the trail as he switched motives. When the three guns he'd hired failed, he ordered Elanore to do it. You know the rest."

Vail said, "No I don't. I thought that gal tried to poison you because you were getting warm."

Longarm shook his head sheepishly and said, "This may come as a great surprise to you, Billy, but every woman in the world don't admire me as much as I'd like. Elanore spiked my wine with cyanide before I confronted her. That was *why* I confronted her. If they'd had sense to quit while I was confused, I'd have likely made love to her and never been the wiser. But his hate got in the way of his good sense. So while he didn't have the balls to go after me himself until just now, with results he must have considered, he let Elanore do his dirty work at close range. He was likely the one who picked off Flash Stubbs, and all the other stuff was self-defense. So the new prosecutor shouldn't arrest us for behaving so unruly back at them."

Vail frowned and said, "I doubt anything will have to come out, official. One hand washes the other, like they say, and the Justice Department will want to keep our domestic quarrels out of the paper. So now that we have everyone in the box, what am I to do with you for the rest of the day?"

Longarm said casually, "I was wondering if I'd earned an afternoon off, Billy. I promised Miss Kathy I'd show her the sights, and I'd like to get an early start."

Vail grimaced and said, "All right, but go easy on the sights you show her. My old woman says she's an innocent gal, old as she is."

So Longarm said he'd treat the redhead right and got up to leave as Vail muttered behind him, "At least the office help will be safe for a spell."

Longarm didn't exactly skip as he made his way back to the hotel, but he was feeling pretty chipper. Next to cracking a tough case, there was nothing that beat loving with a pretty gal in daylight, and he hadn't seen that little redhead naked yet.

As he went through the hotel lobby, the house dick was looking at him with an expression of utter awe. Longarm nodded and went upstairs. He knocked and heard Kathy call, "It's open, dear."

So he went in.

Kathy was in bed. But Kathy was not alone. The late Prosecutor Donovan's wild blond secretary, Nancy, was in bed beside the redhead. Neither had a stitch on as they smiled up at him. Nancy said, "I don't have any work at the office, thanks to you. So when I found a note on poor Mr. Donovan's desk, saying you were here, I came over to, ah, pay my respects."

Kathy piped up, "I let her in and we found we have a lot in common. She says *she* found being a virgin tedious, too! So when she asked me if I'd ever played three-in-a-boat, I said I thought it sounded like a heap of fun, and here we are!"

Longarm couldn't think of a thing to say, so he just turned around and bolted the door behind him. Then he turned back and took off his Stetson and hung it on the hat tree beside the door.

A grin began to spread across his features as he walked slowly toward the crowded bed.

SPECIAL PREVIEW

Here are the opening scenes
from

LONGARM AND THE COMANCHEROS

thirty-eighth novel in the bold
LONGARM series from Jove

Chapter 1

Weariness mingling with reproach in his voice, Longarm asked, "Now you honestly don't expect me to ride a sorry nag like that all the way down through No Man's Land and halfway across Texas, do you Sergeant?"

"Well, Marshal, I'll admit he ain't going to take no prizes for pretty," the remount sergeant major said, looking at the rawboned piebald gelding whose halter he was holding. "But he'll get you there."

"There, maybe," Longarm nodded. "But how about back?"

"He's a better nag than he looks like," the sergeant said.

Longarm shook his head without replying. He walked over to the rail of the paddock and lighted one of his cheroots while he studied the other horses that wandered around the enclosure. There were only eight of them, and of that number, three stood in hang-head dejection, unmoving; two more were sadly sway-backed, and another obviously had sore feet. Turning back to the sergeant major, he pointed to the two that looked to be in the best shape.

"How about one of those two, either that nice roan or the dapple?"

"I'm sorry, Marshal," the noncom replied. "They ain't army stock. One of 'em belongs to the colonel's lady, and the other one's Major Carruthers personal mount."

"If that's the best you can do, I guess I'll have to take it, then," Longarm said. "But it sure don't make me feel easier in my mind to leave for where I'm heading on such a poor-looking animal. What in hell's happened to the cavalry, anyhow, not having any decent horses in the remount paddock in a big place like Fort Dodge, here?"

"Well, right now we got three troops in the field, and they had to take along some reserve horses." The sergeant major looked around and dropped his voice. "To tell you the truth, Marshal, we just don't get the kind of animals we need no more, now that all the Indians has been whipped and penned up on their reservations down in the Nation. There's none of us likes it, but I guess the officers can't do much to cure it."

"I'll take the piebald, then," Longarm told the man. "I don't say I'll be happy about it, but I guess we all got to make do with what we can get these days."

"Yessir. Well, if you'll step over to the stable with me, I'll get one of my men to saddle up for you while I write up a requisition." The sergeant looked at the saddle, saddlebags, and rifle that Longarm had dropped beside the paddock fence. "That's your gear yonder, ain't it?"

Longarm nodded. The sergeant major started for the stable, with Longarm following. While the noncom was filling out the forms, Longarm said thoughtfully, "You know, I ain't been around Dodge City since the moon turned blue, but it was a rip-roaring hell-raiser back then. What's it like now?"

"It's been a pretty dead place since I got posted here about a year ago," the man said, frowning. "I hear it used to be different, when all the buffalo hunters brought their hides here to ship, but there's not all that many buffalo anymore, I guess. I'd say it's coming back to life a little bit, though. A lot of ranchers down in Texas are beginning to drive some cattle herds up to ship East. But it's sure as hell quiet right now."

"I guess there's still a few good saloons in town?"

"Oh sure. There's plenty of saloons. I don't know whether a man in your position would call any of them good or not, but you sure won't have no trouble getting a drink in Dodge."

"What I'm looking for is a saloon that might have a pretty good stock of liquor. I want to buy a bottle or so to carry with me. From what I hear, it can be a long way between saloons up in the unsettled part of Texas where I'm headed."

"If it's just whiskey you want, you can get plenty at the sutler's store right here on the fort."

"No thanks, Sergeant. I've had more'n enough of that raw, cut-down whiskey out of army sutler's barrels to last me a lifetime. More'n I can stand to think about. What I want is some good Maryland rye. Texas ain't too much for rye whiskey, I've found out, and bourbon's a mite sweet for my taste."

"Well, you might try Lonergan's place," the sergeant suggested. "Or the Long Branch, even if it ain't much more'n a hole in the wall. It's got a pretty good liquor stock, and the beer there's the best you can get in Dodge."

"Thanks." Longarm signed his name three times on the requisition forms the noncom held out to him, and returned them. "One more thing, Sergeant, and I'll be on my way. You think I might get a new map of the part of Texas I'm heading for, before I ride out? The one I'm carrying's pretty old, and it don't show too much detail north of Austin."

"You mean North Texas, Marshal?"

"Whatever they call the Llano Estacado down there. It's in the north, all right, but I ain't quite sure where."

"Ask at the engineers' office," the sergeant replied. "That Texas country's strange to me too."

"Strange to almost everybody except the Comanches, I guess," Longarm grinned. "Thanks, I'll see what the engineers say."

In the office of the Corps of Engineers, the young lieutenant shook his head when Longarm asked for a late map of North Texas. "I'm afraid not, Marshal. We've got plenty of maps of the Indian Nation, but after McKenzie whipped the Comanches back in '76, and got them penned up in the Indian Nation, we haven't had much need for maps of North Texas."

"It'd sure save me a lot of riding if I had a map that'd show me where I was at when I get down there," Longarm said regretfully. "But I'll make out without one, I guess. It won't be the first time."

"You might stop off at Fort Elliott on your way south," the

lieutenant suggested. "It's up in the Texas Panhandle, just a few miles west of the Indian Nation boundary line, and—"

"I know about where it is," Longarm interrupted. "I just disremembered it was there, and I never was real close to it on any of the cases I handled in the Nation."

"You shouldn't have any trouble finding Elliot," the lieutenant said. "There's a pretty well-used military supply road that runs from Elliott over to Fort Supply, in the Nation. You can just follow the wheel ruts right to the fort."

"Sure. Well, thanks, Lieutenant. I'll be on my way, then."

Riding into Dodge City from the fort beside the Santa Fe right-of-way, Longarm found that the afternoon sun was now slanting low enough to glare in his eyes under the wide brim of his hat.

Old son, he told himself, *you might just as well make up your mind to stay here tonight, get a barbershop shave and supper in a cafe, and sleep in a real bed. Because it sure looks like it'll be bacon and spuds and parched corn and jerky and a blanket on the ground, once you hit that trail south.*

Riding into the thick dust of the main street, Longarm studied the saloon signs as the piebald gelding picked its way between the jagged, uneven rows of stores. Lonergan's Saloon didn't appeal to him; there were too many loafers sunning themselves on the board sidewalk in front of the place. He rode on until he saw the Long Branch sign, and even though from the outside the narrow building with its sagging batwings fitted the sergeant's description of it as a hole in the wall, Longarm decided to try it first. He pulled the piebald over to the hitch rail and dismounted.

Once inside, he decided that the sergeant's phrase had been even more aptly chosen than the Long Branch's exterior indicated. The place was barely a dozen feet wide, and perhaps three times as long. A scarred and unvarnished bar stretched the length of the interior, brass spittoons spaced along its foot rail. The floor was worn to splinters from the boots that had trodden it. There were plenty of bottles on the shelves of the backbar. Most of them were dusty, and a number of them held only an inch or so of liquor.

A stack of beer kegs stood along the back wall, beside a rear door. Tables crowded the narrow area that remained between the bar and the opposite wall. Only one of them was occupied. At it sat a solitary drinker. His back was turned to the bar, but Longarm judged by what he could see of the man's clothing that he was not a resident of Dodge City, for he wore a neat city suit over a white shirt with a high starched collar, and a derby hat was pushed far back on his head.

Longarm gave the man a casual glance and tagged him as a solitary drunkard just starting on a prolonged spree. Two full bottles of whiskey stood on the table in front of him, as well as a third bottle that was almost empty.

Behind the bar stood a sleepy-eyed barkeep, his soiled apron hitched up around his chest, under his armpits. He looked up without interest when Longarm walked in, and made no move to step up and serve him.

Longarm stopped midway down the bar, in front of the barkeep. "I hope you got a bottle of Maryland rye. Tom Moore, if I got any choice."

"I'm afraid you ain't," the barkeep replied. "I got plenty of good bourbon, but I'm sold outa rye. That fellow over at the table there, he bought what was left in my last bottle of bar whiskey along with the only two other bottles off'n the backbar."

"Who in hell is he, anyhow? One of your town drunks?"

"Not that it's any of your damn business, mister, but I don't know him from Adam's off-ox. I been working here almost a year, and I never set eyes on him before."

"Looks like I'll have to ask him myself, then, if I expect to find out," Longarm commented as he turned and started toward the table. Getting closer, he could see the labels on the two bottles. One was Tom Moore, the other bore Joe Gideon's likeness, as did the bottle the stranger was just emptying into his glass. Longarm waited politely, lighting a cheroot, until the man at the table had sipped from his refilled glass.

Stepping up to where the stranger could see him, he said, "I ain't meaning to be nosy about your affairs, friend, but I was wondering if you're aiming to drink both of them bottles of rye whiskey all by yourself?"

"Sooner or later," the stranger replied, turning in his chair to face Longarm. "Why?"

"Why, I was sort of hoping you'd let me buy one of them

187

full bottles off of you. Seeing as how you got a taste for good rye, and you got two bottles full, and I got none, I figured you might be willing to sell me that bottle of Tom Moore you got there. You see, I'm going down into Texas when I leave here, and it's mighty hard to find good rye whiskey there."

"It's damned near as hard to find good rye here in Kansas, after you get out into the little towns, mister. And I'm going to be working the little towns for a couple of weeks. I'm sorry I can't oblige you, but I'll need both bottles to see me through."

"Well, no harm in asking, I suppose," Longarm said.

"No harm. Sorry I can't oblige you."

Draining his glass, the man stood up, tucked a bottle of the rye under each arm, and started toward the batwings. Just as he reached them, the swinging doors burst open and several roughly dressed men started pushing into the saloon. The first two of them through the doors collided with the man who was going out, knocking one of the bottles from under his arm. He almost dropped the second bottle as he juggled it, catching the one that was falling just before it crashed to the floor.

"Don't be in such a hurry," he snapped at the pair who'd gotten inside the Long Branch. "You damned near made me drop my liquor."

"Well now, ain't that just too bad!" one of the newcomers snorted, as his companions outside crowded up to the still-open batwings to peer in curiously. "Suppose you just step aside now, and get outa our way while we come on in."

"I'll be glad to," the man with the whiskey said. He moved to one side as the three men still on the board sidewalk shoved into the Long Branch. The second man through glanced idly at the waiting whiskey-carrier, took another step forward, then stopped short and turned to face him.

"Well, move on, Abel!" urged the man behind him. "Let's get on up to the bar and get the ballast-dust outten our guzzles."

"Wait a minute," the man named Abel said, frowning. "I know this dude from someplace."

"I'm afraid you're mistaken." The man holding the whiskey shook his head. "Even if you think you know me, I certainly don't recognize you."

"Well now, there just might be a good reason why you don't," Abel retorted. "Because I place you now. It was three years ago when I seen you last, mister. It was right here in Dodge too! You going to tell me you wasn't here then?"

"I don't lie, friend, it's not my style. Yes, I was here three years ago, and quite a few years before that, too. But I did business with a lot of men then, and I can't remember everybody I ran into."

"Well, I can't call your name either, but I never forget a face, mister," Abel said. Anger was growing in his voice as he talked. "And I sure do recall yours. I been waiting for a long time to run into you again!"

It was as obvious to Longarm as it was to the men with Abel that he was working up to a storm of anger.

One of his companions took Abel by the arm and said, "Oh, hell, Abel, pull up on that temper of yours and let's go get the drink we come in for. This fellow don't know what you're talking about, anybody can see that."

"You butt out, Smitty!" Abel snapped. "I got some unfinished business with this lying buzzard, and now's the best time I can see to wind it up!"

"Your friend's right," the man with the whiskey said soothingly. "Three years ago..." He shook his head. "I certainly don't remember having met you before, and I can't think that I've done anything to a man that'd keep him angry for that long."

"Well, I'll just dust off your memory for you," Abel said. "You're the damned cheating hide buyer that turned down the last bunch of flints I brought in here to Dodge to sell before the buffalo run out!"

"That may be true," the other man answered. "I did buy hides in Dodge for several years. And I had to turn down more than one batch of flints because whoever cured them didn't do a good job."

"You wasn't satisfied just turning mine down!" Abel shouted. "You had to go blabbing to all the other buyers that they wasn't cured proper! By God, mister, I never was able to sell them flints after you got through flapping your jaws all up and down the Santa Fe tracks! Cost me a season's take, you did! I ought've got around six thousand dollars for them flint hides!"

"Now look here," the former hide buyer said, "I'm sorry

if you're still carrying a grudge against me after three years, but if I said those flint hides weren't cured properly then, I'll still stand by it. Because I never did cheat a buffalo hunter or the company I was buying for. If a man had good hides, I'd buy them at a fair price. If his hides looked like they'd go soft before they got to the tannery, I turned them down."

Taking a step forward, the fellow brushed past Abel, heading for the door. Longarm was tempted to call out to the man, to tell him that walking away from a quarrel picked by someone like Abel would not only resolve nothing, but could be downright dangerous. On second thought, he decided it was none of his business and that he'd better stay out of it.

"Now, by God!" Abel snarled, "I don't take any man calling me a liar!"

Either the former hide buyer failed to catch the threat in Abel's voice, or he ignored it. He did not turn around, but kept on walking, and was outside the batwings and on the sidewalk before Abel acted. Pulling aside the rough, dusty work coat he was wearing, he began tugging at an ancient sidehammer Colt he wore in a belt holster.

Longarm had no time to reach Abel, but reacted in time to save an unsuspecting man from being backshot. Before Abel's pistol was completely out of its holster, Longarm had his own Colt out and leveled.

Abel was still bringing up his weapon, its muzzle coming up to aim at the departing man's back, when Longarm called loudly, "Abel! Drop that gun! Do it now, dammit!"

For a fraction of a second Abel hesitated while his head turned in the direction from which Longarm's shout had come. His eyes widened when he saw Longarm's Colt covering him, but anger had displaced common sense. Instead of letting his pistol fall to the floor, Abel swiveled to face Longarm, still bringing his gun's muzzle to bear, this time with Longarm as his target.

His move gave Longarm no choice. Like all veterans of many such confrontations, Longarm had learned that when facing a man with a gun aimed at you, shooting to wound can be a fatal mistake; in a second or less, even after your lead has struck, your antagonist can get off a shot that might be fatal.

Longarm fired. Abel's answering shot, triggered with his

dying reflex, tore into the splintered floor of the Long Branch Saloon, ripping a streak of fresh yellow pine from its boards. A look of surprise flashed over Abel's face. The heavy side-hammer Colt seemed to pull him down as his gunhand dropped. He toppled back against the doorframe and slid silently to the floor.

In the first few seconds that ticked off after Longarm's shot, the silence that gripped the saloon seemed as thunderous as the report of the Colt had been. Longarm kept his gaze fixed on the men who'd come in with Abel, but out of the corner of his eye he could see the former hide buyer, frozen stiff in shock, staring at the group from the sidewalk.

Then the dead man's companions began stirring, surprise and anger twisting their faces. Before they could move or speak, Longarm whipped his wallet out of his coat pocket and flipped it open to show his badge.

"You men hold still now," he commanded, his voice coolly level. "I ain't no gunhand. I'm a U.S. marshal, and I shot that man because he was drawing down to backshoot somebody."

"Just the same, you didn't have no right—" one of them began.

"Like hell I didn't!" Longarm said coldly. He held the men's attention with his gunmetal-blue eyes while he took out a cheroot and lighted it one-handed. None of the four men watching him moved or spoke. Longarm went on, "Your friend Abel begun that fuss. Maybe he didn't mean for things to happen like they did, but you was all standing right there watching."

Again there was silence, broken by the man called Smitty.

"I'd say the marshal's right," he told the others. "Abel was as good as being a dead man the minute he pulled out his gun."

"Now wait a minute!" one of the others protested.

Longarm cut him off short. "No, you wait a minute. I'll tell you what your friend's trying to say, if you don't see it yet. You men know better'n I do that a jury here in Dodge City wouldn't waste a minute on a man that backshot somebody who maybe didn't even have a gun on him."

Smitty nodded soberly. "That's about what I was trying to say, Marshal." He turned to the others. "If Abel had gunned that fellow out there, he'd've been dancing a jig at the end of a rope necktie before this time tomorrow."

"Smitty's right," another of the men agreed. "Abel always was a damn fool, anyhow. Never could hold back his temper, once he started gitting riled."

"It don't surprise me none, neither," said the third man. "I guess about all we can do now is see he gets put away proper."

"You do that," Longarm told them. "Now, when I write up my report, I'll explain how it all come about, so you men don't need to worry about a thing but getting your friend buried."

"Which is what we better do," Smitty said thoughtfully. He turned to his companions. "Come on. We'll get him over to old man Wilson. Maybe we can still get him planted today."

With Abel's body sagging between them, the four survivors left the saloon. The former hide buyer, still standing in a state of shock on the sidewalk outside the saloon, moved aside to let them pass. Then he looked at Longarm and said, "I owe you quite a lot, Marshal, and I don't even know your name."

"Name's Long. I work out of the Denver office, not that it makes any difference."

"I'm Carl Werner. And I give you my oath, Marshal Long, if I did turn down that man's load of hides three years ago, I don't remember it."

"Like you said, his wasn't the only hides you turned down."

"No. But nobody ever turned it into a shooting matter with me before. I didn't have any idea that that man Abel would. I'd be a dead man right now if you hadn't done what you did. I owe you quite a lot, Marshal."

"You don't owe me a thing," Longarm replied. "It took me by surprise for a minute too."

"I don't suppose I was very smart," the man said thoughtfully. "I saw enough shooting scrapes begin out of next to nothing when I was here buying hides. I should have known—"

"You ought to've been looking back," Longarm told him. "I've seen men shot over a lot less than what he was blaming you for."

"It seems to me the least I can do is—well, you wanted to buy one of these bottles of rye I've got." He held out the unopened bottle of Tom Moore. "Here. If you want the other bottle too, you're welcome to it."

"Now I wouldn't shoot a man for a bottle of whiskey, Mr. Werner," Longarm protested.

"Hell's bells, I know that!" Werner exclaimed. "But I sure do owe you something, and if I've got you sized up right, you'd take it as an insult if I offered you money."

"You're right about that," Longarm said. "I ain't even real sure I'd be doing the right thing if I was to take your whiskey."

"Nonsense!" Werner said. Then he went on, "Why don't we talk about it over a drink? I was just starting out to get some supper, but I think I need a drink more than I need food right now. How about you?"

"Well, I'll be glad to sit down and have a drink with you." Longarm turned to start back to the table.

Werner put a hand on his arm to stop him. "Not in there, Marshal. In a few minutes the Long Branch is going to be full of men wanting to rehash what happened. I don't feel like I want to be stared at by a bunch of curious strangers. Let's go up to my room in the Dodge House and have our drink in peace."

For a moment Longarm was about to refuse, but it had been a long, dry day and the thought of a smooth-sharp sip of Maryland's best rye whiskey sliding down his throat changed his mind. He'd also remembered his plan to stay over in Dodge that night.

"I'll just take you up on that invitation, Mr. Werner," he said. "I guess I could use a little drink myself, about now."

Chapter 2

Longarm and Charles Werner sat in Werner's room in the Dodge House, the opened bottle of Old Joe Gideon on the small table between them, glasses in their hands. The still-untouched bottle of Tom Moore was on the bureau. In spite of Werner's urgings, Longarm hadn't yet agreed to accept the whiskey. In one corner of the sparsely furnished room, Longarm's saddlebags leaned against the wall, his rifle in front of them. As he'd remarked to Werner when they were leaving the saloon, anybody who tempts thieves by going off and leaving his gear on an unwatched horse at a public hitch rail deserves to have it stolen.

As will most men who have just come unscathed from a period of stress, Longarm and Werner had been unwinding their taut nerves by talking about everything except the events of the immediate past.

Werner was saying, "You know, Marshal, when I take time to look back on it, I don't think I've ever seen anything that I can compare with the way the buffalo-hide trade ended a few years ago."

Longarm nodded. "I've heard it was a sort of sudden thing."

"It just happened overnight," Werner went on. "Why, the last season I was buying hides here in Dodge, there were all the hides in the world, hundreds of thousands of them, stacked up along the railroad right-of-way in rows that were a couple of miles long and maybe a half-mile deep. Then, the next year, there weren't any."

"That's enough to surprise a man, all right."

"Well, it was sudden, but not exactly a surprise. In the office back East, we kept in touch with the Santa Fe for about three weeks before the buying season opened every year. They used to wire us about twice a week to let us know how many hides the hunters were bringing into their different stations, so we'd be able to plan our buying trips. That year they kept wiring that no hides were coming in. I thought maybe it was just the Kansas depots that weren't getting any, so I started checking with other buyers, those who'd been working farther north."

"And they were getting the same story?"

"Exactly. When I found out it wasn't just the southern market that was drying up, I didn't even bother to make another trip to Dodge. That's why I haven't been here for three years."

"But you figure the hide trade's about to open up again?" Longarm asked.

Werner shook his head. "No. From what I've gathered, there just aren't any more buffalo left. Not around here, not farther south, not up in Montana or Dakota Territory. Oh, I suppose there are bound to be some buffalo left. Not many, though. And if my guess is right, they're scattered out here and there in little bunches, fifty or a hundred in one place. But nothing like the herds that would support the kind of hide trade we used to have."

"Funny, ain't it?" Longarm remarked. "Funny how they just went, all of a sudden that way. I never figured there was enough hunters to wipe out all them buffalo."

"It seems they did, though. Pity, too. There'd still be a market for hides, you know. Why, right now I'd be more than glad to pay twelve or fourteen dollars apiece for hides I used to buy for a dollar and a half."

"You're still in that line of business, then?"

"Oh yes. But I buy cattle hides now. It's not as interesting, dealing with slaughterhouse managers instead of buffalo hunters, but it's a living." Werner tipped the bottle over their glasses to refill them, and after he'd waited politely for Longarm to take the first sip and had a swallow himself, he went on, "Now I'd imagine your business is always interesting, Marshal. No two cases are ever alike, are they?"

"Not exactly," Longarm agreed. He'd never enjoyed discussing his work with those who weren't in the same line. He avoided amplifying his reply by pulling a cheroot out of his coat pocket and flicking his thumbnail across the head of a match to light it. He blew a puff of blue smoke into the gathering dimness of the hotel room.

Werner was persistent. "You said you were going down into Texas. A new case, I guess? Or is it something you can't talk about?"

"Oh, there ain't no mystery of any kind about the case I'm on," Longarm replied. "It's only that I don't know enough about it yet to do much talking. I ain't exactly sure where I'm supposed to look, or what I'm looking for. About all I got to go on is that somebody in the Indian bureau had a hunch there's something fishy going on, so I got sent to find out."

"It sounds to me as though you've been sent out on something of a wild-goose chase, then," Werner suggested.

Longarm nodded without replying. Werner's remark had reminded him that he'd said much the same thing to his chief two days earlier, when Billy Vail had assigned him to the case.

Longarm had reported for duty that morning even later than usual. When he'd stuck his head into the chief marshal's office, Vail was reading the last of the overnight wires that had come in on the direct telegraph line between the Federal Building in Denver and Justice Department headquarters in Washington. Without looking up from the sheaf of pink flimsies, Vail motioned with a pudgy pink hand for Longarm to come in.

His suspicions about the kind of case he was going to be assigned were immediately aroused by the lack of his chief's customary remarks about deputies who didn't seem to be able to get to work on time, but Longarm said nothing. He stepped into the office and stood waiting for a moment before pulling up to a corner of Vail's desk the red morrocco-leather chair that stood against the wall. He'd barely settled down into it when Vail put down the flimsies and gazed at him across his paper-strewn desk.

"I hope you're as ready as you generally are to do a little traveling," the chief marshal said without any preliminaries.

"Where you figuring to send me this time, Billy?"

Vail ignored the question and went on, "I've got my clerk writing up your papers now. Travel vouchers, expense money, all the other stuff you'll need."

"Billy, how come you don't want to tell me where this case is at?" Longarm asked.

"Oh, I didn't mention that, did I? It's in Texas."

"Now hold on a minute! You know I ain't right popular with the Texas Rangers, Billy. If they catch me down in what they figure's their country again, they're likely to gang up on me and kick my ass clear back to Denver with them damn pointedy boots they all favor."

"You don't have to worry about the Rangers this time. There won't be any, where you're going."

"Now, Billy, you used to be a Ranger yourself. You know damned well there's no place in Texas I can go where I might not run into one."

Vail ran a hand across his shiny bald head and said nonchalantly, "Even if you did, you still wouldn't have to worry. You're in good standing with the Rangers now. At least that's what a friend of mine who's still on the force wrote me in a letter I had from him a while back."

Longarm frowned suspiciously. "You never mentioned nothing about that to me."

"I think the letter got here while you were handling that case up on the Humboldt. Or maybe I just forgot to say anything about it."

"Well, Billy, even if it was a while ago, I'd sort of like to know what made them Rangers change their minds about me being a first-class, grade-A, number-one son of a bitch."

"Chiefly, it was all the help you gave Tom Dodd when he got shot up down in Mexico. Seems that Tom spread word to just about every Ranger he talked to after he got back. But you won't have to worry about running into any Rangers where you're going, anyhow. There aren't any stationed within five hundred miles of where you'll be."

"Oh, now hold on! Five hundred miles takes in a lot of ground, Billy!"

"And I'll stand by it too," Vail answered. "There aren't any towns, there aren't any people, so there's no use in there being any Rangers stationed anywhere close by."

"Billy, the way you say that gives me the idea I'm going to someplace like the North Pole, not to Texas."

"There'd likely be as many people there," Vail said, no sign of a smile on his florrid face.

"Just where in hell is it in Texas that I'm going? I know it's a big state, but until you started talking, I figured I'd been over pretty much all of it. I sure ain't run into anyplace like you've been telling me about, though."

"Where you're going is what they call the Llano Estacado. That means the Staked Plains, and it's up in the northwest part of Texas, between the Panhandle and the Big Bend. The story is that it got its name because the first men going over the place used to drive stakes in the ground so they'd have landmarks to guide them on their way back."

"Are you real sure it's as godforsaken as you make out to be, Billy?" Longarm asked.

"I'm sure. All you'll see is mile after mile of prairie, as flat as the top of this desk. Oh, there's a lot of gullies you don't see until your horse is about to step off into one, and a couple of pretty good-sized canyons where there's a stream or maybe a puddle of water and a few trees. But mostly it's about as bare as a baby's butt."

"You talk like you seen it for yourself at one time or another."

The chief marshal's eyes narrowed under his bushy black eyebrows. "I have. When I was with the Rangers, I rode over that Llano Estacado a couple of times. It was still Comanche country then, so I didn't waste much time looking at the scenery. I got through it as fast as I could, just going by the compass."

"You sure don't make it sound pretty."

"It's not what you'd call pretty, and there's no farms on it yet, nothing but a few old-time sheep ranches on the far west side, along the border of New Mexico Territory. And as I said a minute ago, no towns."

"What in hell am I supposed to do there, Billy? You said it used to be Comanche country, but I had an idea that all the Comanches is settled down in the Indian Nation by now."

"They're supposed to be."

Something in the chief marshal's voice struck a false note in Longarm's ears. He said suspiciously, "Now wait a minute. I ain't going down there to do the army's work, am I? Rounding up a bunch of Indians that's jumped the reservation? If it is, I say let the army do it."

"I'd say the same thing, Longarm. The army did it once, a few years back, when McKenzie whipped the Comanches and had his men shoot all their horses and mules, then marched them to the Indian Nation and tucked them in. But this isn't an army job or an Indian bureau job. It's ours."

"Don't you think it's about time you told me what the case is about, instead of keeping on beating around the bush?" Longarm suggested.

Vail flipped through the sheaf of telegrams he'd been studying when Longarm entered. he found the pink flimsy he was looking for, glanced at it and said, "It seems that somebody in the Indian bureau's seeing ghosts under the bed. They've got a report that there's Comancheros working down there again."

"Comancheros!" Longarm exploded. "There ain't no such thing anymore!"

"You know what they are, then?"

"Why, sure! At least what they used to be. They was outlaw traders that swapped guns and ammunition and pepper-whiskey to the redskins to ransom prisoners the Indians took off emigrant wagons and homesteads. They'd trade for horses and mules, and I guess for whatever jewelry and gold and other loot they'd managed to get their hands on. But that all begun a long time ago, when most of Texas was Indian country."

Vail nodded. "I thought the same thing you did, that the Comancheros faded away when the Comanches were shut up on their reservation in the Nation. But that might turn out to be what everybody was thinking, and the facts of the matter could be real different, so you'd better go find out what the truth is."

"Billy, are you certain this ain't going to be just a big wild-goose chase?" Longarm asked. "Anybody that's got any brains at all knows the Comancheros can't do business unless they got Comanches to trade with."

"Sure. Even the people at the Indian bureau are smart enough to know that. But there've been more Comanches than usual jumping the reservation lately, and the word's spreading that the Comancheros are back, so that's why the Indian bureau people are getting worried. They don't want the Indians getting their hands on guns and ammunition again."

"Can't say I blame 'em for that." Longarm dropped the butt of his cheroot into the spittoon that stood by Vail's desk. "I don't guess you can tell me anything more about what to look for when I get down to Texas, can you?"

"There's not much left to tell. Just go look, and if you find the Comanchero trade's started up again, do whatever you've got to do to stop it."

"I guess I'm ready to go, then. Look for me back when you see me."

Carl Werner stood up, and his companion's movement brought Longarm's mind snapping back to the room in the Dodge House. Werner stepped over to the bureau. He picked up the bottle of Tom Moore and put it on the table beside the bottle of Gideon.

"I'm not going to let you say no any longer, Marshal," he told Longarm. "You've got the look on your face of a man who's thinking about a job that's facing him, and if you're going to be in Texas for any length of time, you'll need this a lot worse than I do. Now tuck it away in your saddlebag, and let's go get a bite of supper."

"Tell you what, Mr. Werner. I'll buy that bottle off of you, but I won't take it as a reward or nothing like that."

"I'll sell it to you, then. My price is two bits, not a penny more or less."

"Now dammit, that's just the same as giving it to me. A

201

quart of Tom Moore costs a dollar and a quarter most places I've bought it."

"Take it or leave it, Marshal."

"I reckon I'll have to take it, then. Because I'm just fresh out of drinking whiskey, and I've got a long ways to go."